RL

D0476144

THE
SORROWING
WIND

Also by Mary E. Pearce

The Apple Tree Saga:
APPLE TREE LEAN DOWN
JACK MERCYBRIGHT
THE LAND ENDURES
SEEDTIME AND HARVEST

CAST A LONG SHADOW
POLSINNEY HARBOUR
THE TWO FARMS
THE OLD HOUSE AT RAILES

THE SORROWING WIND

Book Three

of

THE APPLE TREE SAGA

WANDSWORTH PUBLIC LIBRARIES

Mary E. Pearce

LITTLE, BROWN AND COMPANY

101135533

A *Little, Brown* Book

First published in Great Britain in 1975
by Macdonald and Jane's Publishers
Published by Warner Books in 1993
This edition published by Little, Brown and Company in 1995

Copyright © Mary E. Pearce 1975

The moral right of the author has been asserted.

*All characters in this publication are fictitious
and any resemblance to real persons, living or dead,
is purely coincidental.*

All rights reserved.
No part of this publication may be reproduced,
stored in a retrieval system, or transmitted, in any
form or by any means, without the prior
permission in writing of the publisher, nor be
otherwise circulated in any form of binding or
cover other than that in which it is published and
without a similar condition including this
condition being imposed on the subsequent purchaser.

A CIP catalogue record for this book
is available from the British Library.

ISBN 0 316 91430 4

Printed and bound in Great Britain by
Mackays of Chatham PLC, Chatham, Kent

Little, Brown and Company (UK)
Brettenham House
Lancaster Place
London WC2E 7EN

Within the woodlands, flow'ry gladed,
By the oak tree's mossy root,
The sheenèn grass-blades, timber-shaded,
Now do quiver underfoot;
An' birds do whissle auver head,
An' water's bubblèn in its bed,
An' there for me the apple tree
Do lean down low in Linden Lea.

William Barnes

Betony and the young Army officer, Michael Andrews, had sat opposite each other all the way from Paddington, but they might never have struck up a friendship had it not been for the scene that occurred between two other people in the compartment: a stout district nurse and a young man who looked like a clerk.

At Paddington the train had been crowded. After Oxford it ran half empty. The nurse got in at Long Stone, the clerk at Milston, and right from the first she fixed him with a stare calculated to discomfit him.

"I wonder you aren't ashamed!" she said, when he was foolish enough to meet her gaze. "A sturdy young man in the prime of life, fighting-fit and full of beans, yet still wearing civvies! *I'd* be ashamed. I would, honest!"

"It so happens I suffer with asthma," the young man said, red with embarrassment, and hid himself behind his paper.

"That's what they all say nowadays, but you look healthy enough to me, young fellow, and if you were a proper man you'd be up and doing like the captain there, and all our other gallant soldiers."

The woman glanced across at Michael. Plainly she expected his approval. Then she leant towards the clerk and rattled the newspaper in his hands.

"It's funny what a lot of asthma there is about lately,

not to mention gastric troubles and the odd cases of housemaid's knee, but I could give it another name if anyone was to ask *me*!"

Michael, in his corner, could bear no more.

"Madam, be quiet!" he said sharply. "Leave the man alone and hold your tongue!"

The woman was shocked. Her mouth fell open a little way, showing teeth stained mauve with the sweets she was eating.

"You've got no right to speak to me like that! If my husband was with me you wouldn't dare!"

"If your husband was with you I hope he'd keep you in better order."

"Well, really!" she exclaimed. "Well, really! I'd never have believed it!"

But she leant back again in her seat and remained silent for the rest of her journey, glaring at the newspaper shielding the clerk. Michael turned again to the window, and Betony looked at him with new interest. Straight sandy hair, rather untidy; beaky face and brown skin; tired grey eyes and tired mouth with lines at the corners: the sort of face, young yet old, which she had grown accustomed to seeing in the fourteen months since the start of the war.

The train was now stopping at every station. When the clerk and the nurse got out at Salton, Michael turned to Betony.

"I'm sorry about that," he said, "but the damned woman got my goat."

"It's the new blood sport, baiting civilians," Betony said.

"If she only knew what it's like over there – if she could see for just five minutes – it would soon wipe the smile from her smug pink face."

"But somebody has to go and fight."

"Yes, yes," he said, with some impatience. "But everyone here is so complacent! So glib and self-righteous and so damnably bloodthirsty!"

"How would you like us to be?" Betony asked, and he gave her a smile.

"Quiet . . . comfortable . . . calm . . ." he said, "talking of cricket and fishing and the crops, and whether the hens are laying at the moment . . ."

Betony nodded. Looking at him, she could feel his tiredness. Her own flesh ached, as his must ache.

"You've been wounded, haven't you?" She could see how stiffly he held his shoulder.

"I've been wounded three times yet up I pop again good as new. A charmed life, apparently. I was gassed, too, on this last tour. That's why my voice is rough at the edges. Not badly, of course, or I shouldn't be here to tell the tale."

"How long is your leave?"

"Until I'm fit. A month, perhaps."

"And then what?"

"Back again to face the music."

"How can you do it?" Betony asked, marvelling.

"No choice," he said, and turned the talk towards her instead. "Do you travel a lot?" He glanced at her brief-case on the rack above.

"Quite a lot, yes, though not usually as far as London. I've been to a sort of conference there. But mostly I travel around the Midlands, seeing to the welfare of women workers in munitions factories."

"Do you enjoy it?"

"Yes. In a way. At least it's something that needs doing. But I'm always glad to leave the towns and get home to Cobbs where it's quiet and peaceful."

"Cobbs? Where's that?"

"In a village called Huntlip, near Chepsworth."

"I live in Chepsworth, myself," he said. "It's a nice walk from there out to Huntlip. Can I come and see you sometimes?"

"Yes, come and meet my family," she said. "I can't guarantee they'll talk about cricket, but someone is sure to mention hens."

"There's one good thing about the war. We can take short cuts in making friends, even with members of the opposite sex."

But he felt she would not have rebuffed him, anyway, war or no war. She was at ease with him; sure of herself; quiet and calm and straightforward. She was also very pleasant to look at: he liked her bright fairness and the clarity of her blue eyes. She had the serenity he longed for.

"Tell me about your family," he said.

At Chepsworth station, Jesse Izzard was waiting for his daughter, eager to take her bag and brief-case, carrying them for her with a sense of importance. His fair face shone, as it always did when he welcomed her home, and his pride increased when she introduced Michael Andrews.

"Captain Andrews will be coming out to visit us, dad. He wants to see the carpenter's shop."

"Why, yes," Jesse said, as he shook Michael's hand. "Very welcome, I'm sure. Are you Captain Andrews of King's Hill House?"

"That's right," Michael said. "Just up there, behind the station."

"I put a new fence round your paddock once. Years ago, now, when your father was alive."

"You'll be glad to know it's still standing."

"Ah, well, it would be," Jesse said. "It was good oak fencing."

His sense of importance knew no bounds. He walked with a very slight swagger. The Andrewses were well-known people. They had lived in Chepsworth umpteen years. But there was a blot on Jesse's day, for, outside the station, instead of the smart little pony and trap, stood the old workshop waggon with sacks of sawdust and shavings aboard and the scruffy horse, Collier, between the shafts.

"It's your great-grumpa's fault," he said, muttering to Betony. "He took the trap to go to Upham." And, clearing his throat, he said to Michael: "Can we give you a lift, captain?"

"No, thanks," Michael said. "I shall enjoy the walk up the hill."

He stood on the pavement and waved them off. Jesse saluted, rather stiffly.

"D'you think he refused on account of the waggon?"

"No, of course not," Betony said. "He's not such a snob as you are, dad."

And, sitting beside him, she squeezed his arm to reassure him. He did not always know when he was being teased.

The old house at Cobbs was quiet under its oaks and elms. There was no noise from the carpenter's shop, for work stopped at twelve on a Saturday now. Only Great-grumpa Tewke found things to do.

"You've had the sign painted," Betony said. They were passing the gate of the workshop yard, and the two names, Tewke and Izzard, stood out black and shiny on the white ground. "The things that happen when I turn my back for a few days!"

"Young Tom done that. He's good with a paint-brush. He gets it from his poor dead father."

In the big kitchen, as Betony entered, her mother was laying the table for supper. She paused, looking up with a welcoming smile, and her flickering glance delivered a warning – that somebody lurked behind the door. Betony pushed it open wide and squeezed her youngest brother, Dicky, who emerged crestfallen, holding his nose.

"Aw, they told you!" he said, disgusted. "And I was going to make you jump!"

"You're too fond of making folk jump," Jesse said. "Here, take this bag up to your sister's room."

"No, don't take it up," Betony said. "I've got things to show you when everyone's in."

"She's brought us presents," Dicky said.

He was young enough, at fifteen, to have waited indoors for his sister's return, but William and Roger, with manly interests to pursue, sauntered in casually a little later.

"Had a good journey?" William asked.

"A slow one, I bet," Roger said, "stopping at every way-side halt."

"What happened in London, when you saw them high-ups?"

"Your sister's been put in charge," Jesse said. "She's to superintend the whole region."

"That'll suit our Betony," Dicky said, "telling folk what to do."

By supper-time, Granna Tewke had come out of the parlour, spectacles pushed up high on her forehead, and Great-grumpa Tewke had returned from Upham, having looked at a stand of timber there and rejected it because of the price.

"Taking advantage!" he said, swearing. "They're taking advantage everywhere you go nowadays but nobody's going to profiteer me!"

"Where's Tom?" Betony asked.

"Late as usual. We'll start without him."

"I reckon he's courting," Dicky said.

"More likely drinking in The Rose and Crown."

"He'll go to the bad, like his father, that boy," said Granna Tewke, looking everywhere for her glasses. "Ferrets indeed! What's a decent boy want with ferrets?"

"Our Betony's made a new friend," Jesse said. "Captain Andrews of King's Hill House. They was talking together on the train and he's likely coming out here on a visit."

"What, one of that lot with all the money?"

"All made out of mustard," said great-grumpa, "and now they live like landed gentry."

"The captain's all right," Jesse said. "A nice young gentleman, straight off."

"He'll think hisself somebody," William said, his mouth already full of food, "being in uniform and all."

"And isn't he somebody?" Betony asked.

"No more'n the rest of us," William said.

"Oh, no, of course not!" Betony exclaimed. "*You* risk your life every day in the workshop, whenever you take up a hammer and chisel!"

"So that's it?" said William. "Now we're hearing a few home truths!" His clear-skinned face became crimson, and his blue eyes glittered. "You want me in uniform, out at the Front, living in trenches like a rat!"

"No, I don't," Betony said. "I just don't like to hear you sneering at those who are."

"No more don't I," Dicky said. "I'd go tomorrow if only they'd have me."

"Me, too," Roger said. "I'm as big as many chaps of eighteen."

"Go and good luck to you!" William said. "You're both too wet behind the ears to know any better!"

He sprang from his chair and would have hurried from the room, but that his mother spoke out sharply.

"Sit down, William, and stop jogging the tea on the table. We'll have no arguments on this subject, nor on no others for the time being. Roger, cut your father a slice of bread."

William sat down, though still in a temper, and the others talked to cover his silence. Often a word was enough from their mother. She had great-grumpa's forcefulness, coupled with a coolness of her own. It was she who ruled within the household, just as great-grumpa ruled in the workshop.

At King's Hill House, Michael had soaked for an hour in the bath, and now, in his bedroom, dressed in grey flannels and a white shirt, he was combing his hair in front of the mirror. Behind him, on the floor, his uniform lay in a crumpled heap, where he had stepped out of it, trampling it underfoot in the process.

His mother knocked and came in. She watched him putting on a tweed jacket.

"Oh, dear! They don't fit you, do they, your old clothes? You've grown so much thinner." She turned to the crumpled heap on the floor and picked up his tunic. "Really, Michael, that's surely no way to treat the King's uniform!"

"The King is welcome to it," he said, "and its livestock, if any."

"Livestock?" she said, and dropped the tunic with a shudder. "You're surely not serious? I don't believe it!"

"Perfectly serious, mother," he said. "Now perhaps you understand why a man likes to get into ordinary clothes."

"Doesn't your servant look after you properly?"

"It's not his fault. It can't be helped. We're all the same over there – lousy as hedgehogs."

"But you've been in hospital. Surely – '

"Oh, I've been deloused, certainly, but the eggs survive the fumigator and live to hatch another day."

"Good heavens!" she said. "I couldn't bear it if it started here."

"Neither could I. It's bad enough over there."

"My poor boy! How thoughtless of me. What must I do with all your things?"

"Leave it to me. I'll take them down to Cook and get her to bake 'em in one of the old wall ovens. A few days of that should do the trick."

Returning a little while later to the bedroom, he found her at work with a spray of disinfectant. She stopped spraying and looked him over.

"Are you going out, dear? You won't forget dinner's at seven?"

"I won't forget. I'm only going down to the town for a drink."

"At a public house?" she said, astonished. "But there are plenty of drinks in the sitting-room."

"I feel like a long cool draught of beer."

"I'm worried about you, going out dressed like that. People are often unkind to civilians, you know."

"I know about that. I witnessed a sample on the train today."

And, having related the incident, he went on to talk about Betony.

"She travels round the midlands, arranging facilities for women working in the factories. It's amazing what girls are doing now. They're really breaking out and showing their mettle."

"A carpenter's daughter, did you say? How extraordinary!"

"She didn't have tin-tacks between her lips, mother, or a pencil stuck behind her ear."

"No need to be so touchy, dear. I didn't think she sounded like your sort of girl, that's all, but if I'm mistaken, perhaps you'd like to invite her to tea?"

"Now you're going a bit too fast."

"Yes, well, perhaps it's not such a good idea. Food is so scarce here now, you know, that meals are becoming quite a problem."

Michael smiled, having seen the dinner Cook was preparing in the kitchen. His mother, interpreting the smile correctly, gently reproved him.

"Today is rather a special occasion. We don't always eat so well."

"I'm sorry, mother. Don't take too much notice of me. I'll be less sour in a day or two."

Walking down into the town he experienced a feeling of well-being so all-suffusing that the pain of his wound almost gave him pleasure. He felt pure and clean and not-of-this-world. Yet his mood was supremely physical, too: the scent of chrysanthemums in people's gardens; the sight of the chestnut trees turning a fiery red-and-yellow; the sound of the great cathedral clock striking as he crossed the close and turned down beside the river: he apprehended all these things in every particle of his body.

And when, drinking a pint of Chepsworth ale in the bar of The Swan, where four farm labourers sat with the landlord and the talk was of turnips and winter wheat, he smiled to himself and listened greedily to every word, till one old man drew him into an argument about the virtues of home-baked bread.

At King's Hill House, his mother, worrying, hoped the war would soon be over. It seemed to be giving Michael a taste for low company.

*

The orchard at Cobbs was at its best, the apples so thick that many branches were borne down low, and Betony, walking among the trees, often had to bend her head. She had never known such a year for apples. She kept touching them with the tips of her fingers: the big green quilters, the rusty red pippins, and the crimson winesaps much loved by wasps. She was choosing a pippin for herself when she saw Michael coming towards her from the house.

"I met your brother William," he said. "He told me where to find you."

"Was he polite to you?" Betony asked.

"Perfectly. Why do you ask?"

"He's in a sullen mood lately. Anti-military. Anti-war."

"Then his feelings run with mine exactly."

"I think he feels guilty at not enlisting."

"It'll all be decided for him soon, when conscription comes in."

"Poor William," she said. "He so loves his home and his family, and the work he does in the carpenter's shop. He so loves everything to be neat and tidy. He'll hate all the mess and confusion and waste . . ." She looked at Michael. "Where will it all end?" she asked. "And when, oh, when?"

Michael shrugged. He knew he ought to say comforting things: that the Germans were beaten and it was only a question of finishing them off. Such was the spirit promulgated by the commanders. But his own feeling was that the war might last for ever and ever. He could see no solution; no victory on either side; no other outcome except complete annihilation. Perhaps it was just that he was so tired. Once he was perfectly fit again, his old optimism was bound to return.

"It's got to end somewhere, sometime," he said. "But don't ask me when. I'm no strategist, God knows. I just obey orders – with my eyes shut mostly – and do my best to stay alive."

They were walking slowly through the orchard and he noticed how, whenever she stooped beneath a low branch, her skirts went out in a billowing flare, sweeping the grass. The dress she wore was a very dark red with black threads running through it in waves, and, watching the way the skirts flared out at every curtsey, he knew he would see the pattern they made whenever he thought of her in future.

"You said you'd show me round the workshop."

"It's shut up on Sundays. Great-grumpa Tewke is strict on that score."

But she took him and showed him the workshop buildings – stables, once, when Cobbs had been a farmhouse, long years before – and the yard where oak and elm planking lay criss-crossed in piles, with laths between to let the air blow through and dry them. She showed him the sawpit and the timber-crabs and the store-yard full of ladders, field-gates, cribs and troughs. And she told him all she knew of the business, founded by Great-grumpa William Tewke in the year 1850, when he was a boy of nineteen and had scarcely enough money about him to buy his first tools. Now the workshop employed twelve men. Or would do, she said, if two had not gone into the Army.

They walked and talked until dusk was falling, when her father came in search of them, saying supper was on the table and would the captain care to stay?

In the big kitchen, under the low black beams and rafters, they sat down to eat at a long table covered over with a stiff white cloth. There were nine in the household.

A clan indeed. Ten, he was told, if they counted Janie, but she was married to Martin Holt and lived at the neighbouring farm of Anster. Michael himself, an only child, was glad to be sitting with this family. He wished he belonged there, sharing the strength their unity gave them. He had often been lonely in his own home.

At the head of the table sat William Tewke, quick of eye and ear although he was turned eighty-four, and next on his left sat Kate Tewke, his dead son's widow, vague and shortsighted, known to the younger ones as granna. At the foot of the table, Beth, Kate's daughter, fresh-faced and comely, her corn-coloured hair in a braid round her head, looked on them all with a calm blue gaze and saw to it they had what they wanted. Next to her, her husband, Jesse, was just as yellow-haired as she, so that it was no wonder the two of them together had produced children of such harvest fairness.

But there was an odd-man-out among them: the boy named Tom Maddox: black-haired and brown-eyed, with the hollow cheeks and smooth dark skin of a gipsy, and the same slender build. He was very quiet, with an almost unnatural stillness about him, and although he was one of the family, he was yet apart from all the rest, watchful, intent, aware of everything that passed yet speaking, it seemed, only when someone spoke to him. He was an oddity indeed; an orphan brought into the family and raised with them from the age of nine; standing out from all the rest like a blackbird in a sheaf of corn.

"You can see he ent one of us, can't you?" said young Dicky, showing off to Michael. "Mother's never been able to scrub him clean."

"Tom is courting," Roger said. "Did you know that, dad? It's Tilly Preston at The Rose and Crown."

"Is that really so, Tom?" Jesse asked, assuming a father's

gravity. "And if it is, shouldn't you be asking my advice?"

"No," Tom said, "it ent true."

"Well, Till Preston is sweet on *him*. She drew him a pint of ale for nothing when we was there on Friday night."

"That's another bloody lie!"

"Now, then, Tom, mind your language in front of strangers."

"Hah!" said great-grumpa. "I daresay the captain's heard worse'n that."

"Yes, indeed," Michael said. "It's a true saying, 'to swear like a trooper'."

"But you're not a trooper," Dicky said. "What are you, exactly, since you ent in uniform for us to see?"

"Infantry," Michael said. "Second Battalion, the Three Counties Regiment."

"Then you've seen some action, probably?"

"Oh, there's plenty of action out in France at present, yes."

"Them French!" said granna, suddenly, adjusting her glasses to glare at Michael. "You give them what-for and teach them a lesson!"

"What're you on about?" asked great-grumpa. "The French are our allies, same as the Belgians."

"Allies?" said granna. "I thought they was meant to be on our side!"

"Let's not talk about the war – Michael gets enough of that," said Betony.

"Don't he like talking about it? – He's different from most, then," William said.

"Let's talk about the chickens and whether they're laying well lately."

"Chickens?" said Dicky. "Why talk about chickens for heaven's sake?"

"It's as good a subject as any other."

And, across the table, Betony exchanged a smile with Michael.

He was often at Cobbs after that. It became for him a place apart. And the family accepted him, even William.

Having done his duty by his mother, going with her to luncheon parties, allowing her to show him off in his new uniform, he would then change into comfortable clothes and escape on long walks into the country, where he ate bread and cheese in quiet pubs, and drank beer. He could not have enough of days like these and often at the end he would come to Huntlip; to the old house at Cobbs; to Betony, whose day's work ended at six o'clock.

One evening they walked in Millery wood, half a mile away, on the north bank of the Derrent brook. It was just about dusk and as they climbed the steep path they passed a figure standing perfectly still in the shadows.

The man's stillness was uncanny, and immediately Michael was back in France, creeping at night along derelict trenches, where at every turn an enemy guard might loom up darkly. His flesh crept. He almost sprang at the man and struck him. But Betony's voice said, "Tom? Is that you?" and her foster-brother stepped out to the pathway. Michael's breathing became normal. The sweat cooled on his lip and forehead.

"Yes, it's me," Tom muttered, and slouched past them, hands in pockets, down the path towards the Derrent.

"Extraordinary fellow!" Michael said. "What does he mean by it, skulking about in the dark like that?"

"It's nothing unusual for Tom. He's always been a night-creature."

"Was he spying on us by any chance?"

"Goodness, no!" she said, laughing. "Badgers, perhaps. Foxes, even. Or he may have been lying in wait for a pheasant. But he'd never bother to spy on people. They don't interest him enough for that."

"Perhaps he had an assignation. That girl your brother Roger mentioned."

"I hope not," Betony said. "Tilly Preston is a slut."

She was rather protective where Tom was concerned. Michael had noticed it often before. And he wondered that she should concern herself with a youth whose manner towards her was always surly and indifferent. He had learnt a little of the boy's history: Tom was illegitimate; granna had spoken of bad blood.

"Bad blood! What rubbish!" Betony said. "I don't believe in all that. Tom's father had a terrible temper. He killed Tom's mother in a drunken quarrel and afterwards he hanged himself. Tom was a baby of twelve months or so, neglected until he was skin and bone. Then he was raised by my Grannie Izzard, well-looked-after but allowed to run wild. Those are the things that have made him strange. It's nothing to do with bad blood."

"You're certainly a loyal champion."

"I was cruel to him at first," she said. "When Grannie Izzard died and Tom came to us, I made his life a misery."

"How did you?"

"Oh, tormenting him about his parents . . . making him feel he wasn't wanted . . ."

"Did your brothers do it too?"

"No Only me. I was horribly spiteful."

"That explains why you leap to defend him. You're trying to pay off a debt of guilt."

"I suppose I am, though there's nothing Tom ever wants from me, and the silly thing is, he bears me no grudge."

"Are you sure of that? He's very churlish."

"He still doesn't trust me," Betony said, "and I can't really blame him."

Coming out of the wood, onto high ground, they were met by a big full golden moon shining on the skyline, and Betony's face, when he turned towards her, had the moonlight bright upon it.

She looked serene. Her glance, meeting his, had a smile in it. But when he put out a hand to touch her, intending to hold her back a while, just as she was, with the moonlight on her, she walked quickly past and swung along the ridgeway path.

"I can hear the trains at Stickingbridge . . . that generally means we'll get a shower . . ."

The orchard at Cobbs presented a different picture now. The apples had been picked and the boughs, relieved of their heavy burden, had sprung back to their proper place. The forked supports had been removed; Martin Holt's sheep had been put in to graze; and now the leaves were falling fast, a luminous yellow in the long lush grass.

Michael was aware that the days were slipping through his fingers. His month's leave was almost over. He wished he could choose a specific moment and call for time to stand still. This moment, for instance, with Betony laughing in the sun, standing on tiptoe under a plum tree, trying to reach a globule of gum that hung on the branch like a bead of amber.

Yet what was the use of asking time to stand and deliver? All living creatures must take what they could. There was no fulfilment otherwise. Betony, with her arms upraised, the shape of her breasts inviting his touch – surely she was aware of herself, aware of the sun going round the sky, faster and faster every day?

Feeling him near her, she turned quickly, letting her arms fall to her sides. She was laughing and breathless and flushed with exertion, but as she looked at him and read the sick appeal in his eyes, her laughter faded away to nothing. His hands touched her face, her throat, her hair, and she stepped back a little, pushing him away. Her eyes remained steady. She tried to think of something to say. But it was Michael who spoke first.

"I want you to marry me. Soon. Straight away. I thought I'd get a special licence."

"No, Michael. It's too soon. I don't really know if it's what I want."

"I know my own feelings. I've no doubts whatever."

"How can that be? It's impossible. We've known each other eighteen days! Afterwards, perhaps, when the war is over – "

"There may not be any afterwards for me."

"You mustn't say that! It isn't fair to say such things."

"It's true all the same. Do you know what the chances of survival are over there? I'm already living on borrowed time."

"So you'd marry me quickly just to go off and leave me a widow?"

"No! That's just it! I know it's silly, but somehow I feel if I had your love, it would keep me safe from everything. I'd damn well make sure I got through safely!"

He knew he was playing on her feelings, but when he saw the pity in her face, he became ashamed.

"This is what it does to us! – Turns us into abject beings, preying on people, demanding their love. I'm sorry, Betony. Don't judge me too harshly. Let's forget about it and try to be as we were before."

He took her hand and drew it into the crook of his arm, and they walked together towards the house, talking quietly of ordinary things. But all the time he wondered about her; tried to guess how she felt towards him; for he had pinned his faith on her and looked to her as his protection.

In the cobbled fold at the back of the house, Jesse Izzard was pumping water, filling two old wooden buckets. He saw Betony walking with Michael through the garden but pretended he had something in his eye. When they had passed, he picked up his buckets and went into the dairy, where his wife was busy bottling honey.

"The captain seems smutten on our Betony. Think it'll come to anything, do you?"

"Maybe. Maybe not." Beth for once had no sure opinion. "But Betony's a girl who will find it hard to give herself heart and soul to someone."

Often when Tom was in The Rose and Crown, someone would bring him a chunk of wood and ask him to carve a bird or a fish or an animal, and today Tilly Preston, the landlord's daughter, had brought out an old maplewood beer-mug, for him to carve her likeness on it.

It took him perhaps half an hour, using only a pocket-knife, but the face on the mug was Tilly's exactly: the wide-set eyes under fine brows; the small straight nose with flared nostrils; the pretty lips parted a little, showing teeth with spaces between them; and the wisps of hair curling down over her forehead.

Tom, as he worked, was shut away from the noise around him, and Roger, watching his clever fingers, wished he had half Tom's skill in carving.

"Why, you've made me look flat!" Tilly complained, when she held the finished mug in her hands. "Still, I reckon you've earnt your pint of Chepsworth."

She filled the mug brimfull, and Tom drank it down in one long draught.

"That's the idea, Tom," said Oliver Rye. "Up with her until she's empty!"

"Is that all he gets?" asked Billy Ratchet. "Don't he get a kiss and a bit of a huggle?"

"Go on, young Tom. Tilly's agreeable, I'll be bound."

"Perhaps he's frightened," said Henry Tupper.

"Perhaps he don't rightly know the motions?"

"D'you want a few pointers, Tom, lad, from one of us old hands that've had some experience?"

Tom said nothing. He wiped his mouth with the back of his hand. His dark face was flushed, and he couldn't look at Tilly Preston. But Tilly herself was leaning towards him, and when Billy Ratchet pushed Tom forward, she put her arms up round his neck. Her small round breasts rested against him, and her face came slowly closer to his, her lips parting as they touched very softly against his own.

The little gathering sent up a cheer. Glasses were thumped upon the tables. Then, abruptly, there was silence. The girl sprang away from the boy's arms and turned to her father who stood scowling in the open doorway.

Emery Preston was a well-built man. His chest was like one of his own barrels. And, going up to the slim-built Tom Maddox, he looked like a bulldog approaching a whippet.

"If I catch you touching my daughter again, I'll make you sorry you was ever born!"

"Father!" said Tilly, pulling at his arm. "You mustn't speak to my friends like that."

"No lip from you or you'll get my belt across your bottom! You're supposed to be courting Harry Yelland. I won't have you meddling with this chap Maddox."

"Why, what's wrong with Tom?" Roger demanded, hot in defence of his foster-brother.

"I knew his father!" Emery said. "He was the nastiest-tempered brute in Huntlip and he once hit my mother across the mouth because she refused him drink on the slate."

"When was that? In the year dot? It warnt our Tom that done it anyway!"

"Like father, like son, so I'm taking no chances," Emery said. "Just mind and keep him away from my daughter!"

"Don't worry!" Roger said. "We'll keep away from you *and* your daughter and be damned to both of you good and all!" And, taking Tom's arm, he led him to the door. "Come on, Tom, we'll drink elsewhere. There's plenty of places better'n this one."

Outside the door Tom pulled away from Roger's grasp and thrust his fists into his pockets. He turned along the Straight and Roger followed.

"Take no notice of Emery Preston. Who cares about him? Or Tilly neither?"

"Not me," said Tom. "I ent grieving over them."

"San-fairy-duckwater, that's the style."

"He was telling the truth, though, all the same. My dad was a bad 'un. There's no doubt of that. He murdered my mother down in that cottage at Collow Ford and then went and hanged hisself in a tree."

"So what? It's all ancient history, over and done with. You don't want to worry yourself over that."

"I don't," Tom said. "It's other folk that worry about it, not me."

Sometimes he tried to picture his father: the drunkard hitting out in a rage; the fugitive run to ground by guilt; the despairer saving the public hangman a task. But no picture ever came to mind. It was just a story, and the man in the story was shadowy, faceless.

Could he picture his mother? Yes, perhaps. For sometimes he had a memory of white arms reaching towards him; of warm hands receiving his body into their strong, safe, thankful grasp. But the memory, if memory it was, always slid away when he tried to catch it, and then there was only a pitchblack darkness.

"Let's go to Chepsworth," Roger said. "We'll have a drink at The Revellers. They've got a skittle table there."

At The Revellers, in Lock Street, a coloured poster hung on the wall, showing the ruins of Louvain cathedral after its capture by the enemy. It was an artist's impression, it said, and it showed the German cavalry stabling their horses in nave and transept. One German trooper was smashing a painted plaster madonna by hurling it against the wall. Another was tearing the sacred vestments. Several others were burning carved wooden statues, including one of Christ blessing the loaves and fishes, to boil a pot of stew on a tripod, while, in the broken doorway, a few Belgian people, mostly old men and women, stood with their faces in their hands.

"I was just thinking," Tom said, "supposing that was Chepsworth cathedral, in ruins like that, with soldiers breaking everything up?"

"You ent religious, are you, Tom?"

"No, not me, but I think it's wicked all the same."

"What about all the people killed? That's a lot more wicked than bosting statues."

"Ah, well, that's right, of course," Tom said. "People is more important than statues."

But he hated the thought of all those carved figures fed to the flames in Louvain cathedral, just to boil a stewpot for German soldiers.

"You've gone and done *what*?" Jesse asked, openmouthed. "You surely didn't say enlisted?"

"Ah," said Tom. "Enlisted, that's right. Three o'clock this afternoon."

"And you?" Jesse said, staring at Roger. "You surely never went in too?"

"They wouldn't have me. They wouldn't believe I was eighteen."

"God in heaven!" said great-grumpa. "Anyone with half an eye could see you was only just weaned."

"They took my name, though," Roger said. "They'll be sending for me in due course."

"Due course," said Jesse, relieved. "Why, it's more'n a year before you're eighteen, and the war will surely be over by then?"

"It'd better be!" great-grumpa said. "It's damn near ruining the business."

"So Tom is to go? Would you believe it! I can't hardly credit it even now." Jesse looked doubtfully at his wife. "Ought we to let him, do you think, or are you going to put your foot down?"

"We can't stop him," Beth said. "He's well past eighteen and a grown man. If all I had to do was put my foot down, this war'd have been over before it started." She looked at Tom, standing before her. "When d'you have to go to the barracks?"

"They'll be sending my papers, the sergeant said."

"You done right to enlist," granna said. "I'm only glad it ent our William."

Tom went off to bed-down the pony in its stall, and there Betony found him later, having heard the news from her father and mother.

"Why did you go and enlist like that, without a word to anybody?"

"I just thought I would, that's all."

"Do you think it's easy being a soldier?"

"I dunno. I ent considered."

"I suppose you were tipsy as usual."

"I suppose I was," he said, shrugging.

She could never get near him, try as she might. He

spoke to her only to answer her questions. It had always been so from the very beginning; from the moment he had come to Cobbs, when she had made him feel an outcast and had driven him into himself like a crab. Nothing would change him now, it seemed. He would never believe that she minded about him.

"I can't imagine Tom as a soldier."

"You seem to be worried," Michael said, "yet it's no different for him that for any other volunteer."

"Tom's known so little happiness. It would be wicked if he were killed."

"He's been happy enough with your family, hasn't he?"

"But he's known no *joy,*" Betony said.

"How many people ever know joy?"

"Not many, I suppose, and then only in fleeting moments."

They were walking in the garden at King's Hill House. Betony had sat through afternoon tea and had weathered his mother's interrogation. But her thoughts, obviously, had been elsewhere.

"There ought to be *special* joys in the world for people like Tom," she said, "though I've no idea what they might be."

"You don't seem to mind that he treats you so boorishly all the time."

"I know I deserve it, that's why."

"Oh, come, now!" Michael said. "You can't have treated him that badly."

"You don't know. You weren't there. Children can be very cruel."

"It was all a very long time ago."

"I still feel guilty all the same."

"I'm glad it's nothing more than that. I was beginning to be afraid you loved him."

"But I *do* love him!" Betony said. "I love him dearly and I wish to God I could make him trust me. He's a creature all alone in the world yet I can't get near him – I can't do anything to help him. Oh, yes, I love him. I love him very dearly indeed."

Then, suddenly, she saw the expression in Michael's eyes.

"Ah, no!" she said. "It isn't like that! Not *that* sort of love. How can I make you understand?"

And because she could not bear to see him unhappy, she reached up and kissed him, holding his face between her hands.

"You mustn't look like that," she said. "You've got no reason to look like that."

"Betony – "

"Yes, yes, I know."

"You do feel something for me, then?"

"Of course I do. How can you ask?"

"Are your feelings the same as mine?"

"I think they will be, given time."

"Time," he repeated. "Ah, time!"

But he had her promise, and it was worth more to him than her surrender. He told her so by taking her hand and raising it formally to his lips. His eyes were not so desperate now.

Mrs Andrews, watching them from the French window, gave a little sigh of resignation. The girl meant to have him. That much was obvious.

Towards the end of his leave, he went before a medical board. The wound in his shoulder had healed well. The effects of gas poisoning were passing away. He was fit for duty.

"You're very lucky," the elderly doctor said to him. "You've got an excellent constitution. Still, I'm taking no chances with those lungs of yours, so it's home service only for at least six months. Then we'll have you along again."

Michael's heart leapt. Six months in England! He could hardly believe it.

"Disappointed?" the doctor asked dryly.

"I think I can bear it," Michael said.

"You've earnt your respite. I wish I could give it to all the men who pass through my hands, but I have to send most of 'em back out there, like so many pitchers going to the well."

Michael went home to enjoy the last few days of his leave and await his posting.

"I'm so relieved," his mother said. "Perhaps it will all be over soon, before you're ready for foreign service."

"Perhaps it will. Who knows?"

That was November, 1915. The war must end sooner or later. Why not look on the bright side?

The new year came in, bringing a new determination. 1916! There was a certain sound about it. Great things were expected from the start, and people in Britain were pulling themselves together again, preparing for a new effort.

Michael was now at Yelmingham, attached to the new Tenth Battalion. He was lecturing recruits on trench warfare.

Tom, in training at Capleton Wick, had a weekend pass every third or fourth week, and the family at Cobbs grew used to seeing him in khaki. Dicky still jeered at his skinny legs, bound tight in puttees, but Great-grumpa Tewke thought him much improved.

"They've smartened you up, boy. They've made you walk straight instead of lolling about like a ploughboy.

There's something to be said for discipline."

Early in April, Tom was at home for the last time, on twenty-four hours' draft leave. There were three other Huntlip boys due to go, and the four were given a noisy send-off at The Rose and Crown. Tilly Preston hung on Tom's arm almost all the evening and her father for once said nothing about it. The family, too, gave him a send-off, drinking his health in a bottle of Beth's strong coltsfoot wine, and presenting him with a pocket-bible.

"Are you sure you don't know where you're going?"

"No, they ent told us, but the chaps think it's France.'

"Well, wherever it is," granna said, "always take care that you air your clothes."

Later that evening, Tom was missing from the family party. Betony went out to the fold, where the cobbles were frosty underfoot, and saw a light in the old woodshed. Tom kept his ferrets in a hutch there, and when she went in, he had the two of them in his arms. His stub of candle stood in the draught, so that his face was lit and unlit ceaselessly, cheekbones and jawbones sharply outlined, deep dark eyes now seen, now unseen, as the flame leapt and flickered, trying to pull itself free of the wick.

"Will you look after my ferrets for me?"

"Why me, for mercy's sake?"

"The boys'd forget. They're not keen on ferrets."

"I'm not keen myself. Nasty smelly things. But yes, I'll look after them, that's a promise."

It surprised her that he should entrust this duty to her. He had never asked a favour in his life before. It pleased her, too, and she stroked the ferrets in his arms.

"I suppose you think you're going on an outing?"

"Ah, that's right, a regular dido."

"Or out poaching with old Charley Bailey."

"I know what it's like. I read the papers."

"You'll write to us, won't you, and tell us how you're getting on?"

"I ent much of a hand at letters."

"Well, I'll write to you," Betony said, "and that's the second promise I've made."

Tom merely shrugged. He was feeling a wart behind Nipper's ear. It might be serious and need a spot of something on it. He showed it to Betony and made her feel it, telling her what she must do about it if it got worse while he was away.

Out there in France, in the trenches, however, letters were precious and were read over and over again. They were kept until they wore through at the folds and even then they were sometimes mended. All except the most intimate letters were passed round and shared, and Betony's letters were great favourites, being full of things that made the men laugh. And because she addressed them to "Private Thos. Maddox" Tom was newly christened "Toss".

"We can't call you Tom," said Pecker Danson. "We're all Tommies out here!"

"What's she like, this Bet of yours? – Is she well-built?" asked Big Glover. "I like 'em well-built, with some shape about them. Fair, did you say, and nice-looking? Soft and sweet and gentle, is she?"

"No," Tom said, and the thought brought a faint smile to his lips.

"Whatya mean, no?"

"I wouldn't call her sweet and gentle."

"Are you saying she's a Tartar?"

"Well, a bit on the bossy side, you know."

"We might've known there was snags in it somewhere.

God preserve us from bossy women!"

But their disappointment did not last long. They would have nothing said against Betony. They had made her their mascot.

"It's a good thing sometimes, being bossy," said Bob Newers. "I wish we had her out here with us. She might get the rations up on time."

"Ask Bet if she'll marry me when I get back to Blighty, will you?" said Big Glover. "Say I'm six-foot-four and handsome with it. Don't mention the mole on my left elbow. I'd sooner keep it as a surprise."

"She's got a chap already," said Danson. "An officer in the Second Battalion. That's right, ent it, Toss? Name of Andrews?"

"Ah, that's right," Tom said.

"Sod hell and damn!" said Big Glover. "The officers get all the luck."

"Stands to reason," said Rufus Smith. "Bet ent like Toss. She's educated. You can tell by the way she writes her letters."

"It makes me laugh whenever I think of it," Pecker Danson said, choking. "What she said last time, about the girls at Coventry writing messages on the shells. It makes me wish I was an artillery man. I might've learnt a thing or two."

Rain was falling steadily. The trenches fell in as fast as the men worked to repair them. They stood to the knees in icy water, filling sandbags with the chalky mud.

"Why don't you never gamble, Toss? Why don't you never cuss and swear?"

"He don't need to, Pecker old son, 'cos you do enough for him and you both."

"He ent hardly human, the way he never grumbles nor

nothing. Don't you feel the cold and wet, Toss, the same as all us other chaps?"

"I try not to think about it," Tom said.

Somehow he was able to shut out the cold teeming rain and the tiredness. He was able to shut himself up inside, with his own thoughts, while his body moved automatically and his arms went on working. Yet when they asked what these thoughts were, he could never tell them.

"The same as yours, I suppose," he said.

"You're a dirty little tyke, then, if you think the same thoughts as the rest of us."

After their spell at Hébuterne, which Danson said was to get them used to shellfire, they marched to billets at Beauquesne. The weather improved. They had ten days of intensive training, mostly in sunshine.

"Why bayonet practice?" Glover said, during a respite. "Are we running out of bullets?"

"I saw a general this morning," said Ritchie, "the first I've seen since coming over."

"You didn't see the C.-in-C.?"

"I wouldn't know him from Adam, would I, except that he'd be wearing khaki?"

"Who *is* C.-in-C.?" asked Pecker Danson.

"Blowed if I know. Does anyone else?"

"Charlie Chaplin," Glover said.

"Mrs Pankhurst," said Rufus Smith.

"Angus Jock Maconochie."

"Alexander's Ragtime Band."

"Here, sarge!" said Bob Newers, stopping Sergeant Grimes as he came by. "Who commands the B.E.F.?"

"I do!" said Grimes. "And next after me, General Sir Douglas Haig."

"Haig," said Newers. "Any whisky coming our way?"

The sergeant fixed him with a pitying eye.

"D'you mean to tell me you didn't know the name of the C.-in-C.? You're ignorant, Newers, that's what you are."

"I am," agreed Newers, nodding sadly. "I'm that bloody ignorant they'll give me three stripes if I ent careful."

"Enough of that!" Grimes said, without rancour. "Too much sauce and I'll make you caper."

Not all the instructors were like Grimes. Sergeant Townchurch, for instance, was out of a different mould entirely. He liked to pick on weaker men and humble them before the others, and one such was a Welshman named Evans, a small thin man with sunken chest who had trouble with his breathing: a man, Newers said, who should never have been in the Army at all.

"Evans?" said Townchurch, during a mock attack one morning. "A Welshman and a miner, eh? In other words, a bloody slacker! We've heard about your lot, going on strike for better pay while we sweat our guts out fighting the Huns!"

Evans said nothing. His eyes were glazed and his skin looked like putty. He was almost choking, for Townchurch had run him about at the double, weighed down by pack, rifle, entrenching tool, and two canvas buckets full of grenades.

"How come you're in the Three Counties? Won't they take slackers in the Royal Welsh? Or even in the South Wales Borderers?"

"Leave him alone," Tom said. He was standing next to Evans and could hear how the man struggled for breath. "If he was a slacker he wouldn't be here."

Townchurch came and stood before Tom. He looked him over from head to foot.

"Are you another bloody Welshman? No? Perhaps not.

A gipsy, then? It's what you look like. And what, might I ask, is your sodding name? Maddox. Right. Be sure I'll remember."

So Tom and Evans became his victims. Luckily their stay at Beauquesne was brief. The party in training broke up, and the Sixth Battalion went into the line, taking over trenches at Mary Redan. Evans was now in C Company, in the same platoon as Tom and Newers, and by a strange unlucky chance, when their sergeant was injured by shrapnel, his place was taken by Sergeant Townchurch.

Tom's letters home were few and far-between, and, although written with immense labour, were never more than half a page long. "I am well. I got your parcel. How are Nipper and Slip and the workshop?" There was not much to say. The censor would only cut it out. So he wrote about the yellowhammer, heard so often in the hedgerows, saying A *little bit of bread and no chee-eeese*, just the same as it did in England. And he pressed speedwell flowers and herb robert between the folded sheet of paper. It astonished him daily that the same flowers grew in Picardy as grew in the fields and lanes at home.

"Things can't be too bad over there," Jesse said to Betony, "if young Tom's got time to gather flowers."

In England, now, the May was out and the wild June roses would soon be coming. The weather was good. Hay harvest had started at Anster and in the evenings Jesse and his sons were out in the fields, helping Janie and her husband Martin with the haymaking. William had now had his eighteenth birthday. Jesse was rather worried about him.

"Won't you get into trouble, boy, stopping at home now conscription's come in?"

"It's no odds to me. I still ent going."

"If William was to work on the farm full-time he might be exempt," Janie said.

"I don't care to be exempt – I just ent going," William said. "I didn't start this damned war so why should I down tools and go fighting in it?"

"Yes, but suppose they put you in gaol, boy?"

"They'll tarnal well have to catch me first!"

One day soon after, William and Roger were delivering ladders at a shop in Chepsworth. Roger disappeared for a little while and returned triumphant.

"I've been along to the recruiting centre. They took me this time. No questions asked."

"Are you gone in the head, you stupid fool? You've got no right! You're still under age."

"If I look eighteen then I'm good enough to be eighteen. I'm a lot stronger than some of the chaps I seen there today."

"I'm going down there to get your name took off their list!"

"If you do that," Roger said, "I'll run away south and join up there."

William saw that Roger meant it. He stood for a moment in a quivering rage. Then, suddenly, he was calm.

"All right," he said, "if one of us goes, we're both going."

"But you don't want to!" Roger said.

"I ent letting you go by yourself. A kid like you needs looking after. Besides, what'd I look like, do you think, with my younger brother gone and not me?"

So William and Roger joined together, and together confronted their parents at home.

"Don't worry, mother," William said. "I'll take care of Roger for you and I'll make certain-sure we don't get parted."

Within a month, they were in camp at Porthcowan, training with the Royal Artillery.

"It's not a bad life, considering," William wrote in a letter home. "In fact I reckon it suits me fine." And at the end, in a casual postscript, "I came out top in the ranging tests yesterday morning. The instructor says I'm a born gunner. I might put in for a stripe directly if everything goes according to plan."

Being William, now that he had become a soldier, he was determined to be a good one.

One Sunday in May Betony went up to London and spent the afternoon with Michael. He was looking better: stronger; more relaxed; yet when she told him so, his eyes darkened and a shiver went through him.

"I'm practically one hundred per cent, which means I'll soon be posted abroad."

"Are you sure?" she said. "Sure you're fit again, I mean."

"You just said so, yourself."

"I said you looked it, but I'm no doctor."

"No, well, we've got plenty of those, and they look me over now and then." Then he said abruptly: "How are things in munitions nowadays?"

"Frightening," she said. "I was in Birmingham yesterday, where they're making shells. The output is tremendous, and it's just the same wherever I go."

"That's the stuff! We might get somewhere if we've got things to throw."

"Is something coming?" Betony asked. "A big offensive?"

"Shush," he said, smiling. "How do I know you're not a spy?"

They were having tea at The Trocadero. He passed his cup across the table and watched her, secretly, as she filled it. There was something about the shape of her face, and her calm expression, that took him by surprise each time he saw her. She seemed so unconscious of herself; of the way she looked, the way she smiled. He had not been mistaken. He wanted her badly.

"Betony," he said, "do you have to go back to Chepsworth tonight?"

"Yes. I've got to be in Gridport at eight in the morning."

"Oh, that work of yours!" he said. "Couldn't you be late just once in a while?"

"No, Michael, I'm afraid not."

"Would you have stayed with me, had you been free to?"

"I'm never free for more than one day."

"You're just trying to spare my feelings. The answer is no, obviously." His gaze fell away and he stared at the sugar-bowl on the table. "I'd like you to know," he said slowly, doing his best to make light of the matter, "that I don't try it on with every young woman I meet."

"Do you meet so many, at Yelmingham?"

"You'd be surprised at the number of homes we officers are made welcome in. It's all meant to sustain our morale and there's a certain titled lady at Gaines who takes her task very seriously indeed."

"Are you trying to make me jealous?"

"Drink up," he said. "We ought to be moving if we're to catch that train."

He drove with her in a taxi to the station, and kept up the same light-hearted conversation till her train pulled out.

"Give my regards to your family," he said. "And don't forget to call on my mother. She's very anxious to get to know you."

Towards the end of May he was pronounced fit for

general service and ordered to rejoin his old battalion. He had forty-eight hours' leave and arrived at Chepsworth at eleven o'clock on Saturday morning. After lunching with his mother he walked out to Huntlip, but Betony was not at home. She had gone to Stafford on a special course and was not expected back until Sunday.

"What time on Sunday?" Michael asked.

"We don't rightly know," Jesse said. "She didn't go by train, you see. She went in a special motor bus, along with some very important people."

"Can I get her on the telephone?"

"Laws!" Jesse said, and his blue eyes opened very wide. "I shouldn't think so!"

So Michael left a note and returned home. His leave slipped away, pointless and empty, with his mother pretending not to notice his silence. She feared for him dreadfully, three times wounded yet returning once more to the battle zone, and she thought it wrong that the same young men should be called upon again and again for duty.

And yet at the same time she took pleasure in the sight of him in his uniform, with the three stars on each epaulette, and the three yellow wound-stripes on the sleeve. She took pride in him because he was her son, and because he had been among the first to answer his country's call for men. She forebore to reproach him for his silence. Her only complaint came at the end, when he refused to let her see him off at the station.

"Is it because of that girl?" she said. "The carpenter's daughter? Will she be there?"

"I don't even know if she got my message."

"If she hasn't, you'll be leaving all alone."

"I'll chance that," he said. "I'd much rather say good-bye here."

"Very well. It's as you wish. I will be praying for you, my son, and thinking of you constantly."

"Good," he said, and stooped to kiss her. "I may be too busy to pray for myself."

His train left at nine that evening. It was drawing out as Betony ran down onto the platform. She saw him at once and hurried forward, trying to take his outstretched hands as he leant towards her, out of the window. Their fingers were joined momentarily, – a brief exchange of warmth and softness – then the train gathered speed and tore them apart. Betony hurried along beside it, and Michael looked down at her with anguished eyes, his lips apart but no words escaping between them. He wanted to open the door and jump out. She was growing smaller all the time. She had come to a standstill.

"Michael, take care, take care!" she called, and he heard her even above the noise of the engine. "Come back safely! I'll be waiting for you!"

Staying in London overnight, he heard much talk of the coming offensive, even among the hotel staff. He mentioned the matter to Morris Tremearne, a fellow captain in the Second Battalion, also staying at The Kenilworth.

"Even the bootboy knows there's going to be a push. And now there are hints in the newspapers. We may as well send the Kaiser a telegram, stating the exact time and place!"

"Ah, that's the beauty of it!" said Tremearne. "The fuss we're making, the Germans'll never believe it's going to happen, don't you know!"

Michael turned away, catching the eye of his new batman. Lovell was discretion personified, but his glance was expressive.

Three days later they were with their battalion in Bethune. Michael was glad to see men he knew. Six months was a long time. He tried not to think of those who had vanished in the interim. He tried not to keep counting them.

"My God, you look smart!" Lightwood said. "I hardly knew you."

"Plenty of new chaps coming up, not all of them hopeless," Ashcott said. "This specimen here is a good man. – He's brought the latest gramophone records." And he waved a hand at the new young subaltern standing beside him. "His name's Spurrey. We call him Weed."

"What's the new C.O. like? Big man or small?"

"Big and fatherly and serious-minded. Has a proper respect for flesh and blood. Treats us almost as human beings."

"What's happening here at the moment?"

"We're up and down the canal mostly. We know it like the backs of our hands. Still, the big push is coming, so they say, and soon we'll be sleeping in the Kaiser's palace."

"Has he *got* a palace?" Spurrey asked.

"I'm damn sure he doesn't live in a dugout!"

"Four miles," Michael said, listening to the guns firing at Givenchy. "It sounds nearer."

"That's because you've been away. You've got used to the hush at home in England. What did you do with yourself, all that time? Pickle the onions?"

"It's mustard, not pickles," Michael said. He was used to jokes about the family business. "But I never go near the factory if I can help it."

"Mustard! Of course! That explains your famous coolness under fire. You've had it hot and strong all your life, what?"

"Besides, I haven't been in Chepsworth all the time."

"No, you've been manning a desk at Yelmingham, you lucky devil. Still, I expect you're glad to be back in the swim. It must be pretty dangerous in England now, with all those women driving the trams."

The next day, they were in the front line, in the Cuinchy sector. Michael had command of B Company, and his sergeant was a man named Bill Minching, a veteran of Mons and Festubert: quiet-spoken; steady-eyed; unupsettable, as Lightwood said. Almost half the men in the Company were new drafts but they looked on Michael as the newcomer.

A working party, under Minching, was out one night digging a new communication trench. Some rain fell and in the morning, when Michael inspected the finished work, there was water at the bottom of the trench. The men slopped about in it, thinking it nothing, but Michael gave orders that duckboards were to be laid down immediately.

"One of those, is he?" a private named Biddle was heard to say. "Believes in giving us plenty to do!"

Minching tapped him on the shoulder.

"You may have webbed feet, Biddle, but the rest of us are not so lucky."

Two men were killed by shellfire that day, and two were wounded. One of the wounded was Private Biddle. He was carried away with a deep jagged gash spouting blood from breast-bone to navel, and, passing Minching, he spoke weakly.

"Seems I'm a goner, don't it, sarge?"

"Oh no you're not!" Minching said. "You'll just be laid up for a bit, that's all. You've got a Blighty one. – Ent that the answer to your prayers?"

Biddle believed him. New hope came into his eyes. He lay back smiling.

"Carry on, my good men," he said to the bearers, "the surgeons are waiting."

"Will he live?" Michael asked Minching later.

"I don't know, sir, but faith can work wonders, so they say."

One afternoon, during an off-duty period in Annequin, a young subaltern, exploring the ruins of a bakery, set off an old enemy shell that had lain there, rusting, for over a year. He was blown to pieces.

"It's a bad place, this," Spurrey said to Lightwood at

mess that evening. "I don't like it. It gives me the creeps."

He was nineteen and had come out in April with his friends Hapton, Challoner, and Wyatt. All three friends were now dead. Wyatt was the man killed by the old "sleeping" shell.

"Don't like La Bassée?" said Hunter-Haynes, as though offended. "You surely don't mean it!"

"How about a stroll down to the brickstacks?" Ashcott said, patting Spurrey's shoulder. "Plenty of souvenirs to be had there . . . such as a bullet in the head."

"You should look on the dark side, young Weed," said Spencer, "then every day is a kind of bonus."

"Blessed are the meek, for they shall inherit the earth," said Lightwood, "though I must say the will is a hell of a long time in probate."

"You're quiet, Andrews," Ashcott remarked.

"He's got inside knowledge, I bet," Lightwood said. "How do you do it, Andrews, old man? Have you got the colonel's ear?"

"I've got Minching's ear. He's good at sorting out the rumours."

"And what does the omniscient Minching predict?"

"A move southwards in the near future."

"Nothing more specific than that?"

"I'm afraid not."

"Ah, well," Lightwood said. "I doubt if Staff themselves know very much more. I don't suppose they've stuck a pin in the map yet."

After their tour of duty in the trenches, they returned to Bethune and had a fortnight's training there, mostly mock battles. They now knew, officially, that the great offensive had begun, thirty miles southwards, on the Somme.

"Shall we be in it?" Spurrey asked.

"Up to our necks," Ashcott said, "but not yet, I hope."

"Why not yet?"

"There's a marvellous girl living near the soapworks, and I mean to have her, that's why."

"You and whose army?" Lightwood murmured.

On July the eighth, after dark, the battalion entrained at Lillers station and travelled southwards through the night. Early next morning they arrived at Saleux, and from there they marched nine miles to St Sauveur.

After the coal-pits and slag-heaps of Artois, Picardy was lovely indeed: a district as yet hardly touched by war: a country of orchards and big sweeping fields full of green standing corn, where poppies flared along the roadsides, and the air smelt sweet and fresh and clean.

At every farmhouse, every hamlet, people turned out and watched from their doors. A very old man bowed gravely, straightened and gave a military salute. An old woman wept into her apron. Children ran beside the soldiers.

"Tommee! Tommee! Soldats anglais!"

"Napoo lay boutons!" the soldiers said, as many small hands plucked at their tunics.

"Napoo lay badges!"

"Napoo nothing! Allay bizonc!"

"Après la guerre finee. Maybee. Ah, and viva to you, too, you cheeky monkey!"

But the men were tired. They grew more silent with each mile that passed. The day was a hot one and they marched in a cloud of thick white dust that dried out their mouths and gave them a terrible raging thirst. So at St Sauveur they stopped for rest, drink, and food, before pressing on another eight miles towards the banks of the River Ancre.

They came at last to Vecquemont, a glimmer of lights

in the dusk now falling, and here they stayed, the men flopping down beside the road while the officers went to arrange billets. The people of Vecquemont were not best pleased. They stood about, blank-faced, unmoving. Yet when a battalion of the Glasgow Highlanders marched through half an hour later, with the pipes playing, they were given a rousing cheer.

"That's what we're here for," one of their officers said to Michael. "The Scots turn-out is good for morale. It gives the civilians a bit of a boost. And you English fellows, too, of course."

"Cocky bastards," Lightwood said, as the Highlander turned and swaggered away. "Strutting about in their fancy dress!"

All next day they remained at Vecquemont, giving the men a chance to recover from their seventeen-mile march and make themselves ready. They left early the following morning, and, determined not to be outdone by the Glasgows, marched smartly out of the village.

"We may not have a howling cat to lead us," Sergeant Minching said to his men, "but there's nothing wrong with the way we march."

"Good old Three Counties!" a voice shouted from the ranks. "Especially Leominster!"

At Morlancourt, eight miles westwards, they rested again for twenty-four hours, and the men handed in unwanted equipment, including greatcoats. They were now within close sound of the guns. No civilians were to be seen. The villages here had all been evacuated some time before. After dark on the twelfth, they marched three miles to Becordel, close to the old front line of 1914. There they met up with other battalions, and the whole brigade went into camp.

In the morning, Michael rode up with the other company commanders to a ridge called Calou, from whence they could see the new battle zone, a mile or so distant, under bombardment by British artillery. The noise was deafening. The enemy line danced and quivered under the smoke. The air was never still for a moment.

"I feel almost sorry for poor old Fritz," a man named Logan said to Michael. "We've been pounding him for three weeks. I shouldn't think he could stand much more. It should be a walkover, when we attack."

As they rode back again, down onto the fields where the whole brigade lay in bivouac, Michael felt an upsurge of hope. There were two thousand men mustered below, and everywhere else along the line the concentration of troops was enormous. Surely the offensive must carry the war? Official communiqués were encouraging. They told of successes further south. And yet, somehow, sneaking in under the official news, there were rumours that spoke of bad setbacks everywhere; of terrible losses; of whole divisions cut to pieces on the enemy wire. How did the rumours get about? he wondered. Were they, as the colonel stated, merely the work of German spies?

That night was cold, and because the encampment was hidden from the enemy by two or three ridges of high ground, the men were allowed to light fires. They flickered up everywhere, small ghosts of fires in the damp darkness, each with its close-packed ring of men. Some groups told stories. Some sang songs. From a few came the sound of a mouth-organ playing. And, going about from group to group, Colonel Nannet in his British warm, with his collar up and his cap pulled well down, stopped to exchange a word or two with the men of his battalion.

Michael, with the other officers of his company, stood

at the opening of their tent. Lightwood was smoking a large cigar. The scent of it wafted on the damp air.

"There goes the old man, dishing out his eve-of-action comfort."

" 'A little touch of· Harry in the night,' " said Ashcott. " 'Oh, God of Battles, steel my soldiers' hearts!' "

"Something the poor devils could well do without," said Lightwood. "Still, he's not a bad old cock, really."

The colonel retired to his quarters at last. B Company officers retired to theirs. Michael sat looking towards the west, where gun flashes lit the cloudy sky, beyond the contours of Calou Ridge. Underneath, in the darkness, the camp fires still flickered, kept alive assiduously with twigs and leaves and bits of grass. Some of the men were still singing.

> "When this lousy war is over,
> Oh, how happy I shall be!
> I will tell the sergeant-major
> Just how much he means to me . . ."

From first light onwards, the Allied bombardment was intensified, all along the enemy lines. It was Bastille Day and the French guns were particularly active. At ten-thirty, the sun was already very warm, shining down on the columns of men marching along the Fricourt road.

They were among the trenches again; on ground that covered, all too shallowly in places, the dead of two years' warfare. All along the old front line, the bodies of those killed in more recent fighting still lay about, and the stench of corruption was everywhere. Sometimes these bodies appeared to heave, because of the flies seething upon them, and because of the movement of scavenging rats.

At the village of Fricourt, now in ruins, the battalion rested for several hours, awaiting orders. They got food and drink from a field kitchen, but every mouthful tasted of lyddite from the batteries of guns firing nearby. Such news as came was so far good. The enemy line was reported broken and the Germans were said to be giving way. Our Indian cavalry had been in action and were at this moment riding the enemy into the ground. Certainly a great many prisoners had been taken. Whole columns of them kept coming down, eyes staring out of blackened faces; exhausted, shrunken, scarcely able to lift their feet.

From Fricourt the battalion marched to the village of Mametz, now no more than a heap of rubble. Among the ruins stood a column of motor ambulance cars, and there were crowds of British wounded awaiting attention at the medical aid post. They seemed cheerful and said the day was going well.

"We've cleared the way for you up there. You've got nothing to do but go round with the mop."

"Jerry is running for all he's worth."

"Bazentin is in our hands . . ."

"Mametz Wood is in our hands . . ."

But one man, with bandaged head, sitting smoking a cigarette, gave a cynical laugh.

"Dead hands, mostly, you'll find," he said.

Leaving Mametz, the battalion moved down a sunken road, then forked off into a valley. On their right rose a long escarpment. On their left the ground sloped, open, all the way up to Mametz Wood. The noise of the bombardment was almost more than they could bear, for, all across the open area, batteries of British field-guns kept up an incessant fire, and beyond the escarpment were the French seventy-fives. The shriek of shells overhead never stopped, for the British heavies were also at work, some way behind.

The rough road was strewn with dead. Michael tried not to look too closely, for it seemed to him there were many more khaki-clad bodies than field-grey, and now the number of walking-wounded had grown to a never-ending stream. Silent men, trudging past as though indifferent; mere shadows of men, hollow-eyed, the same as the Germans; men whose last remaining strength was needed to carry them along the road.

"What lot are you?" Minching asked, as one group passed.

"Manchesters," came the brief answer.

"What lot are you?" he asked another.

"South Staffords – what there is left of us!" a man said, snarling.

Everywhere along the valley lay the carcasses of dead horses, their heads thrown back, their legs in the air. Some were transport horses, and their smashed limbers lay nearby; but some were cavalry horses with braided saddles and gleaming stirrups, and their riders lay only God knew where.

Down the road now came wounded troopers of an Indian regiment, some leading their terrified mounts, others slumped as though dead in their saddles. One elderly Sikh, having watched his wounded horse collapse, was on his knees beside it, and the tears were running down his bearded face. His lips moved as though in prayer. His hands made a little secret sign. He took his revolver from the saddle and shot the dying horse in the head. He knelt, watching, until it was still. Then he turned the revolver on himself and fell across the horse's body.

"Christ!" said a soldier to his mate. "Did you see that?"

"No one saw nothing!" shouted a sergeant, determined to keep the column moving. "Close up, there, Number One Platoon! Keep your dressing by the left!"

The men marched on along the valley, passing between the two flanking storms of the great bombardment, under a sky that shrieked and sizzled with the flying shells.

Logan came up and rode with Michael a little way. He had been talking to a wounded officer of the South Staffords.

"He says he's been here since the big push started. A whole fortnight in the front line. No wonder they all look such wrecks, is it?"

"What's the name of this place, did he say?"

"Seems they call it Happy Valley."

They came out into the open, among fields of tobacco and turnips and corn, the crops all trodden into the ground. It was now seven o'clock in the evening, and the battalion dug itself in for the night, close beside a wood known, from its shape, as Flatiron Copse. Enemy shells were falling all the time. Eight men were killed before the shelter-trenches were dug. Another six were badly wounded.

Nobody slept. The shelling was too close for that. It was also very cold, and the men, having left their greatcoats at Morlancourt, lay huddled close together for warmth, trying to make the most of their groundsheets. Dawn, when it came, brought some relief, and there was breakfast of a sort, with hot sweet tea and a tot of rum.

The battalion fell in, and the whole brigade moved off eastwards in a thick white mist, forward into the battle area. The ground was broken and badly cratered, littered with debris and dead bodies. There were wounded men, too, who had lain out all night and who now reached up with pleading arms as the marching columns tramped by. One or two soldiers, not yet hardened, stepped out of line, reaching for their water-bottles, but were herded back by a watchful N.C.O.

"Leave that to the stretcher-parties! You'll need them water-bottles yourselves directly!"

The brigade formed up in a valley south of High Wood. The Second Three Counties were in reserve. They held a position at Trivet Spur, beside a rough track known as Windy Lane. The Second Worcestershire were nearby.

A mile to the north, the Glasgows and the Queen's formed the front line, and some of the Glasgows had already been in action during the night, in High Wood itself. Now they were attacking the main Switch Line, where the Germans, contrary to earlier reports, were as strong as ever. High Wood was thought to be safe, but as the Glasgows advanced across the open, they were cut down by enemy machine-guns firing from among the trees.

Michael, watching through his field-glasses, could see it all: the double lines of kilted figures advancing up the open slope; the glint of a bayonet here and there; and then the terrible thinning-out as the Maxims raked them from front and rear. He could see the depleted line pressing onwards, with men of the King's and the First Queen's going up to fill the gaps; could see the line faltering again, the bodies thick in the green corn; and now the live men were falling, too, crawling to the cover of shell-scrapes and craters. He saw the Worcesters go up to help: two companies into the wood; two attacking across the open; and he saw the pitiful remnants returning, dragging themselves back to their line.

"What do you think, sir?" Logan was saying to the colonel. "Shall we be sent up to help, d'you suppose?"

Michael put down his glasses and turned a little, waiting for the answer, which was slow in coming. The colonel's face was deep-lined, and his eyes were full of angry tears.

"Is that what you want? – To go the same way as those poor devils out there?" But he quickly relented. "I'm sorry, Logan. I didn't mean to snap your head off. I've no idea what our orders will be. All I know is that it's madness attacking across that space while Fritz still holds that bloody wood. I'm sending along to Brigade H.Q. to tell them so."

At twelve noon, for half an hour, there was another bombardment by British guns, but it short-ranged and the shells fell on what was left of the Glasgows' own forward line. German shells were exploding in the southern half of the wood, driving out the Worcesters and the South Staffords, many of whom were mown down by their own machine-guns before they were able to make themselves known.

At four o'clock in the afternoon, two companies of the Second Three Counties were sent up into the wood: C Company under Logan and D Company under Tremearne: roughly two hundred men in all. The other two companies remained in their trenches, with enemy shells falling close, and at half-past-four orders came for them to advance up the open hillside.

Colonel Nannet delayed. He wanted to be sure the wood was safe. He sent up a runner, who failed to return, and was about to send another when a message arrived from Brigade H.Q.: "High Wood is ours. Proceed as ordered." So, at six o'clock exactly, A Company under Ashcott and B Company under Michael climbed out into the open and began advancing up the slope towards the enemy Switch Line.

The hillside was strewn with the dead and dying, the ground was broken everywhere, and black smoke drifted from left to right as enemy shelling intensified. Visibility was bad, and the slope grew steeper all the time, so that progress was slow, but once up and over the brow, the smoke lessened and it was like coming out into a brighter light again.

Michael turned/ his head, first right, then left, to see how many of his men had gone, falling, unseen, behind the smoke. It seemed to him the line was still strong, the forward movement still determined, and he caught a glimpse of his sergeant's face, calm, intent, open-eyed, under the brim of his steel helmet.

Towards the top of the first slope, crossing a road, Michael turned aside to avoid a deep crater, and as he did so, three men with rifles rose from its shelter and fell in behind him: kilted men of the Highland regiment: survivors of the earlier attack.

"We're wi' ye, laddie! And whoever you are you're doing fine!"

They were out past the corner of the wood now, moving across the wider space, inside the range of the worst shelling, though shrapnel was bursting overhead. A Company was on the right, B Company on the left, the two lines straggling but still moving forward in good order. The ground had flattened out again. The enemy line was only two hundred yards away.

But now, suddenly, from the northernmost boundary of the wood, came a burst of machine-gun and rifle fire, and Michael, glancing back, saw his three Highlanders fall to the ground. Over on his right, A Company had received the first and the worst of the fire, and nearly half its men had fallen. The remainder struggled on, only to meet the same destructive fire from in front, as they tried to reach the enemy line. The task was beyond them and the few men remaining faltered badly, seeking shelter instinctively behind B Company, still advancing. Only Ashcott kept to the front, and, running close beside Michael, sobbed out, swearing:

"The liars said the wood was ours! Why do they tell such lies, the bastards?"

Then, abruptly, he was no longer there. His body was being trampled underfoot. His place beside Michael was taken by Gates. The noise of the Maxims was very loud. Their fire was withering, murderous, keen. Michael felt himself blinking, averting his face as though in a hailstorm, and all the time as he ran forward he felt he was pushing through a great bead curtain of spent bullets. He had the strange fancy that this bead curtain was his protection: that a deadly bullet would not get through: that all he had to do was to keep pushing forward.

Gates was hit and fell with a terrible high-pitched scream. The man who took his place was sobbing and swearing, snorting for breath through wide-open mouth and wide-stretched nostrils. He was hit in the chest and fell headlong, and his rifle was thrown between Michael's feet, causing him to stumble.

Now, whenever he glanced to left or right, there were great gaps all along the line; gaps that were no longer filling up; gaps that grew bigger as he looked. He pressed on, leaping over a huddle of corpses, and as he did so he was hit in the thigh. He fell among the dead bodies.

Twenty yards away lay a crater. He began crawling on his stomach towards it. A man looked over the edge and saw him. It was Alan Spurrey, his new young subaltern, bare-headed, having lost his helmet. Spurrey was wounded in both feet, but he crawled from the crater and wriggled forward, arms outstretched to help Michael.

"Get your head down!" Michael shouted. "Get down and get back, you bloody fool!"

A machine-gun rattled, and Michael pressed his face to the ground. Bullets struck the turf beside him and ripped on in a curving line. When he looked up again, Spurrey was dead, his head shattered. Michael crawled on into the crater.

It was not a bad wound: the bullet had entered the fleshiest part of the right thigh and had passed out behind; but the bleeding was heavy and soon soaked the dressing, so he used his tie as a tourniquet.

When he looked out over the edge, there was no advancing line to be seen, for those few men who were left alive had sought shelter in the broken ground. He could see some of them nearby, crawling on their stomachs, and after a while two men joined him in the crater, one of them wounded in the chest.

The wounded man, Aston, was in a bad way. Michael helped the other, a corporal named Darby, to dress the wound. He gave him a drink from his water-bottle.

"What a mess it all is!" Darby exclaimed. "What a stinking awful bloody mess!" He looked at Michael with bitter defiance. "We never stood a chance of reaching the Germans. Neither us nor the other poor sods this morning. Surely the brasshats should've known?"

"They know now," Michael said.

"If I get back safe I swear I'll get some bloody rednosed brigadier and stick him through with my bloody bayonet!"

"Is Aston your particular friend?"

"He's my brother-in-law. He married my sister before coming out. And what'll *she* say when she hears he's hurted?"

"He may be all right. We must get him back as soon as we can."

"What a hope!" Darby said. "What a bloody flaming hope!"

A burst of machine-gun fire shut him up. He crouched low in the loose earth. Michael was wondering what had drawn the fire when a man rolled over the edge of the crater and lay down beside him. It was Sergeant Minching.

"You all right, sir? I see you're hit."

"Not too badly, though I've bled like a pig. It's Aston here who's in trouble."

Aston was only barely conscious. Minching bent over him, listening to his heartbeats and his breathing. Darby watched him.

"Any hope, sarge?"

"There's always hope," Minching said. "The bullet's missed his lungs, I would say, but we'll have to be careful how we move him. Might be better to leave him here – let Jerry find him and patch him up."

"Hell, no!" Darby said.

"He'd get attention that much sooner."

"What sort of attention, though, by God?"

"The Jerries aren't monsters. They'd take care of him all right."

"I'm getting him back," Darby said, "even if I have to do it by myself."

"All right, we'll do it between us, don't worry, as soon as it's dark enough to move." Minching turned towards Michael. "What about you, sir? Can you walk?"

"If not, I can always crawl."

A shrapnel shell burst in the air nearby, and they pressed their faces into the earth, while the balls blasted the crater's edge. When Michael looked up, the smoke was drifting overhead. He called to Minching, who was looking out.

"What's going on out there? Can you see?"

"I can see a bunch of our men, sir, falling back down the side of the wood. They're making a dash for it, back to the line."

"No sign of their rallying?"

"There's nothing much left to rally, sir. A couple of dozen at the most."

"What happened to our Lewis-gun sections?"

"Copped it, sir, quite early on. A shell got one of 'em – Mr Rail's – and the gun was useless. I know it was 'cos I went to see. The other lot stopped at the corner of the wood, trying to get that bloody Maxim. They were cut down in seconds. They never even got their gun into action."

A rifle cracked from the German line, and a bullet struck the edge of the crater. Minching wriggled back at once.

"The colonel was killed, sir, did you know? So were Mr Lightwood and Mr Haynes."

"And Mr Spencer?"

"Badly wounded in the head. A Company's worse off than us. I reckon they're pretty well wiped clean out."

Michael turned away and closed his eyes.

Just before darkfall, Minching opened their iron rations. They ate corned beef and hard biscuit. Aston, though conscious, could eat nothing. He asked for water all the time. Darby kept giving him his own bottle.

"Hang on, Fred, it won't be long now. We'll get you

back, don't worry. But for God's sake remember to keep mum or we'll have Jerry down on us as sure as fate."

As evening came on, artillery fire was renewed on both sides, and the air above was filled again with the shrieking of shells; but after a while, as night fell, it eased off and became intermittent; and between the two flashing sky-lines, darkness settled along the ground.

"Now," Minching said. "It's time we started."

He and Darby hoisted Aston till he hung with an arm round each man's neck. Aston gave a cry but choked it back quickly, sucking his breath between clenched teeth.

"Easy does it," Minching muttered. "Hold on, my lad, and bite on the bullet. It's a long way to Tipperary."

He turned his face towards Michael, who lay trying to bend his knee.

"You coming, sir?"

"No, not yet. Better for you to go ahead."

"Supposing you was to need help?"

"Don't fuss, man! Just get a move on and do as I say."

"Very well, sir, but don't dilly-dally too long – the Jerry patrols'll be out soon."

"I know that. I'm not a fool."

"All right, sir, and good luck."

"Good luck, Minching," Michael said, and watched as the three men stumbled over the edge, vanishing into the misty darkness.

He crawled to the rim and lay listening. All around in the darkness, wounded men groaned and whimpered, and sometimes he heard slithering noises as somebody crawled along the ground, inching his way down the slope. Sometimes he heard tortured breathing. Once he heard a man praying.

Half a mile below, shells were bursting in High Wood, great yellow flashes splintering the darkness between the trees, while, on the horizons, north and south, as the big guns answered each other, the sky flickered, pulsing whitely. Now and then a starshell rose, green-spiked, beautiful, a manmade meteor rising and sinking like a sigh. And every few minutes the bright Very flares blossomed overhead like Japanese flowers, spreading their light over all the earth.

Michael lay back again, looking up at the throbbing sky. He had lost much blood; he was weak and light-headed; a deathlike weariness numbed his limbs. Somewhere nearby he heard voices speaking in German, and heard the tread of booted feet. The first patrols were going out, picking their way among the dead and wounded. "Ach, Du liebe Güte, was fur ein wüstes Durcheinander!" a voice said, quietly but clearly. Then the voices and the footsteps went further away.

Michael knew he ought to move. His wound was not crippling; he could easily find the strength to crawl; and the doctors at Douvecourt would soon patch him up as good as new, so that he could fight again another day. But his will was paralysed, his soul inert, and his body obeyed its own dictates. So he stayed where he was in the shell-crater and waited for the Germans to come and take him prisoner.

Betony, receiving a letter from Mrs Andrews, went at once to King's Hill House. She was shown into the morning-room, which was full of sunshine and the scent of roses. Mrs Andrews sat straight-backed, her face impassive, but when she began talking of Michael, she broke down and wept and it was some time before she could continue. She felt ashamed, weeping in front of this carpenter's daughter, this girl of twenty whose own eyes were dry, whose manner was strangely matter-of-fact.

"I'm sorry, Miss Izzard, but I haven't yet got over the shock. I didn't expect you to come so soon."

"Have you heard from Michael himself?"

"Yes, but only one of those printed postcards. A letter is following, it said."

"Is he wounded badly?"

"The Red Cross people say not. But he's in a German hospital and I cannot believe they will treat him properly."

"I'm sure they will. The Red Cross are there to see that they do.

"I wish I could share your confidence, but we hear such terrible tales sometimes . . ."

"At least he's safe. That's the main thing."

"My son is a prisoner-of-war with the Germans. I find little in that to comfort me."

"But he *is* alive!" Betony said. "He *will* be coming back again, eventually, when it's all over. Surely that must comfort you?"

And she thought of the thousands of men who had died since the great offensive had begun, for, travelling about England as she did, visiting factories, she met grieving women everywhere and had lost count of all those whose menfolk lay dead on the Somme.

Mrs Andrews got up.

"I'm glad you're taking the news so calmly. I was afraid you might be distressed. I expect you young women are getting quite hardened, which is probably a blessing in its way."

"Is there an address where I can write to Michael?"

"Yes. Of course. I'll give it to you." Mrs Andrews went to her desk. "He'll be very glad to hear from you, I'm sure."

All through summer and on into autumn, fighting continued on the Somme. Pozières. Longueval. Delville

Wood. Morval. Le Transloy. Then, in November, it ground to a halt. A few miles of territory had been gained. 500,000 lives had been lost. The big push had failed. But the Germans, it was said, were demoralized by their own losses. It was bound to tell on them in the end. Meanwhile there was deadlock again; the two opposing armies dug themselves in; and winter advanced upon them both: the worst winter for twenty years.

"D'you think it's as cold as this at home, Woody?"

"Definitely. My missus wrote she was getting chilblains."

"We're practically strangers, my feet and me, not to mention other members."

"Anyone here called Winterbottom?"

"Hey, Toss, remember how hot it was at Monkey Britannia? I could almost wish myself back there now. Or Devil's Wood, say, when the trees was burning. I'd sooner've been burnt like poor old Glover and Verning and Kyte than froze to death by bloody inches."

"How can you talk like that?" asked Costrell, one of a new draft out from England. "As though it was all a huge joke?"

"It *is* a huge joke," said Danson. "A killing joke for some, it's true, and has a lot of the rest in stitches. But you new chaps don't understand."

Costrell was silent. He thought them callous, ghoulish, disgusting. He could never share their attitude. He was always aware of the frozen corpses lying out in no-man's-land, many of them visible from the front trenches, some quite close to the picket wire, only a few short yards away. And when Danson said, as he often did, "D'you reckon old Bill could do with a blanket?" or, "I could swear John Willie has turned hisself over since this morning," Costrell could not help shuddering.

"It's all right, son," Bob Newers said to him. "*They're* all right, the ones out there. *They* don't feel the bleeding cold, or hear the ruddy shells come over, or get told off for san fatigues. They're better off and they bloody well know it."

"Did you notice that subaltern smelling of scent?" said Pecker Danson.

"Poor sod," said Dave Rush. "He's probably plastered with anti-louse cream."

"Get away!" said Privitt, looking up from the letter he was writing. "Do officers have chats, then, the same as us?"

"Not the same, no. The chats they got is bigger and better, with pips on their shoulders and Sam Browne belts."

"What about Fritz? Has he got 'em too?"

"It's him that flaming well sends 'em over. He fires them in canisters, same as gas. It's the Kaiser's most successful weapon."

Privitt, going back to his letter, wrote for a moment or two in silence. He was having a bit of fun with the censor. He looked up again to read what he had written so far.

" 'Dear Brother Humphrey, Last Saturday night I slept with three French girls and their mother. The mother was best though not as good as the Friday before when I spent the night in a high-class establishment kept by a Chinese lady who used to run a laundry in Solihull.' There! That'll make 'em open their peepers! When the major reads that he'll be after me to know the address."

"It isn't true, is it, Privy?"

"Hah! Get away! All I've ever slept with is a woolly rabbit."

A shell came over and exploded, crump, behind the parados. The men ducked low, and a shower of hard-frozen clods fell upon them, bouncing off their steel helmets. Privitt sat up again, wiping the debris from his notepad.

"The way things are here, I shan't get much chance to graduate, neither!"

"The Lord be thanked for tin bowlers," said Pecker Danson, adjusting his helmet. "Or do I mean Lloyd George?"

"Get a move on there!" shouted Corporal Flinders, coming quickly round the traverse. "Clear that mess away, quick sharp, and no sweeping it under the carpet!"

The men got to work with entrenching tools, shovelling up the fallen earth and tossing it onto the broken parados. They filled new sandbags and repaired the gap.

"Entrenching tool," Costrell muttered. "Why can't they call a spade a spade?"

"I'm thinking of changing my name," said Privitt. "It's no joke, you know, being called Private Privitt, nor Privy neither, seeing the privies here ent all that private."

"Say that faster and you'll find yourself in the next camp concert."

"How many shells has he sent over this morning, Toss?"

"I dunno. I ent been counting."

"Seems quiet to me. Perhaps he's busy doing the crossword." Newers, on the firestep, sniffed the air. "He's got bacon for breakfast again this morning. Smoked, I reckon, the lucky sod."

The two lines at Brisle were certainly very close together, and there was a live-and-let-live policy there, so that rifle and machine-gun fire was only rarely exchanged, and that, as Corporal Flinders said, just as a sort of formality. No-man's-land was scarcely fifty yards across, and when some Tommy sneaked out and raised a notice there, saying *Trespassers Will Be Prosecuted,* the Germans, instead of blasting it to smithereens, merely pelted it with snowballs. Even the officers turned a blind eye to these unwarlike pastimes.

One freezing night, when the men were huddled in a dugout, warming themselves at a small brazier, Dave Rush got out his wheezy old mouth-organ and began playing popular tunes. The men sang, swaying together from side to side, for the singing and the movement kept them warm. And then, half way through *There's a long, long trail a-winding,* Burston, on sentry, suddenly pulled aside the curtain.

"Shut up and listen," he said to them, and when they obeyed him they heard the Germans finishing the song.

"Would you believe it!" Rush exclaimed. "They've got a nerve, pinching our songs. But I'll soon fix *them.* Just listen here."

He raised his mouth-organ to his lips and played the first verse of *God Save The King.* At the end he stopped and listened again, and across the way, in the German trenches, there was utter silence.

"That's foxed 'em!" he said. "They're not singing *that,* the saucy buggers!"

"No more ent we," said Pecker Danson, and, taking the brazier outside, swung it about till the charcoal glowed redly again. "The new moon is up," he said, returning. "Anyone got a franc to turn?"

The Germans now, recovering, were singing *Deutschland Uber Alles.* The Sixth Three Counties retaliated and noisily drowned the rival song.

> "Oh, the Kaiser fell in a box of eggs,
> Parleyvoo!
> The Kaiser fell in a box of eggs,
> Parleyvoo!

The Kaiser fell in a box of eggs
And all the yellow ran down his legs,
Inky-dinky-parleyvoo!"

There came a day when Sergeant Townchurch was with them again, after a month in hospital. No one knew what his illness had been, though rumour gave it as "a bout of German measles and a bad cough". He himself gave no explanation. He preferred to forget he had ever been ill. And he reasserted his authority by reporting Corporal Flinders, acting platoon sergeant during his absence, for letting the discipline run down.

One morning, after a heavy fall of snow, two excited German soldiers, fair-haired boys of about seventeen, climbed onto their parapet and began making a snowman there. Tom and Newers, looking through a loophole, watched with amusement as the snowman grew to lifelike proportions and was given a field-grey comforter and cap and a few bandoliers slung over his shoulder.

Sergeant Townchurch came along. He pushed between Newers, Tom, and Evans, and peered out at the two Germans dressing the snowman on their parapet. He unslung his rifle, put it to his shoulder, and took careful aim through the narrow loophole. Newers moved along the bay and apparently tripped on a loose bit of duckboard. He lurched against Townchurch and the shot went wide. The two German soldiers dived for cover.

"Clumsy swine! You done that on purpose! You got friends over there, have you?"

"Sorry, sarge. It's these loose slats. I'll go and get a hammer and nails before someone breaks his silly neck."

A few minutes later, an arm appeared above the German parapet, and a well-aimed grenade exploded inside the British trench. Then a second and a third.

Costrell and Rush retaliated. Six grenades were returned for three. The sector quietened down again. But Burston and Trigg had each lost a hand and Corporal Flinders had been blinded; and Dick Costrell, hearing this news, would have gone for Townchurch with a pick-axe if Tom and Newers had not restrained him.

Quite soon afterwards, the silence in the enemy lines became uncanny. Patrols going out after dark found the trenches deserted. The Germans had withdrawn, noiselessly, to the strongly fortified Hindenburg Line, ten miles or so behind their old trenches.

"Why not to Berlin while they was at it?" said Dave Rush.

"The Hindenburg Line," said Bob Newers. "Is that part of the Great Western?"

"That's right," said Danson. "Paddington, Oxford, Cardiff Docks, and all stations to Haverfordwest."

"If Jerry's gone we can maybe go home – I don't think!" said Dick Costrell.

Two days later they were relieved by the North Warwicks and went into billets at Doudelanville. When they returned to the line again, it was to take over newly dug trenches in the Vermand area.

The weather continued bitterly cold. Men who stood still for a few seconds found themselves frozen to the boards. They could scarcely bear the touch of their rifles, so cold was the metal in their hands, and they fired off round after round at nothing, to warm the barrels and prevent the bolts from freezing up.

But worse even than the cold was when the thaw came, and they lived always in a world of slush, wet through, waking or sleeping. A man named Thompson complained of trouble with his feet. They were badly swollen and had gone numb. He could not get his boots off to rub in the oil that might have brought him some relief.

"Move about a bit more!" Townchurch said. "Of course you'll get trench feet if you never shift yourself, idle bastard!"

Three days later, when their spell in the forward area ended, Thompson was quite unable to stand. He had to be carried out of the line, into the rest camp three miles behind, and there he went for a medical.

His boots were cut away and the feet were revealed, swollen and shapeless, the colour of raw meat putrefying, with the woollen socks darkly embedded, making a pattern in the rotten flesh. Thompson, watching, said not a word. He merely swallowed, making a noise. Then he looked away, into the distance, whistling tunelessly between his teeth.

The doctor took Newers on one side. He said Thompson would probably lose both feet.

"Why wasn't he sent before?"

"Sergeant Townchurch thought he was swinging the lead."

"I must have a word with your Sergeant Townchurch."

But the doctors at Vraignes were busy men. They worked a twenty-hour day. And when the battalion returned to the line, at Gricourt this time, Townchurch went on as he always had done.

"Evans! Maddox! Newers! Rush! I want you in a raiding party. The colonel has asked for a couple of Boche prisoners. It's up to us to try and oblige him."

"Why always Evans?" Newers asked.

"Why always *me*?" Townchurch retorted.

Townchurch himself was without fear. Rush said he meant to get a decoration. He had more than once been mentioned in dispatches, and was held in some regard by the C.O. Townchurch knew it. It was only his due. He worked hard and he had courage. He could do great things if only he were given the chance, and he told his fellow N.C.O.'s that he meant to make the Army his career. He wouldn't go back to being coachman at Capleton Castle. The gentry would never wipe their boots on him again. He was somebody now and his great ambition was to gain a commission in the field.

There was hard fighting again that spring. The British were following up the German withdrawal. They were pushing on towards St Quentin. The bombardment was heavy on both sides.

In the Gricourt sector, shells were falling with great accuracy, aligned exactly with the front line trenches for a length of fifty yards or so, reducing the earthworks to a mass of debris. The noise of the British guns answering was overwhelming. It was like living between volcanoes. And under the storm, human nerves were stretched and broken, human minds were dislocated.

Tom, in a hole scooped out of the trench-side, felt the earth would never stop shaking. He felt it would open and swallow him up. Opposite him was a man named Lambert, who crouched on the firestep with terrible tremors running through him, and who plucked with his fingers at his lower lip till blood splashed down onto his tunic.

Suddenly Lambert sprang to his feet and hauled himself over the parapet. Tom tried to catch him but was too late. Lambert was already through the wire, running towards the enemy, lobbing imaginary grenades as he went.

"Bloody guns!" he shrieked. "I'll soon shut you up! I'll shut you up once and for all!"

Tom was following, running like the wind, when

Lambert fell dead, a sniper's bullet through his forehead. Tom veered and doubled back. He leapt head first towards the trench and rolled over into safety. His left foot felt as though he had hit it with a heavy hammer. A bullet had taken the heel off his boot.

Sometimes, during a period out of the line, housed in a barn or ruined cowshed, a man might throw himself down in the straw and sleep for ten or twelve hours at a stretch. He slept through anything. The world could end for all he cared. The last trump could sound and he'd never hear it.

But in a day or two he would revive. Hot food eaten in safety; hot tea made with clean water; time to sit and smoke a cigarette; and perhaps after all the end of the world had better not come yet. A wash and a shave could make a new man of one who had thought himself played out. There were things to do. Pleasant things. And if he were lucky he could stroll in places where grass still grew and leaves were opening on the trees; where the air still smelt wholesome; and where, from fields of green corn, larks flew up and hung singing in the blue sky.

"It's funny," Tom said, "how many things is just the same as they are at home."

On the farm where they were billeted, there was an orchard of apple trees, and the blossoms were just beginning to open. Tom sat on the ground and watched the swallows building in the eaves of the ruined farmhouse. Some chickens were pecking about in the grass, and a little way off, sitting on a hencoop, a solemn-faced girl of seven or eight was keeping guard over them.

The house was no more than a broken husk, but the elderly farmer lived there still, with his family of women-folk and small children. The younger men were away fighting. The old man was up on the roof, nailing canvas over the beams, a short clay pipe between his teeth, a straw hat on the back of his head. The women were working in the fields. One was ploughing with a team of cows.

Tom got up and walked towards the child on the hencoop. She looked at him with frowning eyes.

"You needn't worry. I shan't steal your hens."

"Comment?"

"Chickens," he said, and pointed to them. "I shan't steal them. Nor the eggs neither."

"Comment?"

"I was watching the swallows, that's all, and looking at the blossoms on the trees. I reckon you'll have a nice crop of apples, so long as there ent no nasty late frosts."

The child said nothing. She did not understand him. She sat with her hands tucked into her apron and frowned at him harder than ever.

"Look at this here," he said to her, and took a snapshot from his pocket. It had come with a letter from Betony and it showed her mother in the orchard at Cobbs, a straw beeskep between her hands, about to take a cast of bees that were swarming on the trunk of an apple tree. "You know what those are, I'll be bound. I see you got stalls of your own up yonder. This is in England. Blighty. *You* know. See the blossom on the trees there? Just the same as you got here."

The child took the picture and looked at it for a long time. She handed it back and her hands disappeared in her apron again.

"C'est la ruche," she murmured, "pour les abeilles."

"Ah. Well. Like I say, that picture was took in England."

Tom walked on. Newers and Danson were coming towards him. So was Evans. They were stopping to smell the apple blossom.

"Hello, Toss, been fraternizing?"

"I was trying to tell her I wasn't after her eggs and chickens."

"*We'd* be after 'em fast enough if it warnt for her grandpa. The old devil keeps a shotgun."

"I wish I could talk to the people here. It don't seem right, not to be able to talk to them."

"What's that to you, Toss? You don't hardly talk much even to us. You was always a silent sort of bastard."

"I talk when I think of something to say."

"Ah, Tuesdays and Fridays usually, ent it?"

"Take no notice of Pecker," said Newers. "He just lost his pay in a game of poker."

Tom had picked up a rounded chump of sweet-chestnut wood, roughly the size of his own fist, and had carved the little girl's likeness from it. Whenever he had a moment to spare he worked away at it, shaping the neatly rounded head, set so gracefully on the fine neck, and perfecting the features from memory.

The battalion was under notice to move. The men were mustering outside the village. Tom walked out to the old farmhouse and met the child driving cows up the lane. He took the carved wooden head from his pocket and gave it to her.

"For you," he said. "A souvenir. I done it myself, see, with this here knife. I hope you like it."

The child looked at the carved head, then at Tom. Her face remained blank. She said nothing.

"Well!" he said. "I've got to go or I'll land in trouble. We're moving in a little while."

He turned and hurried back towards the village, his boots thudding in the dust of the roadway. When he got to the bend and glanced back, she was still standing, a tiny figure, the carved head clutched against her chest.

At ten o'clock that morning, the whole of the battalion was assembled outside the village, fully accoutred and ready to move. The day was a warm one and the air smelt sweetly of trampled grass. The men sat about on the roadside verges, smoking and talking, awaiting orders. Newers and Danson were throwing dice. Tom was adjusting Evans's pack.

"Hey, Toss!" said Newers, nudging him. "Ent these the people from the farm?"

An old man and a small girl were coming slowly along the road, scanning the crowds of waiting soldiers. The old man had very white hair and black eyebrows. He wore a blue cap and smoked a pipe. The child wore a pinafore striped white and brown. They came along the road hand in hand, and one or two soldiers called out to them, making jokes in broken French. Suddenly they came to a halt. The child was pointing a finger at Tom.

The old man nodded, puffing at his pipe. He took something from his pocket and gave it to the child. She in turn gave it to Tom. It was a wooden crucifix, six inches long and four wide, with Christ carved very plainly and simply: the sort of crucifix he had seen so often lately, hanging on the walls of ruined houses throughout the district.

"It is for you," the old man said, in careful English, "to keep you safe from harm in battle."

"Laws," Tom said. "You shouldn't have walked out all this way – "

"The little one wanted so much to find you. It was important. *Very.* Yes. You are her friend and make her a present. She will keep it always, and remember you. Me too. We will remember."

"Ah," Tom said, and rose awkwardly from his knees,

aware of the men listening all round him. "Thank you.
Merci." His hand rested briefly on the child's head.

"Bonne chance," the old man said. "God be with you,
and with your comrades."

He and the child went back hand in hand. They were
soon lost to sight, for the soldiers were moving now,
thronging the road. Tom stood looking at the crucifix,
turning it over in his hands, feeling the smooth-worn corners and edges, and the smooth grain. It was carved from
boxwood and felt very old.

Sergeant Townchurch came along, shouting orders.
He saw the crucifix in Tom's hands.

"What the hell's this? You aren't a bloody Catholic, are
you, Maddox?"

"No, somebody gave it to me," Tom said.

"Some tart, I suppose," Townchurch said, and passed
on, shouting his orders. "On your feet, all you men! What
d'you think this is, a jamboree?"

So the Sixth Battalion marched away, leaving the village of Nobris behind them. Larks sang overhead and
sparrows whirred from the roadside hedges. The sun was
in the soldiers' eyes. They were marching again to the
battle area.

"I *was* married," Evans said, "but my wife died ten years
ago, and our baby with her."

"How long was you married?" Danson asked.

"Two years, that's all."

"Ent you got no family at all?"

"None that I know of," Evans said. "There's no one to
miss me when I'm gone. That's one good thing."

"Gone?" said Braid. "Why, where're you off to, Taff?
Monte Carlo?"

Evans gave a little smile.

"I shan't come through this war alive."

"Oh yes you will," Newers said. "I bet you a pound."

"You got a foreboding, Taff?" asked Dave Rush. "You're all the same, you bloody Welshmen. – All as superstitious as hell."

"You was exempt, being a miner," said Dick Costrell. "Why didn't you stop down the pit?"

Evans looked up at the blue sky.

"I wanted to come up out of the darkness."

"You warnt very clever, choosing your moment."

"It's being afraid all the time, you see. I thought I'd left all that down the pit. I thought, out here, I should either be killed or not killed. I hadn't bargained for *living* with death as though it was a presence in itself. A presence lying in wait everywhere, preying on the minds of men."

"It's time you put in for a spot of home leave."

"I have," Evans said. "But somehow I don't think I'll ever get it. I've got this feeling all the time, that something is about to give."

"We all get that feeling," Danson said. "It means another bloody button going!"

Evans laughed along with the rest. He leant across and punched Danson's shoulder. But the long period out of the line had not built him up as it had the others. He was white-faced and worn, and his hands, when he lit a cigarette, shook like those of a very old man.

There was heavy shelling in the Seiglon sector. The village was soon a heap of rubble. Both the front line trenches and the reserve were blasted in repeatedly, for the enemy had them registered "right to the fraction" a Corporal Stevens said to Braid. One morning, early, a shell fell directly on a forward observation post, and afterwards there was silence there. The post had been manned by Lieutenant Bullock and two men, Bremner and Evans.

Tom and Newers crawled across, under fire from a machine-gun. They reached the post and began to dig. The officer and Bremner were both dead, but Evans, buried under four feet of earth, was still alive when they dug him out. His mouth and throat were full of earth; they had to scoop it out with their fingers; it was almost an hour before his lungs really filled with air.

They thought he would die if he didn't have prompt medical attention and so they decided to run for it, although it was now broad daylight. They lifted him up and started off across no-man's-land. They had about two hundred yards to travel. The German machine-gun opened fire and the bullets perforated the ground behind them. A rifle whipcracked three times. Then, abruptly, the firing stopped. The Germans were letting them cross in safety.

Evans went to the medical post at Rilloy-sus-Coll. Tho doctor pronounced him a lucky man and sent him back to duty again. A fallen rider should always remount at once, he said, and a shell-shock case should face the barrage. Sergeant Townchurch was of the same mind. He carried the principle one stage further. And only forty-two hours later he named Evans for a wiring-party.

"You can't take Evans," said Corporal Stevens. "He's a sick man. He shouldn't be in the line at all."

"All that twitching and jerking, you mean? He's putting that on. He's swinging the lead like he always has done."

"That man was buried alive in the O.P. on Monday. Newers and Maddox had to dig him out."

"So what? It's only when he's buried *dead* that he'll be excused his whack of duty. Till then he takes his turn."

So Evans went with the wiring-party, fifty yards out into

no-man's-land, carrying a coil of new barbed wire. There were ten men including Townchurch and during the night they were fired on by an enemy patrol. The party returned with two men wounded. Townchurch reported another missing. The missing man was Private Evans.

"Was he hit?" asked Captain Edman.

"Not him!" said Townchurch. "He's bloody well skipped it, that's what he's done. I always said he was a slacker."

Some days later, Evans was discovered sitting in the church at Basseroche, and was brought back under arrest. He went before a court martial, charged with desertion. Sergeant Townchurch gave evidence against him. So did the fox-hunting doctor from Rilloy, who stated that Evans was in good health, physically and mentally. Certainly Evans seemed calm enough now. No longer twitching. Only tired. He was found guilty and sentenced to death.

The battalion moved into camp at Berigny. The weather was broken. There were thunderstorms. The men of Number Three Platoon were digging drains to carry away the surface water. Sergeant Townchurch sought them out. He wanted Tom.

"Maddox!" he shouted. "Follow me!" And, as soon as they were out of earshot: "I got a job lined up for you. One of twelve for a firing party. Little matter of an execution, first thing tomorrow morning."

"I won't do it," Tom said.

"Not all the guns're loaded live. You might get a blank."

"It makes no difference. I still won't do it."

"You don't seem to realize – this is an order. D'you know what'll happen if you refuse?"

"I don't care a sod. You've got no right to pick men out from the same platoon. You won't get none of the others to do it neither."

"Somebody's got to do these things. I reckon it's better, keeping it in the family as you might say."

"Let them who sentenced him do the shooting. I came out to kill Germans, not to kill my own mates. Ah, and I sometimes wonder why the hell I should kill *them*, seeing they're people the same as us."

"Maybe you'd like to join up with them? There's sure to be lots like you in their lines. You'd find yourself at home with Fritz. *Don't turn away when I'm talking to you!* Where the hell do you think you're going?"

"I'm going back to my platoon."

"Oh no you're not! I'm putting you under arrest, Maddox, and tomorrow you'll find yourself up on a charge. It's easy enough to disobey orders. We'll see if you like the consequences."

Tom was taken to the edge of the village and locked in a cowshed for the night, next to stables occupied by Evans. There was only a wooden wall between, and Evans heard Tom arrive.

"Who's in by there? Someone I know?"

"It's me," Tom said. "Toss Maddox."

"What you been crimed for, Toss, man?"

"I was late on parade," Tom said. "Third time this week, according to the corporal."

"They're going to shoot me in the morning. Did you know that, Toss? Did you hear what happened?"

"Yes. We heard. The chaps was wanting to come and see you but somebody said you'd asked them not to."

"I'd just as soon be left alone. They weren't offended, were they, Toss? It's just that I need to have time to think."

"They warnt offended," Tom said.

"It's nice and quiet here, considering. I can hear a blackbird singing somewhere."

"You got a window in there, Taff?"

"There's a small round window above the door. I can see the sky, anyway. Looks like we're in for another storm. It'll get dark early tonight, I'd say, but I've got a candle and matches here."

"You got plenty of cigarettes?"

"Diawl, yes! A tin of fifty. But I was never much of a smoker. Just the odd one now and then."

"Me, too," Tom said.

When darkness came, Evans struck a match and lit his candle. Tom sat on his bunk in the shed next door and looked at the cracks of light in the wall. A little while later he lit his own candle. Outside the shed, footsteps sounded occasionally, and men's voices. Further away, north of the village, wheels rumbled on the stone-paved roads as the ration-limbers went up to the line, and further off still was the noise of the guns. In a lean-to shed next to the stable, a few chickens rustled on their perches during the night, querking sleepily now and then and changing places with a flutter of wings.

"Toss?" Evans said. "Are you awake?"

"Yes, Taff, I'm awake."

"Are you sitting up with me till the end?"

"Might as well. Company, like. But you don't have to talk if it don't suit you."

"Have you ever been to Wales, Toss?"

"No, never," Tom said.

"There's a little village outside Merthyr with a stream running through it and an old crooked bridge over the stream and silver birch trees growing beside it. The water in the stream is so clear that if it weren't moving over the stones you would never know it was there at all."

"I should like to see that place," Tom said.

"When I go out tomorrow morning, I shall think I'm going to walk by that stream. It's nonsense, I know, – I've never believed in the life everlasting – but that's what I shall be thinking about, and that's what I'll see in my mind's eye. I'll follow the stream till the ground rises. I've done it often and I know exactly where I'll come to. A green hillside and someone waiting."

Just before first light, the stable door was unlocked, and the padre entered. He sat on a stool at the makeshift table and looked at Evans opposite. The condemned man, he thought, looked quite composed.

"Well, Evans?"

"I told them I didn't want a parson."

"I thought you might have changed your mind."

"I have not changed my mind."

"Are you a chapel man, perhaps? I can find the Methodist padre if you want him, you know."

"No, no. I was brought up Church," Evans said. "But I'm nothing now. I'm an unbeliever."

The padre was silent, looking at Evans in the light of the candle. His hand, with the crumpled prayerbook in it, was long and slender, like a woman's. His face was childlike. He was trying hard to understand the condemned man's mind.

"Obviously, then, it is lack of faith that has brought you to this sorry state."

"Go away," Evans said.

But the padre remained, hesitating. He felt it was his duty to try again.

"You call yourself an unbeliever, yet when you were arrested you were found sitting in a village church."

"It was quiet there."

"If you cannot believe in God, can't you at least have faith in your fellow men?"

"I come from South Wales," Evans said. "I have seen where certain men have laid their hands, and the place is left black and smoking ever after. I have seen where other men have laid their hands, and the place is greener than it was before."

"So? What then? It follows that you believe in good and evil."

"They exist together, and will do always."

"You don't believe that good must ultimately win a victory over evil?"

"It is a victory that good exists at all."

"*I could* give you comfort, you know, if only you'd let me."

"I don't need it," Evans said.

The padre went. The two halves of the stable door were closed and bolted. Light came gradually in at the round hole above and Evans douted the flame of his candle. He put the stump into his pocket.

Tom, in the cowshed, sat on his bunk with his knees up and his arms clasped round them. He watched the daylight growing brighter through the slatted window. Outside, in the yard, the hens had been released and a cock was crowing. Someone was working a chaff-cutter. Next door, Evans was making himself tidy.

When the escort came to take him away, Evans stood up and knocked on the wall.

"So long, Toss. Look after yourself. Thanks for sitting up with me."

"So long, Taff."

Tom got up and looked out through the slats of his window. He saw them marching Evans away. In the straw-littered yard an old woman with a black knitted shawl

over her head was scattering a panful of grain for the
hens. She came to a standstill, crossing herself, as Evans
passed by between his guards. Tom craned his neck and
looked at the sky, overcast with purple stormclouds,
under which the morning light shone out levelly over the
earth. He saw three seagulls flying over, silver-white
against the dark clouds. From somewhere not very far
away came a quick volley of rifle fire. The old woman got
down on her knees.

Tom, appearing before the court martial, was charged
with refusing to obey an order. He admitted the charge
and was found guilty. Townchurch, of course, had been
in the wrong. Tom knew it; the officers knew it; but discipline had to be maintained, so no one asked what the
order had been.

He was sentenced to five days' Field Punishment
Number One. This meant extra fatigues, parading on the
hour in full marching order, and confinement in the
guardroom. It also meant that every evening of the five-
day period he spent two hours tied to the wheel of a gun
limber, stretched crossways with his feet off the ground,
his wrists and ankles strapped to the spokes. Sergeant
Townchurch was there to see that the straps were pulled
tight; he was there again later to see Tom released; and
every evening, as the straps were removed, he would ask
the same question.

"Well, Maddox? Don't you wish you'd obeyed that
order?"

Tom never answered the sergeant's question. He tried
to pretend the man was not there.

At the end of July, the Sixth Battalion left the Somme and moved north into Flanders, up to the martyred city of Ypres, under bombardment day and night. A group of signallers stood watching as they marched in.

"Welcome to the capital of the salient! – Kindly leave it as you find it!"

"Come to Wipers and be wiped out!"

"Hope you're nifty, catching whizzbangs."

"The barracks is over there on your left, or it was this morning."

"The password is knife. You never get time to say nothing more."

That evening, Tom and Newers explored the city, once a place of proud spires. They gazed at the ruins of the old cathedral, the skeleton of the Cloth Hall.

"Someone's going to have to do some building here when it's all over. I wonder how they'll ever have the heart to begin."

"Will you come back?" Tom asked. "Afterwards, I mean, to see how it looks?"

"It's an idea," Newers said. "How about us two coming together? Ten years after the end of the war, say, on a special trip?"

"Right, it's a deal," Tom said, "so long as we're alive to do it."

"If we're dead we'll come in the spirit. There'll be plenty of ghosts wandering through France and Belgium in the years to come."

Throughout the salient, troops were massing for the new offensive. Every acre of open space was packed with men, horses, guns, equipment. And the enemy, occupying the higher ground north-east of the city, could look down over the bustle below as though looking on a human ant-heap. His observation posts were supreme. His gunners could place their shells as they chose. The bombardment intensified every day.

"Talk about sitting ducks!" Dick Costrell said to Newers. "What the hell are top brass waiting for, for God's sake?"

"They're finishing their game of bowls."

"Another day or two of this and there'll be nothing left of us to attack with."

Costrell spoke bitterly. The waiting was getting on his nerves. Rain had begun falling now. The ground was receiving a thorough soaking.

On the last day of July, as first light came, the British guns redoubled their fire, and all along the salient front the British infantry climbed out of their assembly trenches and, following the creeping barrage, advanced towards the enemy lines. The great new offensive had begun.

The Sixth Battalion was in support. They had orders to push through the line established by the Worcestershires and press on to the next objective. Tanks were coming up to assist. But the ground had been thoroughly soaked with rain and the tanks were either bogged down in the ditches or moved so slowly that they were destroyed by enemy shells.

The Sixth Battalion went into the attack but were beaten back by murderous gunfire. They had to dig in short of their objective. And in the evening came more rain.

They lay out all night in shallow trenches full of water. The rain continued all next day, and the day after.

On the fifth night they were relieved by a sister battalion. They marched along the Menin road and went into camp outside Ypres. They were given dry clothes and hot sweet tea with rum in it. Food when it came was bully beef stew ladled piping hot into mess-tins, but, because of the undiminished shelling, it contained a few unwelcome ingredients.

"What's this?" Newers asked, fishing out a piece of shrapnel and showing it to the sergeant cook. "Iron rations?"

"That's something you leave on the side of your plate."

While they ate, they tried to glean news of how the big attack was going, but nobody seemed to know for sure. They heard only rumours and some of these were bad indeed, like the post corporal's story of how the British guns had pounded a position already captured by British troops. They heard, too, of a whole company of the Third Three Counties lost for eight hours in the darkness up near Pilckem Ridge. And they heard – was it true? – that the Fifth Battalion West Mercia had lost three quarters of its strength in the action outside Rannegsmarck.

"The bloody Somme all over again," Pecker Danson said to Tom, "only bloody worse if anything."

August was always a wet month in Flanders, but August 1917 was the worst known for forty years.

"It's the guns that bring down all this rain," Danson kept saying. "I've noticed it time and time again – get a big bombardment and down it comes!"

They were in trenches near Hooge, soaked to the skin for days on end. There was no sleep because of the shelling. Tempers were short and nerves ragged. Only Newers remained cheerful.

"You should've brought your brolly, Pecker."

"I should've brought my bleedin' canoe. I can see why Fritz is so keen on his submarines. He'll be using them in the trenches soon."

"Listen!" said Newers, a finger to his lips.

"What the hell is it?" Danson asked.

"Darkness falling. Stand-to!"

"I'll bloody well brain you in a minute."

The enemy bombardment, heaviest at dusk, gradually lessened as darkness came. Shells were fewer. More widely spaced. "Fritz is getting ready for bed," Newers would say, as the shelling eased. "He's putting the cat out and leaving a message for the milkman." *Womp. Womp.* Away on the left.

"Two pints," Newers said.

Womp. Womp. Away on the right.

"He's fallen over the milk-bottles."

Womp. – Womp. – Womp. – Womp.

"Now he's going upstairs to his missus. She's lying there listening to his steps on the stairs. She's been warming the bed like a good wife should."

There followed a silence. Newers sucked at his empty pipe.

"I don't like to think what they're doing now."

Womp. Womp. Very close.

"Seems he's fallen out of bed."

"Don't you ever shut up?" Costrell shouted suddenly.

"Sometimes I do," Newers said.

"I'm sick to death of your endless clacking! For God's sake let's have some peace and quiet!"

"All right, keep your hair on," Newers said. "I can take a hint as well as the next man."

Costrell was in a state of nerves. He twitched and trembled all the time. Tom was reminded of Lambert and Evans. He leant across the tiny dugout and offered Costrell a cigarette. Costrell knocked it out of his hand.

"Steady on," Danson murmured.

The next night, wet as ever, Tom and Danson were on sentry. So was Costrell. Tom heard a commotion in the next bay and went along to see what was wrong. Costrell lay stretched out on the duckboards, a rum-jar beside him, and the other sentries were trying in vain to wake him up. "He's dead to the world! Where'n hell did he get that jar?"

"What shall we do?" Rush whispered, and there was panic in his voice. "If Townchurch sees him like this he'll end up the same as poor Taffy Evans."

They raised Costrell and slapped his face, but he remained lifeless in their grasp. Tom ran back to his own bay and called Newers out of the dugout. Newers came, turning his pipe-bowl upside down, and lifted one of Costrell's hands. He put his thumb-nail under Costrell's and pressed down hard into the quick. There was a sudden loud cry. Rush put his hand over Costrell's mouth and Danson rubbed the boy's wrists. They stood him on his feet and ran him quickly to and fro. He was soon sick and began to recover.

"Where'n hell did you get that jar?"

"I dunno. I won it somewhere."

"Can you stand now? Can you walk about?"

"Think so," Costrell muttered.

"You better had!" Danson said. "You know the penalty for being drunk on sentry, don't you?"

"Christ!" Costrell said, and began crying. "I feel so ill!"

"Pull yourself together, lad. Townchurch'll be along in a minute."

"Oh, Christ!" Costrell said, but he stood up straight and took his rifle from Dave Rush.

"If it wasn't for Newers you'd still be out cold," Danson said. "We couldn't do nothing to bring you round."

Costrell's glance slid to Newers.

"Thanks, chum. I'll buy you a drink in 'Pop' on Friday."

"Chew some of this," Newers said, and handed him a plug of tobacco. "It'll maybe soak up the smell of rum."

Newers went back to his own dugout, taking the half-empty rum-jar with him. A few minutes later, Townchurch came by with the platoon officer, Mr Coleby. All the sentries were up on the firestep. Everything was as it should be.

The low-lying land north of Ypres had long ago been reclaimed from the sea; it was kept drained by a series of dykes; but these dykes had been broken down by the British bombardment and the waters, overflowing, were turning the area back to swamp. Over this swamp the Allied forces were attempting to advance, against the Germans firmly entrenched on the ground above.

"Talk about Weston-super-bloody-Mare!" said Dave Rush, dragging one leg from the mire as he spoke. "It's only sheer will-power that's keeping my boots on my bloody feet."

"The continong is not all it's cracked up to be," said Pecker Danson. "I'll stick to Skegness in future."

"I'll stick to everything after this!"

Newers had been caught in a shell-blast that had bowled him over into the mud, yet he still had his empty pipe in his mouth and was blowing through it to clear out the muck.

"A mud-pack is said to be good for the complexion. We'll come out looking like the Oxo Boy. There's ladies in London who spend a mint of money to get what we're getting here for nothing."

"I bet their mud-packs don't smell like this."

"You mustn't mind that – it's only the smell of rotting bodies."

"Yes, my pal Jim Baker's buried here, somewhere. He was out in 1915."

"Well, we won't stop and look for him now, Pecker. We got an appointment with Fritz in the morning."

It was towards the end of August, a night of rain and intense darkness, and they were moving up to the line, feeling their way yard by yard into the forward assembly trenches, ready for the engagement next day.

"What we need," said Dave Rush, "is an electric torch with a black light."

"No smoking!" came the order, passed along from man to man.

"I ent ready for this engagement," Pecker Danson said to Tom. "I haven't bought the bleeding ring."

"No talking from now on!" shouted the corporal, just behind them.

The columns of men filed forward very slowly, slock-slock, through the mud. It was still raining. The assembly trenches were all flooded. The water reached above their knees.

Dawn, when it came, showed itself first in the flood-water lying out in front. No-man's-land was a waste of puddles and the light in the water seemed paler, brighter, than the light in the heavily clouded sky. Rain was falling steadily, a grey curtain reluctantly letting the daylight through, to reveal the desolation on the ground. Ruined field-guns lay lopsided in the mud and smashed tanks were bogged to the turrets. One great tank had lost its tracks. Dead men and horses lay everywhere, sunk in black slime, unrecognizable except that in places, here and there, a hand or a hoof stuck out and pointed to the sky.

"If I get out of this war safely," Dave Rush said to Tom, "I never want to see another dawn as long as I live."

Communications were difficult. They lay out all morning in the rain waiting for orders. At two o'clock the British guns opened up an intense fire. The attacking platoons crawled from their trenches and began pushing forward through the mud, following the barrage as it moved slowly up the slope.

Weighed down as they were with battle equipment, moving through mud which in places reached to the very thighs, their progress was dreadfully, painfully slow.

"It's all right for Jerry," Danson said. "He's got the best place up there on that ridge."

"Then you know what to do – take it from him!" said the young lieutenant commanding the platoon, and pushed forward, his rifle held high.

"Easy, ent it?" Danson said, as Newers drew alongside. "Nothing to it, if Jerry'll just wait while I get my bleeding feet up, out of this bleeding rotten muck."

Townchurch, ahead, had stepped up onto a slab of concrete and was urging the men to make more effort.

"Come on, you grubs! Shift yourselves and get a move on! I want some progress bloody forward! I want my platoon up there in front!"

"We know what *you* want!" Costrell shouted, hardly aware of what he was saying.

"Yes, Costrell, what do I want?"

Costrell was struggling in the mud. Townchurch splashed across to him and helped him on with a shove from behind. Costrell fell forward onto his face.

"I said get a move on!" Townchurch bellowed. "I said to shift yourselves and show some spunk! You'll get on forward up that slope if I have to push you all the way!"

Costrell floundered onto his knees, choking and crying, trying to wipe the mud from his rifle.

"Just look! Just look! How the hell can I use that? I can't go on without a rifle! What the hell am I going to do?"

"You've got your bayonet!" Townchurch said. "If you ever get close enough to use it! Now get on or I'll bloody well put you on a charge!"

Tom and Newers helped Costrell up.

"Keep with us," Newers said, "and if one of us falls, grab his rifle."

Townchurch was now splashing forward to another group stuck in the mire.

"Shift yourselves, can't you? I want you up there behind that smoke! If I can move, so can you!"

The barrage, creeping forward, was gradually leaving them behind. They could not keep pace with it, slow as it was, and now, as the smoke around them drifted away, there was nothing to hide them from the enemy. They were out in the open, in a sea of mud, though the enemy lines were still some way off, under the smoke and the driving rain.

"Which way? Which way?" a man was screaming, off his head. "I don't even know where the Germans are!"

"Nor me neither," Newers said. "I'm following them two up there." He pointed to Townchurch and the subaltern, moving twenty yards ahead. "Let's hope *they* know where we're going!"

Tom, sharp-eared, heard an order shouted in German, somewhere on the right, not far away. A Maxim opened fire from there, followed by another on the left, and the men in front went down like ninepins. A few that were left crept into shell-holes. Others, stuck, unable to move, burrowed into the mud where they were. Tom found himself treading on a man's shoulders.

The Germans had set up machine-gun posts in shelters of sandbags out in the open, and now the barrage had moved over, they came into action everywhere. The attacking platoons were in an ambush, receiving fire on both flanks, and the second wave went down like the first. D Company had suffered badly: all its officers had fallen and the remnants, pushing on, followed a subaltern of B Company, who had lost touch with his own men. He was calling to them and waving them on when a Maxim opened fire from the main German line, now visible a hundred yards off. He fell, wounded, and lay on his elbows watching men falling all round him.

"It's no good!" he shouted, as the stragglers reached him. "Save yourselves! We can't get through!"

But Sergeant Townchurch was urging them on.

"Don't listen to him, he's raving!" he said. "Of course we'll get through! Follow me!"

Then his arms flew up and he toppled over into the mud, and everywhere behind him men took cover in the broken ground.

Fighting continued all day: fierce little battles conducted from shell-holes; and all the enemy machine-gun posts were at length destroyed. But the main attack was not renewed. Those men who were left were too few and too tired; there was no hope of reinforcements; and early darkness put an end to the day. Orders came to dig in. Rain fell harder than ever.

All next day, stretcher-parties were out from both sides, retrieving their wounded. The big guns exchanged some token fire, but all along the forward area an unofficial truce was observed, and the bearers moved across the open, searching the shell-holes. Enemy losses had not been great, and sometimes the German stretcher-bearers, having rescued British wounded, would set them down near the British lines.

Tom and Newers, with Braid and Costrell, worked on until after darkfall. They moved about the battalion aid post, doing what they could to help the wounded until the doctors could get to them. Townchurch lay groaning out in the open. He was asking for water. Costrell passed him many times, ignoring him, refusing to help him. Pecker Danson did the same. Tom fetched water and took it to him. He held the bottle while Townchurch drank. The man was in great agony. His face was contorted, his eyes glazed. He looked at Tom with slowly dawning recognition.

"Currying favour?" he whispered hoarsely. "You're wasting your time – I'm a dead man."

Late that night, Tom was sitting with Newers and Danson, drinking tea from a field-kitchen before going off to get some sleep. A young doctor came out to them.

"Your Sergeant Townchurch has just died."

"I'm not surprised," Danson said. "He was pretty far gone."

"He was saying some rather strange things."

"He was always like that, sir, even when he was in the pink."

"He wasn't delirious," the doctor said. "He knew what he was saying and he claimed he'd been shot from close behind."

"Well, we had Jerry on both our flanks, sir, and if the sergeant was turning round – "

"The hole in his body was definitely made by an

English bullet. I can guarantee that."

"Would you believe it!" Newers said. "He must've got in somebody's way. One of the accidents of war, sir. I've seen 'em often in the past year."

"I'll have to make a report of the matter. I can't just let it go at that."

"No, sir. Of course not, sir. Very sad thing to happen, sir."

The doctor looked at them each in turn, and went away without further comment. Newers took a drink of tea, breathing heavily into his mug. He was sitting between Tom and Danson.

"It wasn't me, chums, if that's what you're thinking."

"Nor me," Danson said.

"Nor me neither," Tom said.

"Accident of war, that's what it was. Lots of chaps've copped it that way, not all so deserving as Townchurch, of course, but there you are. Pity he never got his V.C."

Three months later, on a foggy night late in November, Tom and Newers, with Danson and Rush, were in an estaminet in Poperinghe.

It was much patronized by British and Colonial troops and the wall was covered with their scribblings. "Lost, stolen, or strayed: one Russian steamroller," someone had written, and another: "On August tenth, at the new St Wipers nursing home, to the B.E.F., 12 baby elephants, all doing well." There were other jokes, too, less pure, that Danson said made him blush.

Newers ordered four glasses of wine. Neither he nor the others would touch Belgian beer. They had drunk better stuff from shell-holes, they said.

"Have you seen the Americans yet?"

"I dunno. What colour are they?"

"Much the same as Canadians, really, but maybe more so," Danson said.

"Watch it, Limey!" a Canadian said from the next table.

"Sure, sure!" Danson answered, through his nose. "Whaddya know! Ontario!"

"Here, Toss," said Dave Rush. "There's two chaps looking in at the window, making ugly mugs at you. I reckon they're trying to get your goat."

Tom turned in his chair and saw two faces pressed against the glass.

"It's William and Roger! My foster-brothers! Glory be, can you beat that?"

He went to the door and yanked it open. William and Roger sauntered in.

"Catched you, ent we, drinking as usual?"

"We heard your outfit was up here somewhere so we took a chance of tracking you down."

"Ent that a masterpiece?" Tom said. He could not get over it even now. "Come over and meet my mates."

The two Izzard boys were now big men. Even Roger had grown thickset. But they were as fresh-faced and snub-nosed as ever, bright fair hair brushed sleekly down, eyes very blue under colourless eyebrows, wide awake, missing nothing. William was now a bombardier but pretended to think it nothing much when Tom, amazed, touched the stripes on his sleeve.

"Picked 'em up cheap," he said, shrugging, "from a chap that didn't need 'em no more."

"You artillery chaps is full of swank," said Danson, rising to shake hands. "So you're Bet's brothers? Fancy that."

"You know my sister?" William said.

"We know her from snapshots," Newers said. "And her letters, of course, that she writes to Toss. She writes a good letter, your sister Bet. We always like it when Toss hears from her."

The six of them sat at a small table. William ordered a bottle of wine. It was brought to them by a fierce old woman with frizzled hair who glared at them, scowling, as she set the bottle on the table.

"Six francs," she said, one hand held out to William.

"Get away!" said Newers. "We've never paid more'n five before, and that's five too many, you old bundle, you!"

"Six francs," she said, and tapped her palm with an impatient finger.

"Don't pay it, mate," Pecker Danson said to William. "She's trying it on 'cos she thinks it's a party."

"Five francs," William said, and put the money on the table.

"Non-non-non-non! Six francs! I insist! I insist!"

"Five!" William said. "And bring two more glasses if you please. You don't expect us to drink from the bottle?"

"Six! Six! I must insist!"

"Bring two glasses, please, madame, and not so much of your ruddy nonsense."

"Toot sweet," Newers said, "and the tooter the sweeter."

"Non-non-non-non! Six francs. I insist! I insist!"

The argument was attracting attention. The Canadians were laying bets on the outcome, and a group of Gloucesters were shouting abuse at the old woman. She had grown purple in the face and was threatening to remove the bottle when a younger woman appeared on the scene. She came to the table, placed two glasses in front of William, and picked up the five francs.

"Drink up, Tommees, and kill a few Boches for me tomorrow."

"I'd sooner get rid of your old woman."

"Don't mind the old one. She is greedy for money to

ransom her son. He is a prisoner with the Boches. She thinks she'll be able to buy his freedom."

"Tell her from me it'll soon be over."

"Never! Never!" the old woman said, and there were tears in her eyes. "I do not believe it will ever end."

"That's cheerful, that is! Are there more like her around these parts?"

William poured out the wine and raised his glass to the old woman.

"Viva la victoree!" he said. "Viva the happy smiling faces!"

The old woman went, still grumbling, led away by the young girl. William and Roger grinned at Tom.

"If mother and dad could see us now!"

"How come you're here?" Tom asked. "I thought you was down in the south some place."

"That's right. Lafitte. But we had to come up to Armchairs on a course and we thought we'd take the long way back."

"How're things with you, Tom?" Roger asked.

"All right," Tom said, and could think of nothing more to say.

"Your lot's been copping it again lately, I heard. Have you been in the new push?"

"We was at Steenbeek," Tom said.

"And the Menin road," said Pecker Danson.

"And Passchendaele," said Dave Rush.

"What was it like?" Roger asked. "Was it as bad as people say?"

"People!" said Danson. "What people?"

He and Newers drank their wine.

"I'm going on leave directly," Tom said. "Any message for them at home?"

"Wish them all the best, Tom, and say you found us in

the pink. Rog and me ent going on leave. Not till we've finished this bloody war. It'd mean splitting up if we went on leave and I promised mother we'd stick like glue."

"The truth is," Roger said, "they can't fight the war without us gunners."

"Why, are you the only two they've got?" Newers asked, lighting his pipe. "No wonder it's quiet in Picardy lately."

"We're two of the best, that's all."

"You're all the same, you artillery blokes," said Pecker Danson, "but seeing how I'm drinking your vin I can't hardly tell you what that is."

When the party left the estaminet, they met two girls just coming in.

"You buy drinks for us, yes, Tommee? Plentee monee! Buy café rhum?"

"Après la guerre!" William said, walking on, and then, to Tom: "If mother and dad could see us now!"

Outside the town the group split up, William and Roger going to their train, Tom and the others going to scrounge a lift back to camp. Their voices echoed across the street.

"So long, Bill! So long, Rog! We'll be thinking of you when we hear them guns of yours lousing off down there at Lafitte."

"So long!" Tom said, watching the two boys walking away. "All the best!"

"So long!" they said. "Be seeing you, Tom."

Home for ten days' leave at Cobbs, Tom strolled about the carpenter's shop, kicking the shavings that littered the floor and sniffing the old familiar smells of timber, putty, paint and glue. The carpenters watched him with some curiosity.

"Well, young Tom? I suppose you find it pretty tame at

home here now? Quiet, like? Nothing much happening in the old place?"

"Ah. Quiet. Just like always, or very nearly."

"Have you been having a good time? Making the most of things? Getting a bit of experience, eh?"

"A good time?" Tom said.

"Well, you're only young once, that's what I say, and you might never get the chance again."

"The mademoiselles, that's what Sam means," said Bob Green.

"Oh, them!" Tom said, and stooped to pick up a knot of wood. "They're just after your money, that's all."

"Well," said Sam, "you don't expect to get it for nothing?"

"Get what?" Tom said, and went a dark red as their laughter sounded along the workshop.

"Laws, Tom, you ent as innocent as all that?"

"A chap like you, turned twenty, and a soldier in the Army, too! Don't they teach you nothing at all?"

"You ent your father's son, boy, if you're as green as all that."

"Tom is keeping hisself nice for Tilly Preston. *She's* the mademoiselle for him. Ent that so, Tom?"

Tom merely shrugged and walked away.

In the big kitchen, Beth Izzard sat at the table with writing-pad, pen, and a bottle of ink set out before her. Her husband, Jesse, stood behind her, smoking his pipe. Opposite her, a mug of tea in mittened hands, sat Mrs Clementina Rainbow, a handsome old gipsy from Puppet Hill, where the gipsies had always camped in winter ever since never, people said.

Mrs Rainbow could not read or write. She had there-fore come to Cobbs for help. Her son, Alexander, was in the Army, serving somewhere on the western front, and a letter must be sent without delay to his commanding officer, requesting that Alexander be sent home at once, for his poor ma and da had received an enormous order for pegs and Alexander's help was needed.

Beth sat, somewhat self-conscious, aware of her husband standing behind her and the boy Tom sitting quiet in the chimney corner.

"My daughter Betony's the scholar by rights. If you wait till this evening, Mrs Rainbow, she will write your letter for you."

"You can do it, Mrs Izzard. I seen you writing oftentimes. You done that notice for Georgie's waggon."

"Very well," Beth said, and took up her pen. "What shall I say?"

"Well, about the pegs, Mrs Izzard, please. An immendous great order we've had, tell him, and can't manage without Alexander."

"They won't send him home," Jesse said, "just to make pegs, Mrs Rainbow."

"You think not, Mr Izzard?"

"I'm certain of it, Mrs Rainbow."

"Then put in we've had an order for baskets as well, Mrs Izzard, and must have'm ready in time for Christmas."

"Anything else, Mrs Rainbow?"

"Tell the gentleman-colonel, please, that I seen things last night in the smoke of the fire that mean he's coming into money."

Beth, straight-faced, finished the letter and wrote Mrs Rainbow's name at the bottom. She put it in an envelope and wrote the address.

"Silly fella!" the gipsy said. "Going to the Army and 'listing like that. He'll never be the same again, Mrs Izzard, getting mixed up in this old war."

"No one'll be quite the same, Mrs Rainbow."

When the gipsy had gone, Beth looked up and met Tom's eye.

"I'd like to be there," he said, smiling, "when Alexander's colonel gets that letter."

"How was William and Roger?" asked Jesse. "Was they keeping hale and hearty?" He had asked the question a dozen times.

"They was fine," Tom said. "They've growed pretty big, the pair of them. William is nearly as big as a house."

"Ah, well, he's a bombardier now, remember."

William and Roger had had their photograph taken in Rouen and had sent it home. Then, in December, an old soldier had come through Huntlip, walking on crutches, having lost his left leg in the fighting at Mons in 1914. He eked out his pension by painting portraits from photographs of absent soldiers. He travelled about, knocking on doors.

"Husbands, fathers, sons, lovers. – If you've got a photo I'll copy it for you, a proper portrait, done in oils."

Beth had given him the photograph of William and Roger, together with details of their colouring, and he had copied it, true to life. The portrait hung in the front parlour, on the wall above the fireplace, and the two boys looked out on all the family gatherings: sitting side by side, fair hair greased down, faces glowing, keen blue eyes looking straight ahead; proud to be sitting together in khaki, William with his two stripes, both with their buttons polished to perfection.

"You should get your photo took as well," Jesse told Tom, "and we'll get the artist to paint you too."

He thought perhaps Tom might feel left out, because Granna Tewke, always knitting for William and Roger, never knitted anything for Tom.

"Not that you miss much," he whispered once, " 'cos granna's knitting is none too gainly nowadays."

"What's wrong with my knitting?" granna demanded, sitting up and glaring at Jesse. Her sight might be poor, but her hearing was perfect. "What's wrong with my knitting I'd like to know?"

"Why, that glove you made last week had a finger too many, and there was a cap as I recall that was half purple."

"Young Dicky done that. Changed the wools when I warnt looking." Granna leant forward and touched Tom's arm. "I'll knit you something. What'd you like? Socks or gloves or a comforter?"

"Don't you bother. I'm all right."

"You never did seem to feel the cold."

"I'm all right," Tom said. "I've got plenty."

Beth and Betony sent him woollens. They saw that he was kept supplied.

"What's the *best* thing to send?" Betony asked him. "What would you find really useful?"

"A big Dundee cake, like your mother sent in a tin one time. It was packed with fruit and had almonds on it."

"Don't you know there's a sugar shortage? It's going on ration in the new year."

"I thought maybe Beth could spare some honey."

"My mother says she's never known so many people ask so kindly after her bees as they have done lately since sugar got scarce. But no doubt she's got some to spare for you."

The two of them were alone in the kitchen. Tom sat staring into the fire. Betony watched him.

"You never used to like fruit cake."

"We're glad of it, though, out there."

"What do you mean by 'we' exactly?"

"The chaps," he said. "They always like Dundee cake."

"And must I make cakes to feed the chaps?"

"Not just them – we share things," he said. "We always share what we get in our parcels. It's good stuff, you see, and we're pretty nearly always hungry."

"But why?" she exclaimed. "Why on earth don't they feed you properly?"

"A lot of the food gets flogged," he said. "There's chaps that sell it to the shops and cafés. Or so I've heard, anyway, and I reckon it's true."

"But that's terrible! It makes my blood boil to hear such things! There ought to be better supervision."

"There ought to be, but it ent easy, out there."

The fire collapsed in the open stove, and Tom leant forward to put on more logs. He looked at her for a while in silence.

"I was sorry," he said, awkwardly, "to hear the captain was a prisoner."

"Yes," she said. "I hope the Germans don't treat him badly. He says in his letters he's all right, but I can't help wondering all the same."

"I don't think the Germans is all bad. Some of them must be, but not all. He'll be all right, Bet, don't you worry."

"I wish you wouldn't keep calling me Bet! You never used to in the old days."

"Sorry," he said. "I've got the habit off the chaps." And he went on to explain to her about the letters. "We share *them* as well. We read each other's. Except when they're private, from wives and that. The chaps always like it when I hear from you. Your letters go round like hot buns. You cheer them up and make them laugh. They always say it's a real tonic."

"I shall have to be careful what I write."

"You don't mind, do you, Bet? I didn't think you'd mind about it."

"No," she said, "I don't mind."

In fact the knowledge gave her pleasure. She felt herself closer to the men out there, suffering, enduring as they were. It was little enough, in God's name, and she must try to write more often.

"Tell me about them, these mates of yours," she said, and, seeing him smile: "What's the joke exactly?" she asked.

"I was thinking about Big Glover. He was always talking about you. He said once to ask if you'd marry him."

"Tell him I'd have to see him first."

"Big Glover is dead now. He was killed last summer on the Somme. He came from outside Bromyard somewhere. So did Ritchie and Flyer Kyte. Kyte was clever with a jew's harp. Ritchie was always full of tales. They was both good chaps, Kyte and Ritchie, but they're dead now."

And so it went on: Tom's own roll of honour: Cuddy; Evans; Mustow; Braid; Verning; Reynolds; Privitt; Smith; all good men but dead now.

"Good God," Betony said, "are none of them left alive at all?"

"Not many," he said, "but there's new chaps coming up all the time."

"It's all wrong," she said, "that so many men should be sent out to die, cut down like cornstalks in a field."

"Yes," he said, "it's all wrong."

Looking at him, she thought him changed. He had always had a haunted look, but now he was old before his time. His eyes had seen things no eyes should see.

"Dicky'll be called up next spring," she said.

"Ah. I know. He was telling me."

"Where will it end, Tom? Where will it end?"

"I dunno, but it's bound to end somewhere, I suppose."

"Shall we beat the Germans, do you think?"

"I reckon we've got to," Tom said, "or all them lives will've gone for nothing."

"Take care of yourself," Betony said, "and tell your mates the cake will be coming."

"Don't let the war be over yet," said Dicky, " 'cos I want to be in it and have some fun."

"Dicky, be quiet!" Beth exclaimed. "You've got no notion what you're saying."

"Ah, you jus be quiet, son," Jesse said, "and give Tom a hand with that there kitbag."

"I'll be knitting you something," granna said, "just as soon as I find the time."

"I hope you ent losing your touch as a craftsman," said Great-grumpa Tewke, thumping Tom's back as he climbed up into the trap. "You should practise carving whenever you can, to keep your hand in for when you come home."

And Tilly Preston, waiting outside The Rose and Crown, watching for the pony and trap, ran out into the road and threw a knot of ribbons, red white and blue, into Tom's lap.

"Keep them, Tom, and they'll bring you luck."

Tom stuffed the ribbons into his pocket. Jesse, driving, glanced at his face.

"D'you like Tilly Preston, Tom?" he asked.

"She's all right," Tom said, shrugging.

The Sixth Battalion, having moved south into France again, was re-forming, absorbing men of the Tenth Battalion, disbanded after heavy losses, and being made up to strength again with new drafts just out from England. Tom and Newers were now old sweats. They felt entitled to give themselves airs. They were veterans. Men of experience. It was their duty, Newers said, to take the new recruits in hand especially when they got to the trenches.

"See as much as you can, hear as much as you can, and do sod-all about either," he said. "It won't be long now. We're dying of boredom on both sides. And what's left of the B.E.F. will all go home in the same boat."

The new men were teased without mercy.

"Have you brought your sugar card?"

"The sergeant likes you to call him dad."

"Six months as san-man and you get the D.S.O. Twelve months and you get the V.C. Two years, you retire on a pension."

One young lad, entering his dugout, was horrified at the number of rats scampering and fighting there.

"Ugh!" he said, drawing back. "I don't like rats."

"You'd better get to like 'em," Newers said, " 'cos they bloody well think the world of us!"

"Hey, Toss," said Danson. "There's a chap here asking to see Jack Johnson!"

"That's nothing," said Rush. "I've got one here complaining about his thigh-boots. He says he never takes nothing but number nines!"

The weather turned cold. There was deep snow. The men had been issued with leather jackets. They sat huddled close in the tiny dugouts, woollen comforters pulled down over their ears, sandbags tied like gaiters round their legs.

"I find myself thinking of featherbeds, and my missus beside me, warm as toast, tickling my back," said Chirpy Bird. "Pathetic, ent it?"

"I think of my furnace," said Bert Moore, an iron-worker from Wolverhampton, "and the heat in my face as I push a load in on the jib."

"I think of summer days and cricket on Pitchcroft," said Bob Newers, who came from Worcester, "sitting in the sun in my white flannels, waiting my turn to go in and bat."

"I think of damn-all when I'm cold," said Baines, " 'cos my brainbox is froze and won't work."

It was very quiet along most of the front during the cold spell early that year. Too quiet, Newers said, and they feared the worst.

"Nip and see what Jerry's doing and tell him not to, will you, Cox?"

"D'you think it's true he's getting ready to give us hell?"

"Nasty rumours are always true. He'll have a go at smashing us before the Yanks get organized. It won't be much use his trying after."

The rumours became established fact. German prisoners, coming in, all spoke of a big offensive, and from the forward observation posts, German reinforcements could be seen massing behind their lines, just out of range of the British guns. The weather was improving. March winds were drying the ground. In the little salient near

Cambrai, British troops, working to strengthen the defences there, were caught unawares by a heavy bombardment of mustard gas. Two men in three were incapacitated.

Tom, delivering a message at Montevalle, saw a long string of these gassed men, blinded, voiceless, filing hand-in-hand along a zig-zag communication trench, making their way to the rear line. He counted a hundred and thirty-three.

"Will they recover?" he asked an ambulance man at Chesle.

"After a fashion," the man said.

On the night of the twenty-first, the Germans began an intense shelling of the British line, all the way from Croiselle to La Fère. It was heavier than anything known before, and in the forward defences the British garrisons crouched low under the storm, deafened, concussed, as the earth split around them on all sides.

"This is it," Newers said. "Once this stops they'll be all over us like flies on a cowpat, God rot their wicked souls."

From where they lay they could see British shells exploding in St Quentin. Gunflashes turned the night to day. Some distance away, on their right flank, a machine-gun post was blown sky high, and, further on still, three shells in a row fell into a trench sector.

"Poor bastards," Newers said. "That's Wilkie gone up with them emma gees. I liked old Wilkie. I'll miss him a lot. He owed me a shilling from a game of poker."

First light came, struggling through a thick fog, but the German bombardment continued all morning. Then at nine-thirty it moved over and the German infantry were seen advancing, grey-clad men coming out of the grey fog. The forward posts opened fire.

The fog was helping the enemy, and they came not in waves but in separate groups, working their way through the weakly manned British defences, then turning on them from flank and rear. The forward posts were soon overwhelmed. The few survivors were falling back.

In the main line, there was confusion. Officers strode up and down the trench, calling to the men to keep their heads. One young subaltern ran to and fro several times.

"Keep calm! Keep calm!" he shouted to the men on the firestep. "Keep quite calm and choose your target carefully."

"Hark at him," Newers muttered. "He's the one that's getting excited."

But Captain Highet, their company commander, watching over the parapet, was calm and quiet to a degree, ready to give the order to fire. A group of Germans emerged from the fog out in front, coming across at a steady pace. The order was given and there was a burst of rifle fire. The group of Germans disappeared, its place was taken by another, and other groups loomed up behind. Elsewhere, in many places, they had broken through the main line.

The Sixth Battalion, in Artichoke Trench, had the enemy strong on both sides and was in danger of being cut off. Bombers were posted in shell-holes at either flank, to cover withdrawal, and Tom was in the party on the right, with Newers, Danson, Grover and Coombes. The battalion fell back, fighting fiercely as it went, till it reached the safety of Sandboy Redoubt. The bombing parties were the last to leave. They stayed until all their grenades were thrown, and then made a dash for it, every man for himself.

On the way, Tom came under fire from a German machine-gun, and was hit in the calf of each leg. He crawled to a shell-hole and lay low. The machine-gun was firing from the rim of a crater fifty yards off. There came an explosion and the machine-gun stopped. A well-aimed bomb had found its mark.

His puttees and trousers were ripped from the back of each leg and hung in tatters, sticky with blood and fragments of flesh. He was trying to open his field-dressing when a voice spoke and there was Newers, coming towards him, crouched low, unlit pipe between his teeth.

"Bloody fool!" Tom said. "Coming back through all this!"

"I thought you might have a match," Newers said.

He knelt beside Tom and broke a phial of iodine over each wound. The dressings were soaked with blood instantly, so Newers took off his own puttees and used them as extra bandages. Tom then fainted and knew nothing more.

Newers gathered him up in his arms and set out across the stretch of open ground now overrun by enemy troops. His only cover was the fog, but he reached the rear lines unharmed and carried Tom to the medical aid post at Vraine St Marie, a distance of almost two miles. When Tom recovered consciousness, Newers had gone.

Tom spent three weeks in the field hospital at St Irac, and was then put on a long period of light duty, in the stores at Aubrille. He fretted, rather, away from his mates, for the news coming in was grave indeed. The Germans had broken through everywhere, and the Allies were falling back all the time, fighting desperately over every mile of ground yielded. The Commander-in-Chief had issued a message to all his troops. They had their backs to the wall, he said, and every man must fight to the end.

By the end of May, however, the German offensive was losing its force, and the British line began to hold. Hope was reviving, growing strong, and soon there was confidence in the air.

In the middle of June, Tom rejoined his own battalion, in reserve at Chantereine. Three months had passed and many friends had disappeared, killed or sent home badly wounded, but Bob Newers was still there, and Pecker Danson, and Dave Rush was back again.

"And we've still got Fritz with us, of course. That's him over there, across the way, but don't provoke him if you can help it 'cos he's lost his sense of humour lately."

"I thought you'd got a Blighty one," Pecker Danson said to Tom.

"Not Toss," said Newers. "He's a lot tougher than he looks."

Twice in June the Germans attacked nearby Bligny, but were beaten back. Afterwards, the attacks died down in that sector, and things were quiet for the Sixth Battalion. Away on their right, the besieged city of Reims still held, and away on their left, the enemy advance had been stopped in the woods on the banks of the Marne. In the middle of July the Germans attempted another thrust, but were checked by Foch and thrown back to the Vesle, and by the end of the month the German offensive had come to a halt everywhere.

In the lull that followed, the Allies had time to nurse themselves back to strength again. They counted their losses and re-formed. Soon they were ready to strike the blow that would end the war. The American forces were building up. The French spirit was on fire again. This time it really *would* be over by Christmas.

August and September saw the turning of the tide. The Allies were advancing, driving the enemy back across

France. By early October the Hindenburg Line was in Allied hands.

"What'll you do when you get to Berlin, Pecker?"

"Dance the Blue Danube with the Kaiser."

"And then what?"

"Catch the next train for Blighty, of course."

The Sixth Battalion was on the march. They had seen little action in the past six weeks, but now, after careful and strenuous training, they were on their way to the front line again.

At a small town called Vaillon St Jacques, the people turned out to watch them march through. Women ran forward with cups of coffee for the soldiers to drink; old men wanted to shake their hands; children waved small tricolour flags. At one house, plainly a brothel, a group of women stood on the iron balcony, blowing kisses and baring their breasts.

"Tommees, come in! We give you good time! Soldats anglais, we surrender to you!"

"On our way back!" the soldiers answered. "Mind you keep the offer open!"

And, marching on, they sang their own version of a popular song.

> "Keep the red lamp burning . . .
> We shall be returning . . .
> Though a soldier's pay is poor
> He can spare two francs . . ."

Outside Vaillon, as they marched through, they could hear the noise of guns some miles away towards the east, reminding them that the war was not quite over yet.

"Here we go!" Danson muttered. "Back to the bloody mincing-machine."

"Only one more river," Newers said in a comforting way.

In pouring wet weather in late September, they marched through Les Boeufs, Le Transloy, Rocquigny, Chenay. It was a district they knew all too well. Many friends were buried there. They knew the kind of weather too. Did it never stop raining in this country? It was worse than Manchester, Shuttleworth said. A few days later they passed through the ruins of La Bouleau, and, on another dark rainy night, went into trenches in the front line.

Their objective was called County Point, a strongpoint in the enemy line. C and D Companies were to attack together and press on to the sunken road known as Bull's Alley. A and B Companies were to follow up on their right flank and take the position called Cock's Spur. At five in the morning, first light, the British guns opened fire and the four attacking companies advanced behind the creeping barrage, over slippery ground that rose slightly.

In front hung a curtain of thick choking smoke as the barrage fell, moving forward, perfectly timed. The first wave of troops was now straggling, thrown out by the broken ground, unable to see because of the smoke drifting past in coils. Orders were shouted but were lost in the noise.

Coming out of the smoke, Tom found himself stumbling against a thicket of barbed wire surrounding a German machine-gun emplacement. The gun was in pieces behind the shattered breastwork and the gun-crew were lying dead. He swung to the right, going round the entanglement, and half a dozen men went with him. Two of them fell, hit by snipers hidden somewhere in no-man's-land, and the others went forward at a trot. But the rest of the line had disappeared, somewhere under the drifting smoke, and in front of the few lay a water-logged wasteland rising to an empty sky. Rain was falling heavily. Visibility was bad. It seemed to Tom they had gone past their mark. The little group stopped to confer.

"If this is the Cheltenham racecourse," said Bird, "it seems there's no meeting today, lads."

"Do we go back or go on?" asked Tom.

"On," said Brownlee, "and hope for the best."

They had gone perhaps three hundred yards when a shell exploded in front of them. The five lay low, then went on again, and now they could see the enemy line, in the dim distance away on their left, marked out by the flash of guns and the puffs of smoke hanging in the rain. They could also see their own men, like ants in a swarm, seething on the slopes there.

"Jesus wept!" Newers said. "We *have* gone astray and no mistake."

They changed direction and began to run, the rain now blowing in their faces, and as they stumbled through the mud a machine-gun rattled from a sandbagged emplacement on their right. Brownlee fell dead, and Bird doubled over, hit in the stomach. The three remaining men dived for the cover of a shell-crater and Newers got a bullet in the arm.

Tom and Thurrop looked over the rim, trying to locate the machine-gun post. A chance British shell located it, one of six fired from a battery of field-guns at Souane-la-Mare, and the watchers saw it go up in smoke. Tom and Thurrop went out to help Bird, but found him dead, his face contorted. They crawled back to Newers, who sat in the crater, blowing through his empty pipe.

"Don't tell me – I know – we're in a hole. We'll be mentioned in dispatches for this and asked to lecture to the rookies. 'How to lose your way in a direct charge.' Oh, well, I daresay the chaps'll manage without us."

"You all right, Bob?"

"No, half of me's left, Toss."

"Let's see that arm. I'll do you up."

"Go easy, then, 'cos that's the arm I shall use for bowling when I play for Worcestershire next year."

Tom dressed the badly torn arm and gave Newers his water-bottle. Thurrop was up at the edge of the crater, looking out, his rifle at the ready. There came a sharp crack and he fell back, dead, rolling over and over down the slope till he splashed into the pool at the bottom. Tom went quickly up to the rim and lay looking out. There was a movement in the next hole and he took aim. The sniper heaved and then lay still. Tom stayed where he was, watching.

"Did you get him?" Newers called.

"Yes, but I reckon there's more of 'em out here somewhere."

"Our own chaps've got it in for us as well. We'd better get to hell out of here as soon as we can find another hole."

The field-guns at Souane were firing again and the shells were falling very close.

"Stupid sods," Newers said. "You'd think they'd know a British-held crater when they saw it, wouldn't you?"

Tom was just turning when a shell exploded within the crater and he was knocked over by the blast. Debris covered him and he felt scorched. He got to his knees and shook off dirt that weighed a ton. Everything now seemed very quiet and when the smoke cleared away he saw that Newers had been blown to pieces. Nothing remained that could be called a man. Yet the pipe from his mouth was quite undamaged, lying in the mud some yards away. Tom crawled towards it and picked it up. He put it in his pocket and buttoned the flap. And then without warning a shell exploded in front of him, a fireworks show inside his head, followed by darkness.

When he became conscious again, he thought it was night-time, but after a while he realized he was blind. The darkness was in his own head. It was not lit by stars, or Very lights, or the distant flashes of guns. It was darkness thick and absolute, and he was at its mercy.

The upper part of his skull felt numb, yet inside it was full of pain. When he put up a hand, there were hard splinters embedded in his flesh, all over his face and scalp and neck. His uniform hung in ribbons in front, and his body felt small, as though it had first been scorched then crushed; and everywhere, when his fingers explored, he encountered sharp chips of metal and stone, driven into his skin by the hot blast. He had an open wound in his chest, sticky with blood, and he held his field-dressing pressed against it.

He crawled from the crater, out onto flat land. His eyes were hurting him, hot in their sockets, and whenever he blinked he could feel the gritty fragments in them. He crawled on his belly; he had no strength to raise himself up; and he pushed himself on with one arm. His mouth was shrivelled and he drank from puddles, water corrupt, evil, stinking, for dead men had rotted recently in this ground and cordite vapours had spread their poison everywhere.

He came to a trench and wriggled down into its bottom. It was an old German trench, long deserted, and in many places its sides had collapsed. He crawled along it for some way, and then sat still, listening. The sound of gunfire was very faint, and he thought his hearing had been affected. He felt very cold and knew he ought to keep on the move, but before he could make another effort he had passed into a deep faint.

He awoke to a small scrabbling sound, somewhere close at hand. A rat, perhaps, scavenging among the bones. But then he heard a human footfall and the click of a rifle bolt being drawn back.

"Who's there?" he called. He could see nothing.

"Stehen bleiben oder ich schiesse! Hände hoch, Du englischer Tommee, keine dummen Geschichten. Du bist mein Gefangener. Verstanden?"

God in heaven! He had crawled right into the enemy lines. How had he managed to travel so far? But the German, it seemed, was all alone: a man like himself, cut off from his comrades, seeking shelter where he could. He saw that Tom was hurt and unarmed, and there was a sound as he leant his rifle against the wall.

"Du lieber Himmel! Du siehst ja schlimm aus. Trink einen Schluck Wasser."

"Water," Tom said. "Yes. Thanks."

He felt the bottle at his lips and drank from it weakly, his head back. It was muddy stuff, tasting of petrol, but might have come from a clear mountain stream, so cool was it in his aching throat. He was too weak to move and lay where he was, shivering, while the German touched him, looking at his wounds.

"Blown-up? Stimmt's? Dich hat's da draussen irgendwo erwischt?"

"Blind," Tom said, and put up a hand to touch his eyes. "My eyesight's gone. Napoo! Kaput!"

"Tut mir leid! Armer Kerl! Sehr unangenehme Sache. Wenn mein Kameraden kommen, können wir uns vernünftig um Dich kümmern. Wir haben gute Arzte, die Dir wieder auf die Beine helfen."

"Kamerad," Tom said. It was the only word he understood.

The German had opened his ragged tunic and was cleansing the open wound in his chest. The unseen hands were quick, sure, gentle, as they put on a dressing and tied it in place.

"Thanks," Tom said. "It feels a lot better, that's a fact."

"T'anks? Hast Du Dich etwa bedankt? Vielen Dank?"

"Ah, that's right, danke schön."

"Ich heisse Josef. Und Du?"

"I dunno. Search me!" But after a moment he understood. "Tom," he said, wearily.

"Tom? Tommee? Führst Du mich etwa an der Nase 'rum?" The German was chuckling, slapping his leg. "Fritz und Tommee! Tommee und Fritz! Merk' Dir – ich bin nicht Fritz, sondern Josef." Then, as Tom shivered again, he gave an exclamation and got to his feet. "Ich werd' Dir was zu essen holen, und veilleicht was zum Zudecken."

He was gone a long time. Tom thought he had gone for good. But he came back with a German greatcoat and helped Tom into it, wrapping it round him and turning the collar up to his ears. He also brought food and a stoneware bottle full of liquor.

"Käse," he said, and placed a small piece of cheese in Tom's hand. "Was heisst das auf englisch?"

"Cheese," Tom said, putting it whole into his mouth and sucking slowly. "Danke schön."

"Brot," Josef said, and this time he gave Tom a crust of bread. "Was heisst das?"

"Bread," Tom said. "I hope you've got some for yourself. Eh? Have you? Brot for Josef?"

"Richtig. Ordentlich was zu essen für uns beide und natürlich 'ne Menge Schnaps."

When Tom had eaten, Josef took his hands and placed them round the stoneware bottle, helping him raise it to his lips. The drink was warming and brought some life into Tom's veins.

"Schnaps. Was heisst das auf englisch?"

"I reckon that's brandy," Tom said. "It's good. Very good. It's made me feel a lot better."

"Schmeckt's Ja? Freut mich. Du solltest Dich jetzt aber mal ordentlich auspennen." Josef was making snoring noises.

"Ah," Tom said, his head aching. "Yes, you're right, I'm about done."

"Leg' Dich hin – so geht's gut. Ich halte Wache. Bisschen später kommen meine Kameraden und wir sehen zu, dass wir Dich zur Sanitäts-Station hinkriegen."

"Is it night-time?" Tom asked. "Nacht, is it?"

"Nacht? Ja, es ist zehn Uhr."

"That's just what it feels like," Tom said.

He lay on his back, staring upwards, but could see nothing of the night sky. Only a kind of throbbing blackness. His eyes were ruined and he was too numb to think about it. He fell asleep like a dead man.

He awoke to a smell of hot coffee and sat up, looking around him. Surely his eyes were not quite ruined after all, for when he looked downwards at the ground, the darkness was greater than when he looked upwards into the sky, and there was the hint of a shadow moving, where Josef was busy preparing breakfast. Only a blurred featureless shape, it was true, but it made his heart leap up with hope. Yesterday, blackness. Today, a grey fog. Tomorrow, perhaps, there would be light.

"Morgen!" said Josef. "Trocken, sogar."

"My eyes are better!" Tom exclaimed. "I can see! I can see!"

"Was war das? Ich versteh' Dich nicht. Kannst Du mich sehen? Kannst Du mein Gesicht erkennen?"

"Eyes," Tom said, and pointed to them. "They seem a lot better than they was."

"Dir geht's besser – Willst Du das sagen? Schön, gut. Gott sei Dank!"

He brought Tom a breakfast of black coffee, faintly sweetened, and a hunk of rye bread with a slice of stale cold sausage on it. They sat opposite each other, with the fire between them, and Tom peered at the German's outline, a darker shadow against the greyness. He wished he knew what the man looked like. He wished he could touch the unseen face. And he put out his hands in such a way that the man understood him, and, laughing a little, guided the hands towards his face, allowing Tom to feel his features.

"Bin ich nicht schön? Ich find' mich wunderschön! Bin ein Bild von Junge, findst Du nicht?"

He laughed again, deep in his throat, and Tom smiled, guessing the nature of the joke. He now had a picture of the German's face: square in shape and broad-browed, the flesh shrunken on the strong bones, the stubbled skin tightly stretched; and he let his hands fall into his lap.

"You ent been getting enough to eat. You shouldn't have shared your food with me."

"Na? Was war das wieder? Was sagst Du da?"

"Have you got a wife?" Tom asked. "Frau? Kinder? Family?"

"Ja, klar. Ich habe Bilder von ihnen. Ach, stimmt ja, Du kannst ja nicht sehen. Ich hab 'ne Frau, Margarete, und zwei Kinder, Peterlein und Lottchen. Ausserdem noch einee Hund Waldi." He made a noise like a dog barking. "Hund!" he said. "Was heisst das auf englisch?"

"Dog," Tom said.

"Dog. Waldi. Er kommt gut mit Schafen zurecht." He made a noise like a sheep bleating. "Schafen!" he said. "Was heisst das?"

"Sheep," Tom said.

"Ja. Ja. Gut-dog-mit-sheep. Dann werd' ich wohl bald prima englisch sprechen!"

So the man was a shepherd and lived on a farm. Why had he left it and come to fight? Were German shepherds under conscription? Tom had no way of asking these questions. He picked up his mug and drank his coffee.

Suddenly there was a noise. Voices talking not far away. Josef sprang up with an exclamation and went running off along the trench. Tom remained sitting, ears strained, trying to interpret the sounds that reached him. Then came the loud-bouncing crack of a rifle, followed by several cracks close together, and, after a pause, footsteps coming to the edge of the trench. An English voice spoke, and Tom answered.

"Good God, there's one of our own lads down here!" said the voice, plainly that of an officer. "And in pretty bad shape by the look of things. What's your name, man, and which lot are you from?"

"28233 Maddox, Sixth Battalion, Three Counties."

"I thought you were a German, wearing that coat. It's lucky you spoke up quickly like that or I might have shot you. Can you walk, Maddox?"

"I reckon I can. The only thing is, I can't see too well."

"Hang on a minute. We'll give you a hand. Cunningham! Dodds! Come and give this man a hand."

"Where's Josef?" Tom asked.

"What, that bloody German?" said one of the men who came to help him. "He's bloody well dead, with three or four bullets in his rotten carcass."

"But he was my friend! He saved my life! He gave me his coat and let me share his food and drink."

"Did he, by God?" the officer said. "Well, I'm sorry, Maddox, but he *did* open fire on us first, and he got my man Ross straight through the heart. That made me see red, I can tell you, because Ross was the best servant I ever had."

As they led Tom away they told him that the battle of La Bouleau had been successful. County Point had been taken, so had Cock's Spur, and eight hundred Germans had surrendered. The whole of that sector was in British hands.

In the crowded hospital at Rouen, a doctor came every morning and evening and examined his eyes, looking into them with a tiny torch.

"Will they get better?" Tom asked.

"Oh, yes, I think so. They're improving already, aren't they?"

"A bit. Not much. I still can't see nothing but shapes and shadows."

"It's early days yet. That shell must have been a pretty near thing. I'd say you were lucky to be alive."

The hospital was never quiet. There were over a hundred men in the ward with Tom, many of them in great pain, groaning, whimpering, crying out. The nurses were terribly overworked. Their voices were often loud and impatient, their hands ruthless, plucking dressings from torn flesh. Tom, still in darkness even by day, was often confused by the bustle around him. It hurt his head and made him feel dizzy. He had nothing to say to these brisk white presences talking across him. He was all alone at the centre of a world of noise and movement.

But one day, out of the commotion, a more restful presence, a gentler hand, and a girl's voice speaking in quiet tones beside him.

"Private Maddox? Somebody said you came from Chepsworth, where they blow on the mustard to make it cool."

Tom smiled. The girl's voice was a voice from home. Her accents were his, though not so broad, and she called the town "Cheps'orth" in the local manner.

"You must come from there yourself, knowing that saying."

"I come from Blagg, a tiny place four miles out. Do you know it?"

"I should just think I do, for I come from Huntlip, right next door. Why, we're practically neighbours, you and me."

"The people of Huntlip are either foxes or hounds, they say, so which are you?"

"And the people of Blagg all go in rags!" he answered back, enjoying himself.

"Not me," she said, "I get my uniform free of charge." And he could hear that she was smiling. "Whereabouts in Huntlip do you live?"

"Place called Cobbs, out towards Middening. There's a carpenter's shop – Tewke and Izzard's."

"Oh, yes, I've passed it often."

"What's your name?"

"Linn Mercybright."

"I don't remember you at school in Huntlip."

"We've only lived at Blagg these past five years. Before that we lived at Stamley and before that at Skinton Monks. My dad's a bit of a wanderer. He works at

Outlands Farm at present and has a cottage in Stoney Lane."

"I know Outlands. I've been there a lot. But I'd better not say what I was up to."

"Poaching?" she said. "You needn't worry. My father's only a labourer there. He'd very likely give you his blessing."

Tom leant forward a little way, but could see her only as a white shadow.

"I wish I could see you properly."

"You will be able to soon, I'm sure, but I must go now or Sister will have me on the carpet."

"Nurse," he said, anxiously. "Nurse! Are you there?"

"Yes?" she said. "What is it?"

"Will you come and see me again?"

"Yes, of course, every day."

She had been in service at Meynell Hall before volunteering as a nurse. She would go back there when the war was over.

"God willing, of course."

"It won't be long now, from what they're saying."

"God grant they're right."

"Linn?" he said. "How old are you?"

"Close on twenty-two."

"Six months older'n me, then."

"I see you've had a letter from home. And a parcel too."

"Trouble is, I can't write back. Not a proper letter. All I could do was get someone to fill in a card."

"I'll write a letter for you, when I get time. Tomorrow, perhaps. It's my easy day."

Next day when she came, he was sitting out on the terrace. There was bright sunlight and he could see it on her hair, which was reddish-gold and shone like copper, for now, off duty, she wore no cap.

"I can see you better today," he said. "You've got red hair."

"Mrs Winson at Meynell Hall always used to call it auburn."

"Auburn, that's right. I couldn't think of the right word."

"I was only teasing you," she said, laughing. "Of course it's red, and who cares? The main thing is that you can see it. Has Dr Young been to see you today?"

"Early this morning," Tom said, and, after a moment: "Strikes me he's bald."

Linn, delighted, laughed again. He had never heard laughter quite like hers. He could see her leaning back in the chair.

"You *are* improving, aren't you?" she said. "Soon you'll be able to see our warts."

"Warts?" he said. "What, you?"

"That was just another joke."

"Are you going to write my letter?"

"Just this once, yes, but soon you'll see to write your own."

At the end of the week he *could* see. His sight was almost back to normal. He could see that Collins, in the bed beside him, who had lost both his legs, was only a boy of eighteen, and that Beale, in the bed on the other side, was jerking with tetanus. He could see the many men poisoned by the fumes of gas, who lay with faces discoloured and burnt, breathing painfully, with a terrible noise, drowning with their lungs full of foul bubbling foam, whose dying was drawn out day by day.

He could see, too, that the wound in his chest had now

healed, leaving a dark empurpled scar; that his face and body were criss-crossed all over with smaller scars; that the dressing on his foot had concealed from him the loss of two toes.

"Seems I came off lightly," he said, "compared with most of the chaps here."

"You'll be going to hospital in England soon."

"Ah. I know. The doctor told me."

He could see now that Linn's eyes and eyebrows were dark brown; that her features were small and neatly made; that, suffering as she did with the mutilated men in her care, her cheerfulness often cost her dear.

When his transfer came, he was given only an hour's notice. He packed his few belongings quickly and hobbled off in search of Linn. He found her in the last ward, renewing the dressing on a man's neck.

"Seems I'm for off. Marching orders. They're putting me on the next train."

"I heard there was a contingent going. I wondered if you might be among them."

"They don't give much warning, do they?" he said. "I've been running round like a scalded cat."

"Hoi!" said the man whose wound she was dressing. "You go ahead, nurse, and say goodbye to your chap here. I shan't hurt for a minute or two."

"No," Linn said. "I mustn't leave you half done. Besides which, Sister's watching."

"I'll say goodbye, then," Tom said. He could see the ward sister, three rows away, frowning severely across at him. "Maybe I'll see you back at Blagg."

"Sure to," she said, and turned to smile at him, looking at him in a searching way. "You might go to Outlands and look up my dad. Tell him I'm well and looking forward to coming home."

She turned back to what she was doing, and her patient gave Tom a sympathetic wink.

"I'd let you take her back to Blighty, cock, only my need is greater than yourn, I reckon."

Tom nodded and walked away.

A month later, after treatment at the military hospital in Sawsford, he was home in Huntlip, discharged from the Army and wearing civilian clothes again.

It felt very strange, sleeping alone in a room of his own, after the crowded hospital ward, and the crowded billets. Often he lay wide awake, listening to the silence, till the small sounds of the household at rest came to him through the deafening stillness. He would look at the window and wonder at the steadiness of the sky outside: its unbroken darkness when there was mist; the constancy of moon and stars when the night was a clear one. He expected the lightning of gunflash and flare to whiten the sky and set it pulsing. It took a long time to get used to an earth so dark, so hushed, so perfectly still.

"Why've you been discharged?" Dicky asked. "If your eyes is all right again, why don't they want you back in the Army?"

"Seems I ent quite up to standard. My papers've got 'shell-shock' on 'em."

"Is that all that's wrong with you?"

"Leave Tom alone," Beth said to her son. "Just be thankful he's back safe."

"Ah, don't ask so many questions, boy," said great-grumpa. "Tom may've lost a few bits and pieces."

"I've lost the tops off two toes," Tom said.

"There!" said granna. "And I was going to make you some socks."

"He'll still need socks, granna," Betony said, impatiently.

"What gets me," Dicky said, "is Tom's being hurt by a British shell."

"Them things happen," Tom said.

Dicky himself was in khaki now. He was based at Capleton and had a weekend pass every month. He had lost all desire to go to the front. Such a muddle it all seemed. He wouldn't have minded dying a hero, but to get blown up by your own side! People said it would end soon, and he hoped they were right.

At The Rose and Crown, when Tom went in with Dicky one evening, Emery Preston was quite friendly.

"A drink on me for you two lads. I always believe in treating soldiers."

"I knew you'd come back, Tom," Tilly said. "I never doubted it. Not once. Have you brought me any souvenirs?"

"No," Tom said, "no souvenirs."

"Show her the scar on your chest," Dicky said. "That's a souvenir, ent it?"

"How long d'you think it'll be before it's over?" Emery asked.

"Not long now," Tom said.

One Monday morning, Tom and Jesse were up on the slopes of Lippy Hill, repairing a field-barn for Isaac Mapp. The day was a cold one, with drizzle blowing on the wind, grey and drenching. Jesse was sawing a new beam, inside the barn, where he was sheltered. He stopped work, thinking he could hear music, and went across to the door to listen.

Brass-bands on a weekday? There must be something

wrong with his ears! Yet somewhere down in the greyness
below there was certainly a banging, clanging noise of
some kind and, as the explanation came to him, a bright
sunrise dawned in his face.

"It's the Armistice!" he shouted to Tom. "That's what it
is! It's come at last! The war is over!"

He dropped his saw, snatched up his jacket, and went
hurrying down the steep track, leaving Tom behind. He
reached the road at the bottom of the hill and there,
sure enough, the villagers were out from Otchetts and
Peckstone and Dugwell and Blagg, and were marching
on Huntlip, armed with pots and pans and biscuit-tins, –
anything that would make a din – gathering more people
as they went.

"The war is over!" they said to him. "The Armistice was
signed at eleven o'clock. The Kaiser has skipped it and
gone to Holland. Our boys'll soon be coming home!"

"Glory be!" Jesse said. "I knowed what it was the very
minute I heard the rumpus! I've got two boys of my own,
you know, William and Roger. They'll be coming home!
They'll be coming home!"

He fell in with the noisy procession and danced along
with it, clapping people on the back and telling them
about William and Roger.

"My eldest boy, he's a bombardier, and my second,
well, he's a gunner, see. But God bless my soul! To have
them back again after such years!"

And, growing impatient to reach home, he took a
short-cut across the fields, sending sheep and cattle in all
directions.

In the kitchen at Cobbs, when he stumbled in, Beth sat
at the table, a cabbage half shredded on the board before
her. Great-grumpa Tewke stood at the window. Granna
Tewke sat by the fire.

"Ent you heard the news?" Jesse demanded. "It's the Armistice! The war is over! Everyone's out in the roads, creating, and the din can be heard from here to Scarne. Ent you had word of it down here?"

"Yes, we've had word of it," Beth said.

"Well, you don't seem too bucked," he said, laughing. "I thought you'd all be over the moon."

Her stillness stopped him, brought him up short, and he saw the telegram on the table, lying open, under her hands. William and Roger had been killed in action. Sunday the tenth. Eleven A.M. Twenty-four hours before the signing of the Armistice.

Only two days before, there had been a letter, written by William: "We're in the pink, Rog and me, still washing behind the ears and sticking together like you told us to do."

They had died together, serving their gun, when an enemy shell had fallen directly into their gunpit.

The carpenter's shop stopped work that day. The men were sent home. Dicky, coming on special leave, entered a house of terrible silence. Betony was there and broke the news. He went at once to look for his father and was shocked to hear him weeping aloud in the empty workshop. He crept away, unable to face such open grief, and returned later. His father stood hunched against the workbench.

"Why should my sons've been took from me? Why? Why?"

"You've still got *me*, dad. You've still got me."

Jesse made no answer, and Dicky went away again, hurt and baffled.

A few days later, a small package came, containing the two dead boys' effects: cap-badges, passbooks, letters, snapshots. Jesse was angry at sight of these things. He wanted to hurl them into the fire.

"What use are they without the boys?"

"No use," Beth said, "except just to remember them by."

She put the badges up on their portrait, pinning them to the ledge of the frame. Jesse gave a groan and left the room, pushing Dicky aside in the doorway. Beth turned and saw the boy's eyes as he looked at the portrait of his brothers.

"You mustn't hate them for having died."

Dicky was ashamed. How did his mother know his feelings? His father knew nothing. He had shut them all out.

"My dad don't want me nowadays. I reckon he wishes me dead like them."

"Your father's not hisself at present. It's up to you to be patient with him."

Betony, seeking to comfort Dicky, went with him to Chepsworth Park, to the special ceremony held there. A part of the grounds, about fifteen acres, had been given to the public by Mr Champley to commemorate the signing of the Armistice. A plaque was unveiled on one of the gateposts; a drinking-fountain was switched on; doves were released from the old stone dovecote. It would be known as Polygon Park and would be a place of recreation for the people of Chepsworth. The house itself, with the rest of the grounds, was already a home for disabled soldiers. Mr Champley's only son had been killed in the battle of Polygon Wood.

"Is it wrong for us to be gadding about?" Dicky asked.

"No, of course not," Betony said.

"My dad seems to think so," Dicky said.

Huntlip itself had almost a week of celebrations, ending after dark on Saturday night with a torchlight procession through the village, up onto the open common. A straw-stuffed effigy of the Kaiser, with a realistic withered arm and wearing a genuine pickelhaube helmet, was carried up with a rope round its neck and hanged from the old gibbet. A fire was lit underneath it and fireworks secreted in the dummy's body went off with loud bangs as the dummy burned.

Tom, alone in the outer darkness, stood watching the yellow flames leaping and the rockets fizzing towards the sky. The Kaiser had dropped from his rope now, and the gibbet itself was burning fiercely, beginning to topple into the fire. The dancers and singers were cheering its fall.

Tom felt withdrawn, a living ghost. The merrymakers were strangers to him. The night was unreal. Though the fire burnt, it could never warm him. Though the voices shouted, the words meant nothing. And although a great many people were gathered there under the moon, reaching out to one another, there were no pale arms reaching out to him. He was wrapped in a caul of darkness and aloneness.

"Tom?" said a voice, and Tilly Preston stood beside him. "I've been looking for you everywhere. Dicky said you was here some place. Why ent you dancing like the others? Harry Yelland's arrived now and brought his accordian."

"I ent much good at dancing, Tilly. I'm none too steady on my pins. But you go ahead and dance if you want to. I'd just as soon stand by and be quiet."

"I don't care about dancing neither. Great lumping louts they are here. I'd just as soon go for a walk, away from the noise, wouldn't you?"

She slid her arm into his and leant against him, looking into his thin dark face, lit by the bonfire, now burning red. She wanted to touch him, tenderly. She wanted to kiss his poor scarred eyes.

"What're you thinking about, Tom?"

"I was thinking of William and Roger," he said, "and all the other chaps that're gone."

"Don't be unhappy, Tom. Don't look like that. They wouldn't want you to grieve for them, would they, specially not on a night like tonight?"

"I was only thinking, that's all." And he turned his head to look at her. "You sure you don't want to join in the dancing?"

Tilly was wearing a hand-crocheted cap of fluffy red wool with a pompon on it, and a long scarf to match, with a similar pompon at either end. She looked very small, in her long winter coat and buttoned boots, like a child going skating on an icy pond.

"Don't you want my company, Tom?"

"I never said that."

"Wouldn't you sooner go for a walk?"

"All right," he said, "let's go for a walk."

She took him to a barn at New Strakes, her uncle's farm on the edge of the common, and led him up into the hayloft. She undid her coat and was warm against him, taking his hands and guiding them slowly till they covered her breasts, as she drew him down with her into the loose-tumbled sweet-smelling hay. Her breath was quick and hot on his lips. She ached for him and knew she could easily make him love her.

The church bell at Eastery, cracked for more than thirty years, had been recast in honour of Eastery's war dead, and on the fourth Sunday in November, when people from neighbouring villages came for the rededication service, it rang out tunefully over their heads, in celebration of the new peace.

"When your mother and me was married here," Jesse said to Betony, "that there bell made sorry music, but now it's something to hear, ent it?"

Old memories had unlocked his tongue. He was almost himself again.

"That's a wonderful thing to hear the church bells ringing out, after being stopped for so long, and to know they're ringing all over England. Ah, and that's a wonderful thing to know the captain is coming home, too, ent it? Are you sure you don't want me to drive you to the station?"

"No, father. I'd sooner go alone."

Betony was nervous, meeting Michael after two and a half years. She felt she hardly knew him at all; hardly remembered what he looked like; and could not, however hard she tried, pin down exactly what she had felt for him before the enforced separation.

But when at last he stepped from the train, helped by his mother, and she saw his starved face, with its slow-twisting smile and burning gaze, she knew that even if he were a perfect stranger he would still have a claim upon her love. She had seen so many men like this, their faces sculpted by suffering, and she felt that love should be theirs for the asking, given freely, without meanness.

"Betony," he said. "I thought this journey would never end. The train stopped at every station."

"Michael. Darling. You look so ill."

"I've had this damned 'flu. It's left me feeling as weak as a kitten."

When he took her in his arms, she could feel the tension thrumming in him, as though he were wound up tight like a spring.

"Will you marry me, Betony?"

"Yes," she whispered. "Yes. Oh, yes."

"Thank God for that. I have wanted you so. I think I would die if you said no now."

"I haven't said no. I've said yes."

"It was the one thing that kept me going. Thinking of you. Knowing you loved me. I remembered the way you looked at me, that last time, on this very station, when you got here just as the train was leaving. Do you remember?"

"Yes," she said, "I remember."

"If you hadn't been here today," he said "looking at me in just the same way, I don't know what I would have done."

"Michael. Darling. I *am* here."

And she felt the tension easing a little, as he let her go and looked directly into her face.

"Come along, both of you," his mother said. "There's a car waiting."

Their engagement was soon made public, and Betony was often at King's Hill House. Mrs Andrews gave her blessing, but thought they ought to wait a while before marrying. Six months, perhaps, or even a year.

"Don't you think I've waited long enough?" Michael said.

"You're a sick man. Is it fair on Betony to marry her before you're quite well?"

"I shan't take that long, getting well."

Alone together, he and Betony talked it out.

"My mother says it's unfair on you. Am I such a wreck?"

"Your mother thinks we're not really suited. She thinks if we have to wait a while we shall change our minds."

"In that case we'll wait!" he said grimly. "If only to prove how wrong she is. I don't really mind, so long as I can see you often."

"I don't mind, either. With my brothers only recently

dead, it would be better not to have a wedding in the family just yet. Also, there's so much work crying out to be done."

Her work in the factories had come to an end. She was now at Chepsworth Park, helping at the home for sick and disabled ex-soldiers. There, under the direction of volunteer doctors, men were learning to use new artificial limbs; nervous cases were learning to talk again; husks of men with burnt-out lungs were coming to terms with the remnant of life that was left to them; and those who had nothing left at all were being nursed through their last days of pain.

Betony travelled about the three counties, raising funds, recruiting helpers, buying equipment. And often she worked with the men themselves: washing and feeding those who were helpless; giving her shoulder to a cripple hobbling on metal legs; wheeling men in bathchairs out to a sunny place in the orangery. There were men who stammered very badly and men who spoke only gibberish, and Betony would sit with them, trying to interpret their crazy, tortured utterances.

There was a boy named Johnny Clegg whose brain, it seemed, was tied in knots. He had no family or friends; received no visitors; and frightened everyone at the home by dashing at them, shouting unintelligibly at the top of his voice. He was very wild-looking and, failing to make himself understood, would hurl himself about in a frenzy.

He came to Betony one day, took hold of her arms, and shook her savagely to and fro. He dragged her towards the piano.

"Lanno!" he shouted. "Lanno! Lanno! Midder-orders-plidder-chewing!"

"Tune?" she said. "Your mother always played a tune?"

"Assit! Assit! Plidder-chewing-obesit-obing!"

Betony went and sat at the piano and played *Home Sweet Home*. Johnny, beside her, stood perfectly still, listening intently to the end. Then when she turned round on the stool, he threw himself onto his knees before her, hid his face in her lap, and burst into tears.

He was always calmer after that. He had managed, just once, to make himself understood, and Betony, becoming attuned, was able to teach him to speak more clearly.

Tom stood at the bend in Stoney Lane, looking at the small neat redbrick cottage. The door was open, held back by an iron dog, and a few bits of matting lay out on the path. Blue smoke rose from the chimney.

A cloud of dust appeared at the doorway, followed by a man with a long-handled broom. He looked a lot older than Tom had expected and his face was half covered by a crinkly grey beard. He swept the dust out to the garden and stood leaning on his broom, staring at Tom who stood, hands in pockets, outside the gate.

"I seen you before. What're you up to, hanging about round my cottage?"

"I was looking for Linn," Tom said. "I wondered if she was home yet."

"If Linn was home," Jack Mercybright said, "I wouldn't be doing my own sweeping."

He came out onto the path and picked up the mats. Tom saw that one leg was lame at the knee.

"How come you know my daughter?"

"I was in France. In the hospital at Rouen. I live in Huntlip and Linn said to call and say how-do."

"Then why hang about instead of coming straight to the door? Did you think I'd eat you?"

"No," Tom said, "I didn't think that."

"Well, if you've come to tell me how she is, you ent making a lot of headway."

"She's all right. She said to tell you not to worry."

"No message besides?"

"I don't remember nothing else."

"Well, it's soon delivered, I'll say that!"

Mercybright was turning indoors. He seemed about to shut Tom out. But he paused briefly and spoke again.

"I had a letter from her this morning. Seems she'll likely be home tomorrow. Who shall I say was asking for her?"

"Tom Maddox."

"Well, you call again," Mercybright said. "In a day or two, when she's got settled. I'll tell her you're coming."

He went inside and closed the door.

Three days later, when Tom was again loitering in the lane, Linn saw him from the cottage window and ran out to meet him. She wore a dress of dark green, with a collar standing up at the neck, and above it her hair was bright red-gold, neatly twisted into a coil, but with finespun strands curling down over her nape. Her dark eyes were shining. She laughed at him in the way he remembered.

"Why don't you come to the door and knock? You surely don't think you aren't welcome?"

She took him by the arm and led him into the cottage kitchen. Her father sat beside the hearth, smoking an old-fashioned clay pipe, the bowl of which was shaped like an acorn. He motioned Tom towards the settle, and Linn sat there, too, perched sideways, watching Tom's face.

"How're your eyes since you've been home?"

"Pretty good, considering."

"Not giving you any pain?"

"I wouldn't say pain. Not exactly. My head beats a bit now and then, but nothing special."

"And your foot?" she asked. "How's that?"

"Pretty good, considering."

"Seems to me," her father said, "you must've been through the mill, young fella."

"I came out alive, though, that's something."

"Only just, by the look of you."

"Take no notice of dad," Linn said. "I never do. It's bad for him."

"Ent there some beer we can give this boy?"

"How should I know?" she asked, laughing. "I've only been home five minutes."

But she went out to the back kitchen and returned with two mugs full of frothing beer.

"That's what I like!" her father said. "Being waited on and mollied after. I missed that a lot while you was away, girl, and I reckon I bore it pretty well."

He took a deep drink and wiped the froth from moustache and beard. He looked at Tom with keen eyes.

"That'll come hard on me," he said, "when my daughter leaves me to get married."

When Tom had gone, and Linn was left alone with her father, she sat with her hands folded in her lap, laughing at him. He looked back at her, straight-faced.

"I been making enquiries about Tom Maddox."

"There, now!" she said. "Fancy that!"

"Seems his parents warnt never married."

"You surely don't hold that against him?"

"No. Surely not. But it's always better to know these things. And there was worser stories than that."

"What stories?"

"His father was a drunkard and killed his mother in a fit of temper. Then he hanged hisself in a tree. Your Tom was a babe about twelve months old."

"Poor boy," Linn said.

"There was good things told me as well as bad. They say the lad's a clever craftsman. Does carving and such, at Tewke and Izzard's, as well as first-rate carpentry." Jack leant forward to light a paper spill at the fire. "So it's just as well his sight warnt ruined by that shell."

"D'you like him, dad?"

"It's early days to answer that. He ent got a lot to say for hisself, has he?"

"Not as much as some I could mention."

"You ent growed less cheeky, since being out in foreign parts."

"Puff, puff, puff," she said, watching him as he lit his pipe. "Old tobacco-face! Always smoking!"

"The real question is, whether *you* like him."

"I think I do."

"But you ent sure?"

"He's a strange boy. He reminds me, somehow, of a wild animal. Oh, I don't mean wild in a fierce way, but awkward and shy, like a deer in the forest."

"I bet they wasn't all shy, them soldiers you nursed over there."

"No," she said, "far from it."

"It makes me boil!" Jack exclaimed, striking his chair with the palm of his hand. "It makes me boil that a young girl like you should've had to nurse a lot of rough soldiers the way you been doing these past two years. I'm a man and I know what they're like. They don't deserve to be mollied for by nice young girls of your sort."

"Father, be quiet, you don't know what you're saying!" she said, and her eyes were suddenly full of tears. "You've no idea what these men had to go through."

"I was a soldier once, remember, for a short while back in the eighties – "

"You still don't know what *these* men went through in *this* war. Nobody knows, except those who've seen for themselves, and it's wrong to say they're undeserving. It's wrong, very wrong, and I won't have it! You know nothing at all about the matter."

"H'mm. It's a fine thing, I must say, when a man is told he knows nothing by his chit of a daughter who knows it all!"

"I saw so much courage . . . so much unselfishness . . . and so much love, among these men. The work I did was nothing at all, and I won't have you grudge it to them, father."

She leant across and touched his knee. She had thrown off her sadness and was laughing again, teasing him, the tears still glistening on her cheeks.

"Own up," she said. "You were only cross 'cos I went and left you to fend for yourself. Now isn't that so?"

"Things ent much improved now you're home, neither. – My mug's been empty this past half hour."

Often when Tom was at Lilac Cottage, he would fall into a kind of dream, watching Linn as she ironed clothes at the kitchen table or sat by the fire with her knitting or mending. Sometimes his gaze was so intense that she felt herself growing uncomfortable.

"How you do stare!" she said to him once. "You really oughtn't to stare at people so hard, Tom, especially saying nothing for hours on end."

"Sorry," he said, and looked away, frowning at the fire in the stove.

But at sight of the colour rising in his face, and the fraught expression in his eyes, Linn regretted her little outburst, humbling him in front of her father, and wanted to put the matter right.

"You can stare if you want to. You can stare at me as much as you like! I know what it is. It's my red hair. It's enough to make anyone stare, I'm sure."

Tom smiled. His glance rested briefly on her face, then flickered away again. He tried to think of something to say.

"Won't be long now. Christmas, I mean. I reckon it's just about eighteen days."

"You'll have to do better'n that," Jack said. "We thrashed that one out an hour ago. Not to mention the chances of snow."

"Father, please," Linn said.

"I know I don't talk much," Tom said. "The chaps used to say so in the Army. Betony always says so too."

"I met Betony at Chepsworth Park. I told her I knew you and she said, 'So that's where Tom's been spending all his evenings lately.' "

"Ah. Well. Now she knows."

"Is it such a secret, Tom, that you come out here to see us?"

"Not a secret exactly. I wouldn't say that."

"You haven't told anybody?"

"No. Maybe not."

"Then it must be a secret, mustn't it, unless Betony's told other people?"

"She wouldn't do that," Tom said.

"That's all right, then. – The secret is kept."

"I reckon you're teasing me again."

"Good gracious!" she said. "As though I would!"

Later that evening, when Tom had gone, Jack spoke to Linn in a serious manner.

"What's your feeling for that boy?"

"I don't rightly know. It's hard to say. I haven't known

him very long . . . yet I feel I've known him all my life."

"Do you care for him?" Jack asked.

"Oh, dear! What a catechism! Must I make up my mind tonight?"

She was looking at him with her head on one side, laughing into his bearded face, making fun of his fierce eyebrows. But Jack was not to be deflected.

"It's as well for you to know your mind, 'cos he cares for you a mighty lot, just as sure as God's in Gloucester."

"Yes," she said, becoming serious. "Perhaps he does."

"You must mind and not lead him on for nothing."

"D'you think I'd do that?"

"No, I don't, but I reckon you ought to consider the matter and sort out your feelings as they are so far."

"Yes," she said, "perhaps I should."

Every evening now, immediately after supper at Cobbs, Tom made himself tidy and left the house. And today, Saturday, he hurried off after midday lunch.

"Where's he get to?" Jesse asked. "Is he courting, Dicky, do you suppose?"

"I dunno, dad. He don't say nothing to me about it."

"It's none of our business, anyway," Betony said.

"Ent it?" said Dicky, and rose, grinning, from the table, a piece of bread pudding in his hand. "Supposing I think it is?" he said. "Supposing I go and try to find out?"

He left the house and followed Tom to Millery Bridge, taking care to keep out of sight. Just past the Malthouse, Tom turned off along the road to Blagg, and when Dicky got to the corner, he had already reached Shepherd's Cross. There, as he passed the old ruined cowsheds, a girl stepped out and ran to meet him, and Dicky, watching from the Malthouse doorway, saw that it was Tilly Preston.

He returned home in triumph and told his father what he had seen.

"Oh, well," Jesse said, "she was always sweet on him, warnt she, that girl?"

But Betony was extremely puzzled.

"Are you sure it was Tilly Preston?"

"Laws!" Dicky said. "I've seen her often enough, surely?"

Tilly had waited for Tom at the old cowsheds. She was shrammed with cold and shivering. Her face was pinched, red, miserable.

"Are you avoiding me, Tom Maddox?"

"No, not exactly," Tom said.

"I think you are!" she said, hugging herself and rubbing the upper parts of her arms. "Oh, yes! I'm certain of it!"

"You'll catch your death of cold, Tilly, hanging about in this weather without a proper coat on."

"Whose fault is it I'm hanging about? You've got no right, avoiding me, not after all that's happened between us, and I shouldn't have to come looking for you. *You* should ought to be calling on *me*."

"It was all a mistake," Tom said. "It shouldn't never've happened by rights."

"A mistake? Really? Well, that's nice, I must say! You've made my day for me now, ent you, telling me a thing like that?"

"It *was* a mistake, though, all the same."

"It's a bit late for saying that, and it don't get us no further forward, does it?"

"No. Maybe not. But I dunno what else to say."

"You was glad enough the night it happened. You was quite content and don't you deny it, taking advantage like you did. But now you've got other fish to fry, ent you, and don't care tuppence what happens to me?"

Tilly was crying, her eyes almost closed, the tears squeezing out between reddened lids. She was shivering violently, cold to the bone, and she cried with little gasping noises, holding both hands against her mouth.

"You ought to get home," Tom said, "or you'll get a chill as sure as fate."

He put out a hand to touch her gently and she took it eagerly in her own, holding it close against her chest.

"Why not come home with me and see my dad? Why not tell him we're going to be married? I'm sure he'd be pleased. – He's quite changed his mind towards you ever since you went as a soldier."

"No," Tom said, and drew back his hand.

"Why not?" she asked. "Why shouldn't we get married?"

"It wouldn't be right for us, that's why."

"Supposing we had to?" Tilly said. "Supposing I was having a baby?"

Tom was silent. He looked at her for a long time.

"You ent, though, are you? No. Surely not."

"I don't know. It's too soon to say. But I think about it all the time and it makes me so scared I could nearly throw myself into the Derrent."

"You can't be," Tom said. "No. Surely not."

"Why can't I, for goodness' sake? These things do happen, as well you should know, seeing it's how you come to be born your own self."

"I know it happens, but is it happening to you, that's the point?"

"I don't know. We'll just have to hope for the best, shan't we? It certainly won't work out that way if I can help it."

"Don't you go doing nothing foolish!"

"It's too late saying that."

"You know what I mean."

"No. I don't. What do you mean?"

"Well, if it should happen there is a baby, you won't do nothing to harm it, will you?"

"No," she said. "I won't do that, I promise, honest." And she looked at him from under her lashes. "You do care what happens to me, then, after all? I knew you did, deep down, underneath. I knew you couldn't be horrid to me."

"I reckon I'd better see you home."

"And speak to my father while you're there?"

"No!" he said. "I got nothing to say to him at all." And he thrust his fists into his pockets. "I've got to have time to think things out. I shall need to know about that baby."

"Meantime, perhaps, you'll be making up to that Mercybright girl who lives with her dad in Stoney Lane? Oh, yes, you may well look surprised, but *I* know what takes you out to Blagg every moment you got to spare!"

"I've got to go," Tom said, and walked away, making towards Puppet Hill.

"You'll be hearing from me!" she called shrilly. "You can't just drop me like an old glove. Not after all that's happened between us! I won't take it. I won't! I won't!"

One evening, a week or so later, Jack Mercybright was in The Rose and Crown, buying a pint of Chepsworth ale and four new clay pipes.

"Quiet this evening," he said to Tilly, for he was her only customer.

"Too many folk ill in bed with the 'flu, including my dad and two of my brothers."

"You ent sickening for it, I hope?"

"I hope not indeed. I've got troubles enough already."

"I'm sorry to hear it," Jack said.

"You might be sorrier," Tilly said, leaning her elbows

on the counter, "if you knew the other party concerned."

"What're you on about, girl?"

"I happen to know that Tom Maddox is a friend of yours, made welcome in your home."

"That's right. He's a friend of my daughter's."

"You ought to warn her," Tilly said, "or she might end up the same as me, carrying his baby."

Jack, smoking, looked into Tilly's watchful eyes. His own face was blank. She would read nothing there if he could help it.

"Does Tom know you're having his baby?"

"I wasn't too sure of it last time I saw him, and he ent been near me since I mentioned the matter."

"What about your father? Does he know?"

"Lord, no! My father would kill me. He would, honest. He don't think a lot of Tom Maddox. I dare not mention it till the wedding day is fixed between us."

"You're very free in airing your troubles, young woman."

"I wouldn't air them to no one else. But you've got a daughter to consider. You wouldn't want no harm to befall her."

"It ent likely to," Jack said. "My daughter is no slut."

He drank his beer and left without speaking another word.

He went straight home to Lilac Cottage, and there, when he entered the bright, warm, comfortable kitchen, Tom was helping to wind Linn's wool, holding the skein on outstretched hands while she wound it up in a soft ball.

"Gracious," she said, as Jack stood on the hearth between them, "you look like murder, dad, you do, really."

"I've got good reason," Jack said. "I've been talking to Tilly Preston and she says she's carrying this chap's baby."

Tom and Linn were facing each other, sitting close, their knees touching. Linn had stopped winding and was looking at him with unbelieving eyes. He could see the laughter dying in them; could see her face growing slowly cold; and inside himself there was a similar coldness and deadness, together with an immense shame.

"Well?" Jack demanded, angrily. "Is it true or false that you've been lovering with this girl?"

"What a word," Tom muttered. "Lovering!"

"Choose what word you better prefer. I'm only asking if it's true."

"Yes. It's true. That ent disputed."

"And you knew," Linn said, staring at him, "that Tilly was going to have a baby?"

"Not for sure, no. She was afraid of it, but she wasn't sure."

"You didn't go to her to find out?"

"No," he said, and looked away.

"How long is it since you saw her last?"

"A week. Ten days. I dunno."

"And said nothing at all about it? Came here every evening the same, behaving as always, knowing Tilly was in such trouble? What did you think would happen to her?"

"I reckon I put it out of my mind."

"How nice for you, having a mind so *very* convenient!"

Linn leant across and took the skein of wool from his hands. She held it loosely in her lap. Her face was pale, and she still looked at him as though she could scarcely believe what she heard.

"Well?" Jack said. "What d'you aim to do about it? Tilly expects you to marry her."

"I dunno why," Tom said. "I reckon she knows I don't love her."

"But you must do!" Linn exclaimed. "Surely? Surely? At least a little? Or are you the sort that takes every girl that comes along?"

"It was the night of the bonfire," he said. "A lot of folk was mad that night. But it don't mean I love her. Not enough to marry her. Nor she don't care tuppence for me neither. I'm pretty damn well sure of that."

"How d'you know? Have you ever asked her?"

"I don't need to. I just know."

"You haven't thought of her feelings at all. It's too inconvenient. It's something else you've put out of your mind!"

"The way you're talking to me," Tom said, "I reckon maybe I'd better go."

"Yes!" she said. "Go to this Tilly Preston of yours and do what you know is right by her!"

Tom got up and stood for a moment as though lost. Then he walked out and they heard his footsteps in the lane. Linn sat staring with hurt, angry eyes. Her father watched her, aching for her.

"And I thought I knew him!" she said with sudden self-scorn. "It was silly of me, after so short a time, but I thought I knew him through and through."

"I told you before, you're a lot too trusting where other people is concerned, and men ent altogether quite the way you see them."

"Then no doubt you're pleased, being right as usual!"

"No, I ent pleased. Far from it. In fact I feel sorry for that boy Tom."

"It's the girl I feel sorry for, poor soul."

"You needn't worry on that score. Tilly can look after herself pretty well."

"It's a good thing she can," Linn said.

*

Tom went to The Rose and Crown and found Tilly still alone in the taproom.

"You got my message, then?" she said.

"Yes, I got it. That's why I'm here."

"I've been so worried these past two weeks, I'm nearly going out of my mind."

"It's definite, then, about your having the baby?" he said. "Have you been to see the doctor?"

"What, and let the whole district know about it?"

"No," he said, "I suppose not."

"It's definite, you take my word. So what're you going to do about it?"

"Get married, what else? It's the only solution. I'll ask Jesse if we can have the old Pikehouse to live in and a few bits and pieces of furniture."

"A house of our own?" she said, glowing. "Oh, Tom, won't that be lovely? Won't that be grand?"

"I'll see the vicar in the morning. If we get a move on, we can be married just after Christmas."

"My word, you're in a hurry, ent you?" she said.

"There's no point in hanging about."

At Cobbs, later, when the news was known, only Betony felt surprise. She took Tom aside and asked him about it.

"What happened to Linn Mercybright?"

"Nothing happened. I'm marrying Tilly."

"But for God's sake why? I don't understand."

"We've got a baby coming," he said. "He's forced our hand, as you might say."

"Oh, you're such fools, you men!" she said. "Getting yourself into a mess like that with a little trollop like Tilly Preston! I thought you'd more sense."

"Tilly's all right," he said, shrugging. "It ent just her fault she's having a baby and it's him we got to think of now."

*

He had lived at the Pikehouse as a boy. It was strange to be back there again now, with some of the same furniture, given to them by Beth and Jesse, and some of the same old crockery hanging up in the tiny kitchen.

"I lived here with my Grannie Izzard. She wasn't my proper grannie, really, but she brung me up from about a year old. That old rocking-chair was hers, and the footstool there, and that little old Welsh dresser."

"I bet you never thought," Tilly said, sitting beside him on the settle, "that you'd be bringing your bride home here and setting up house the way you have."

"No," he said, "I never did."

"I reckon we're lucky, don't you, having a nice little home of our own, miles away by ourselves like we are, with no nosy neighbours poking in?"

"Yes," he said, "I reckon we are."

"I shall try my best to be a good wife to you, Tom."

"And I shall try to be a good husband."

"Oh, I know you will! I know. I know."

"I put some wood aside in the workshop yesterday, ready for making a cot," he said. "I shall start work on that when I've got a bit of time to spare."

Tilly moved closer and put her arm through the crook of his, squeezing it hard against his side. She rested her face against his shoulder.

"The men'll see it if you do that. You know what gossips they all are, specially Sam Lovage."

"They've got to know sooner or later. You can't keep a baby secret for ever."

"Tom," she said, twisting the button on his cuff, "I've got something to tell you about that."

"What is it?"

"I made a mistake about having a baby. I'm not going to have one after all."

"Mistake?" he said. "How could you have made a mistake when so many weeks is gone past by?"

"You know what I mean. I was frightened to death! I thought you was going to let me down."

"There wasn't no baby. It was all a lie. Is that what you're trying to say to me?"

"I really don't see it makes much difference. We have been lovers, after all, and men so often need a nudge before they come up to scratch, the wretches."

Tilly felt the change in him. She sat up straight and looked at his face, and what she saw there made her afraid.

"Tom?" she said, in a small voice. "Don't look at me like that, Tom. It gives me the creeps. It does, honest. It makes me go icy all down inside."

Gently, her fingers plucked at his sleeve.

"Surely it's better to be by ourselves for a bit? We're only young once and babies'll come soon enough I daresay. Why not make the most of things while there's a chance?"

Tom got up and reached for his cap. His shadow leapt, huge in the firelight. His face was that of a graven image.

"Tom, where are you going?" Tilly demanded. "You can't go out on our wedding evening! You can't go out and leave me alone!"

Tom made no answer. He was already on his way out. A blast of cold air blew into the room, the door rattled shut, and he was gone. Tilly put her face in her hands and rocked herself to and fro, giving vent to small choking sobs. Then she took out her handkerchief and wiped her eyes, aware that her tears were washing the face-powder from her cheeks and would stain the front of her wedding-gown.

The fire had burnt low. She threw on three logs and wiped her hands on the rag-made hearth-rug. She was feeling hungry and she thought of the joint of cold mutton lying on the platter in the pantry. Ought she to wait till Tom returned or would his sulks keep him out past midnight? If so, that was his own fault. It was no reason for her to starve.

She got up and went to the pantry.

Sometimes, at night, Tom would slip quietly out of bed, put on his clothes, and creep downstairs, out of the house. He rarely slept more than three or four hours at a time, for his head ached and there was a splitting of coloured lights immediately behind his eyes. Even his breathing gave him trouble. He had to get out in the keen night air.

Tilly, luckily, was a sound sleeper. She never knew when he left her side. She was still in bed when he set off for work at seven. But one morning, while he was eating his breakfast, she came downstairs in nightdress and shawl.

"You been out poaching again?" she said. "Brevitting about in them old woods?"

"I went for a bit of a walk, that's all."

"In the dark?" she said. "On cold winter nights like they are now? You must want seeing to, really, you must."

"It wasn't dark last night. There was a big full moon about three o'clock, and a sky full of stars."

"Respectable folk are warm in their beds at three o'clock in the small hours."

She came behind him and put her arms around his neck, and her face, close to his, was soft and warm like a sleepy child's.

"Don't you love me no more, now, Tom? Aren't you

going to try to forget that I told you just that one little
lie?"

"I shall get round to it, given time."

"And will you be nice to me again?"

"I ent aware that I been nasty."

"I could make you love me again if only you'd give me
half a chance. I could make you my slave. I know I could.
There was plenty of chaps who was always after me in the
old days. Harry Yelland for one. I could twist them all
round my little finger."

"Then why ent you married to one of *them*?"

"I chose you instead, didn't I? Though I sometimes
wonder why I did!" She was holding him back against her
body, her arms tightening across his throat. "Tom?" she
said softly, into his ear. "I know I can make you love me
again if you'll only let me. I'm your lawful wife. You've
got no right being nasty to me."

"I've got to go. I'll be late at the workshop."

He rose from his chair and Tilly released him. He began getting ready and she studied him with growing anger.

"Don't forget to ask Jesse Izzard about that new stove. I
can't cook on this open fire. I've never been used to it, all
my life."

"My grannie cooked on that open fire. She never
found it gave her trouble."

"Oh, your old grannie was a proper wonder! But I'm
not cooking at that there fireplace all my days and you
may as well make up your mind I mean it!"

"All right," Tom said. "I'll ask Jesse's advice about it."

One evening when he got home, he saw a new broom
with a brown-painted handle standing in the corner of
the kitchen, and a new metal dustpan, painted green.

"Where'd they come from, all new and shiny like that?"
he asked.

"A man came selling them at the door. From Birmingham, he said he was. I can pay bit by bit for that broom and dustpan, and anything else I care to buy."

"From Birmingham? And comes all this way?"

"He's got a motor-car," Tilly said. She looked at Tom with a little smile. "He offered to take me for a ride round. That's 'cos I said there was no buses. But I told him no, my husband wouldn't like it."

"It's no odds to me," Tom said, "though it's maybe wiser to watch your step with chaps of that sort."

"Chaps of what sort, I'd like to know? Mr Trimble's a very nice man. He was in the Army the same as you. Out in Egypt with the engineers."

"All right. You go for a ride if that's what you want. I ent raising no objections."

"What fun do I get, stuck out here all by myself, miles away from other people? I see old Mould from the lodge sometimes and I see Mrs Awner going past, but otherwise not a single soul do I ever talk to from one day's end to the next."

"I reckon it is pretty lonely out here, after your being right in Huntlip, with all the folk at The Rose and Crown. Why not go in now and then and give your father a hand like you used to?"

"Oh, no!" Tilly said. "Why should I work in my father's taproom, now I'm married with a home of my own? What'd people say, seeing me back there, serving beer? What d'you think I got married *for*?"

"Look!" Tom said. "You do whatever it is you want to do and stop going on at me. All I want is peace and quiet."

"And nothing else matters!" Tilly said. "You don't never think of me at all!"

She turned away and began crying, great heaving sobs

that wrenched her body. She leant against the back of the settle and hid her face in her folded arms. She looked small and frail, and it seemed she would never be able to stop crying.

"I wish I was dead! I do really! You're always so horrid nowadays. I never thought it'd be like this! Hating me, hating me, all the time!"

"Ah, no," Tom said. "You mustn't say that 'cos it ent true. You must stop crying or you'll make yourself ill. I never meant to make you cry."

He put out a hand and touched her shoulder, and straight away she was in his arms, clutching at him and pressing her body against his. The shivering sobs ceased abruptly and when she looked up at him, into his face, he saw she was laughing.

"I knew I could do it!" she said, exultant. "I knew I could make you love me again if I put my mind to it properly. Men are as soft as dough, really, but they have to be kneaded to bring them round." She put up her hands and entwined her fingers in his hair, trying to make him bend towards her. "Your *face!*" she said. "When I turned just now! If you could've seen it! I had to laugh!"

Tom pulled away from her, jerking his head back, free of her grasp. She clutched at him and he pushed her aside.

"Now what's the matter, for goodness' sake? You're not going out without your supper?"

"Damn the supper and you too!"

The door slammed and she was left alone again, strands of his hair still entwined in her fingers.

"I get the feeling," said Sam Lovage, toasting his cheese at the workshop stove, "that marriage don't agree with our butty here."

"He's quieter than ever lately, ent he?" Albert Tunniman agreed. "And his work's gone off something terrible."

"What've you got for oneses, Tom? Don't Tilly feed you, the bad girl?"

"He's got bread and dripping, same as always," said Fred Lovage, winking at Sam.

"Oh no I ent!" Tom said. "It's fried bacon."

"You ent got a motor-car, have you, Tom? A smart little Austin with a hood? No, well, it ent hardly likely, I don't suppose. Yet my girl Lilian swears she seen one, outside the Pikehouse on Friday morning, when she was going to sew at Scoate."

"It's a traveller-chap, selling brushes. He calls every Friday for his money."

"I shouldn't like that," Tunniman said, "a stranger calling on my missus when I ent there to see what's what."

"I know about him," said Sam Lovage. "He's been through Huntlip, door to door, and tried to sell Queenie a new mop. She sent him packing and a good thing too. There's too many salesmen going about bothering people since the war. Somebody ought to up and stop it."

"Tom should ought to speak to Tilly. I wouldn't stick it if I was him."

"It's no odds to me," Tom said. "Tilly must do as she thinks best."

He finished his lunch and went back to the bench, where the screen he was carving lay half done. He selected a chisel from the rack.

"Don't you never rest?" Lovage shouted. "It wants ɩwenty minutes to one o'clock."

"I've had all I want," Tom said. "I'd just as soon get on."

The next day, Saturday, Tom had work at Crayle in the morning and finished it by eleven o'clock. The workshop was closed in the afternoon so he went straight home, thus arriving early, perhaps an hour before his time. And, seeing a motor-car in the roadway, he went across to the woods opposite and stood among the trees, waiting for the visitor to depart.

At one o'clock, a fair-haired man came out of the Pikehouse, glancing at his watch, and Tilly followed him to the gate. They stood talking for a little while, and the man had his arm round Tilly's shoulders. Then he got into the motor-car and drove away towards Norton. Tilly turned and went back indoors, swinging the end of the silken cord which she wore tied about her waist. Her heels click-clicked along the path.

When Tom walked in, she was combing her hair before the mirror.

"You're early today, aren't you?"

"Ah. Well. Maybe I am."

"I've been busy this morning. You'll have to make do with bread and cheese."

"Suits me," Tom said.

It was true, as Albert Tunniman had said, that his work was not so good lately. Great-grumpa Tewke said the same.

"You've lost your touch, boy, that's your trouble. You've been too long with a rifle in your hands instead of the tools of your proper trade. You can't go off for three years without it showing in your work."

"I reckon that's right," Tom said . "I shall have to practise all the harder."

But however hard he tried, it would not come: there was not the old unity between hand and eye; there was not the mastery over the chisel; and often his judgment played him false.

The work he was doing was for Mr Talbot of Crayle Court. A fire had occurred there in December and some old oak furniture had been badly damaged. Tom's task now was to make two replica doors for a cupboard, each one carved with a Talbot hound, surrounded by oakapples, leaves, and acorns, the initials E.B.T. among them. One of the old burnt doors lay before him and he was copying it, using oak great-grumpa had given him, taken from an old oak pew.

One day, while carving the second door, peering closely to follow the delicate pencil-lines, he had trouble in keeping to the tiny detail. His gouge seemed too big, the tracing too small, and the whole design seemed to swim hazily before his eyes. He stood up straight and looked out of the window. The workshop yard was covered in frost; the cobnut bushes were white-fuzzed; a blackbird quivered on a slim stem. When he looked back again at his work, the tracery seemed smaller than ever, and he suddenly threw down his gouge and hammer.

"I can't do it," he said to Jesse. "George Hopson'll have to do it."

And, pulling his jacket on as he went, he walked out of the workshop door.

"What's up with him?" asked Great-grumpa Tewke, coming to Jesse.

"I don't rightly know," Jesse said, frowning. "I reckon maybe he feels it, you know, your telling him he'd lost his touch. It ent like Tom to leave a piece of work unfinished. I must speak to him about that in the morning."

But Tom was not at work the next morning, nor the morning after, so early on Saturday afternoon, Jesse took the pony and trap and drove to the Pikehouse. His knock brought no answer. The door, amazingly, was locked, and when he peeped in at the window, he could see no sign of life whatever. He returned to Cobbs puzzled and worried and spoke to his wife and daughter about it.

"Nobody at all?" Beth said. "Not even Tilly?"

"Neither hide nor hair of either of 'em."

"If Tom's there alone and in one of his moods," Betony said, "he may have been lying low when you called, just to avoid talking to you."

"Why should he do that? To me of all people? Ent I as good as a father to him?"

"I was thinking of him as a little boy and how he always ran off to the woods whenever we called on Grannie Izzard."

"But he ent a little boy now," Jesse said. "He's a grown man. I should like to know what it is that's upset him."

"So should I," Betony said, "and I mean to find out."

She went that very afternoon, going on foot to give no warning, and arriving just as dusk was falling. The house was in darkness, silent as the grave, lonely beside the old turnpike road, with only a handful of Scoate House sheep grazing on the surrounding wasteland. She opened and closed the gate with care, walked on tiptoe along the path, and stood for a moment in the porch. The door when she tried it opened before her and she stepped straight into the unlit kitchen.

"Tom?" she said. "It's me. Betony. Are you there?"

"Yes, I'm here," Tom said, and got up from the rocking-chair. "How did you come? I never heard no sound of the trap."

He struck a match and lit the oil-lamp on the table. The room came to life and Betony closed the door behind her.

"What's wrong with you? Why haven't you been to work? Why didn't you answer when dad called earlier today?"

"I'm taking a bit of a holiday."

"Just look at the mess in this kitchen! It can't have been cleaned in a month of Sundays. Whatever does Tilly think she's doing?"

"Tilly ent here, she's gone," he said.

"Gone where, for God's sake?"

"I dunno where. She didn't say."

"Has she gone back to her father in Huntlip? No, surely not, or we should have heard."

"I reckon she's gone with another chap."

"Don't you *know* what's happened to her?"

"I came home from work one day and there was a note to say she'd gone. I dunno no more'n that."

"What makes you think there's another man?"

"I seen him," he said. "A traveller-chap, selling brushes. Once he was here when I got home. I saw them laughing and talking together. Then he went off in a little car."

"Well, that's a fine thing, I must say, after only a few weeks of marriage! Don't you care where she's gone? Aren't you going to try and find her?"

"No. Why should I? It's no odds to me."

"It's cold in here," Betony said, shivering. "Don't you think you should light the fire? There's plenty of sticks and logs there and I don't like freezing even if you do."

"All right," he said, and began at once pushing the wood-ashes back in the hearth. "Maybe it *is* time I boiled a kettle."

"What about the baby?" Betony asked.

"There wasn't no baby after all. Just a mistake, Tilly said."

"You mean she led you up the path?"

"That's about it, I suppose, yes."

When the fire was burning, piled high, and the kettle hung above the flames, Tom rose from his haunches and crossed the room to hang up his jacket. On the way he stumbled, sending the little footstool flying, and almost sweeping the lamp from the table. Betony gave an exclamation and set the lamp in its rightful place.

"You can't be drunk at this time of day! What's wrong with you for heaven's sake?"

Tom stood quite still, his hands in his pockets. He was looking past her, into the fire.

"Seems I'm going blind," he said.

After a while, when the kettle boiled, Betony made a pot of tea. There was no milk to be found anywhere; nor any sugar; only a jar of her mother's honey; so she stirred a spoonful into the mug of milkless tea and sat opposite, watching him drink it.

"How long is it since your sight began failing?"

"I dunno. It's hard to say. It comes and goes, like, and sometimes it seems better than others."

"Have you seen a doctor?"

"Not since leaving the hospital at Sawsford."

"Then you must!" she said. "Where's the point in losing time?"

"Will they be able to do something for me?"

"We won't know that till we get there," she said. "But it's no use burying yourself away out here, without a word to anyone. What did you hope to achieve by it?"

"I wanted time to sort things out."

"How did you think you were going to live, stuck out here and not working?"

"I hadn't got as far as that. I just wanted to be by myself and make the most of what sight is left me."

"And afterwards?"

"I dunno. I hadn't decided. End it, maybe, somehow or other."

"Do away with yourself, you mean, the same as your father did before you?"

"I'd just as soon die, as go through life in the dark," he said.

"What rubbish you're talking!" she said, with scorn. "This is something you've got to fight! You fought over there for nearly three years. You didn't give in so easily then and you certainly mustn't give in now. You must fight back like a proper soldier."

Tom sipped at his hot tea, and the steam rose, moistening his face. His dark skin was smooth and shining, but still white-flecked in many places, where the shell-blast had scarred him. His deep dark eyes were bright, steady, contemplative, and looked at her with childlike hope. It was hard to believe those eyes could fail him.

"All right," he said. "Tell me what I ought to do."

Her family, when she broke the news, could scarcely believe what she was saying. Tom's injury was four months old. They had thought his sufferings were over.

"Ah, no, not our Tom!" Jesse said. "After all this time? And what he's been through?"

"Did Tilly know he was going blind when she left him?" Beth asked.

"No, mother. He told no one until today."

"He shouldn't have married her," Dicky said. "I said all along she was nothing worth it."

"Damnable war!" great-grumpa said. "Is there no end to its consequences, even now?"

"No, there's no end," Betony said. "I see its evil every day when I visit the men at Chepworth Park."

"I'll go out and see him," Jesse said. "I'll knock this time till he lets me in."

"No, don't go yet," Betony said. "I think he's better left alone."

On Monday, early, she travelled with Tom by train to Sawsford. The military hospital stood on a hill and had a fine view out over the town. To Betony it seemed very busy but to Tom it was quiet compared with when he had been there last. He was seen by three doctors and spent half an hour with each in turn. They were strangers to him but had his medical details before them and asked him a great many questions. He was then given X rays and told he would have to wait some time before they could tell him the results.

"I suggest you have lunch," the surgeon, Major Kerrison, said, speaking to Tom and Betony together. "The Fleece round the corner is good. Tell the waiter I sent you."

After lunch at The Fleece and an hour spent walking over the hill, they returned to the hospital and sat waiting. The day was a mild one, with a premature hint of spring, and in the gardens outside the window, heliotrope flowered, pink and mauve.

A nurse came into the waiting-room, and Tom stood up. He was white to the lips and a pulse was throbbing in his cheek.

"The doctor would like to see Mrs Maddox."

"I'm not Mrs Maddox," Betony said. "I'm his foster-sister. My name is Miss Izzard."

"Oh. Well. Come this way, Miss Izzard, please."

So Tom had to wait again, sitting on the bench with his back against the wall, while nurses in white and patients in blue passed to and fro along the corridor. When Betony came back at last, he knew from her face that she brought bad news.

"What'd they say? You may as well tell me straight out."

"They say there's nothing they can do."

"No operation nor treatment nor nothing?"

"The optic nerves are too badly damaged. There's nothing they can do about it. They say it's only a question of time."

"Total blindness?" Tom asked.

"I'm afraid so."

"How long?"

"They don't know."

"Six months? A year? They must have some notion, I'd have thought."

"No. They're uncertain. It could happen soon . . . or it could be as much as two years."

"I knew it was going to be bad," he said, "when they asked for you."

"The doctor wants to see you too. He has some advice he wants to give you and a letter for Dr Dundas at home. He says you're eligible for a pension."

"A pension!" he said, hollowly, and went away down the corridor.

Betony sat with her hands on her handbag. She had not told him everything, even now, because she and the doctor had decided against it, and she closed her eyes for a brief moment, seeking in herself some untapped spring of strength and courage. By the time Tom returned, she thought she had found it. She rose and went to him with a calm face.

When they reached Chepsworth and were on their way to The Old Plough, where they had left the pony and trap, Tom stopped suddenly and said he would prefer to walk back home across the fields.

"It's a nice afternoon. You don't mind, do you, Bet?"

"Promise you won't do anything silly."

"It's all right," he said, and a rare smile just touched

his lips. "I'm taking it like a proper soldier."

"You may never lose your sight at all," she said briskly. "Doctors have been known to be wrong sometimes."

She drove home without him, and as she turned into the fold, Michael came out of the house to meet her.

"You're very late, Betony. We're due at my uncle's by half past five but I doubt if we'll get there much before six."

"I'm sorry, Michael, I'm not coming. There's something important I have to do."

"More important than keeping an engagement?"

"I hope you'll make my excuses to your uncle and explain that it just couldn't be avoided."

"I suppose it's something to do with Tom? Your mother said you'd both been down to Sawsford today."

"Yes, I went with him to the hospital there."

"How much longer, may I ask, are you going to play nursemaid to that young man?"

"Tom's going blind!" she said bluntly. "I suppose you'd admit he needs help?"

"Betony, I'm sorry, I'd no idea. Your mother and father should have said. But still, even so, I don't see why you should take the responsibility. Not now that he has a wife."

"Tilly's left him," Betony said.

"Good God! What a mess it all is!"

"The longer you wait here, the later you'll be getting to Ilton."

"Yes, yes, I'm going," he said, but continued to stand there, watching her as she fed the pony. "You don't seem able to get away from Tom, do you? He haunts you like some guilty dream. You're always trying to pay off a debt for something you did or did not do to him in childhood."

"Yes, well, perhaps I am."

"In my opinion, it can't be done. I feel you're only wasting your time."

"It isn't only my debt. Tom was hurt while fighting in France. I think we all owe a debt to men like him."

"That can't ever be paid either."

"No, I don't think it can," Betony said, "But I think we should try all the same."

An hour later she drove to Blagg and called on the Mercybrights at Lilac Cottage. Jack was sitting reading his paper. He put it aside as Linn showed Betony into the kitchen, but he made no attempt to stand up, and she saw that one leg lay resting across a stool.

"I wanted to talk to you both about Tom."

"You'd better sit down. I'm willing to hear what you got to say, and so is Linn, though I doubt if his business can interest us much."

"Tom's wife has left him. He's all alone. It wasn't true she was having a baby. She led him up the garden path."

"I ent too surprised," Jack said. "She struck me as a sly piece. But it don't alter the fact that he'd been monkeying with her in the first place."

"One fall from grace," Betony said, "and you'd hold it against him all his life?"

She turned from him to look at Linn, who sat on the edge of an upright chair, her hands still nursing a cup and a tea-cloth. The girl was beautiful, Betony thought: delicate features, neatly made; colouring vivid and unusual; dark brown eyes full of thought and feeling. There was a gentle warmth about her, yet plainly she had a resolute will.

"Would you hold it against him for ever?"

"I'm not his judge," Linn said.

"I'm hoping you might be his salvation."

"Look here," Jack said. "That young man made my daughter unhappy. He hurt her, Miss Izzard, and she done right to send him away."

"He must have meant something to you, then," Betony said, still looking at Linn, "if he had the power to make you unhappy."

"He chose someone else. It's not my fault if it didn't work out."

"He never cared tuppence for Tilly Preston."

"He told me that, but I didn't believe him."

"You ought to have done. Tom doesn't tell lies."

"Why have you come to us, Miss Izzard?"

"I've come because Tom is going blind."

"No," Linn said, and turned her face away, hiding her pain. "No! Oh, no!"

"Can't something be done for him?" Jack asked.

"No, nothing," Betony said. "He saw the doctors this afternoon. Now he's out at the Pikehouse, alone, facing up to it the best way he can. But there's something else – something Tom himself doesn't know – that nobody knows except myself – and I hope to God I do right to tell you."

Betony paused. She was trying to read the girl's face.

"He's only got a short time to live," she said. "Twelve months at the most, and that only if he takes things quietly. If he had an illness of any kind, or too much strain, death could come sooner, the doctor said."

Linn sat perfectly still. It was some time before she spoke.

"I remember. . . at the hospital in Rouen . . . they were afraid of brain-damage . . . but then it seemed as if everything was all right after all." She was perfectly calm, though white as ashes, and she drew a deep, controlled breath. "I wish I could have known . . . when I first came home and met him again . . ."

"Linn, do you love him?" her father asked, and when she turned to look at him, giving her answer silently, he said, "In that case, I reckon you'd better go to him, don't you?"

"Yes," she said. "I think so too."

"I'll take you there," Betony said. "I'll wait outside while you get ready. Don't be too long. I've already kept the pony standing and the evening is getting a lot colder."

She went out to the trap and sat waiting, and after a while Linn joined her, carrying a small canvas bag. It was dusk by the time they reached the Pikehouse, and a small rain was sprinkling down, out of a sky the colour of charcoal. The house was in darkness, and Betony sat waiting again while Linn found her way to the door. A few minutes passed, then the lamp was lit and shone through the window. Betony turned in the narrow roadway and drove home through the drizzling rain.

It was a Sunday, and the family at Cobbs were about to sit down to their midday dinner when the back door burst open and Emery Preston walked in, followed by his eldest son, Matthew.

"What's all this?" granna demanded, bringing a pile of plates to the table, and Great-grumpa Tewke, carving-knife poised against the steel, said, "This ent The Rose and Crown, by God, and I'll thank you to knock before lifting the sneck of decent folks' doors."

"Decent folks?" Emery shouted. "Decent folks, did you say?"

"What d'you want?" Beth asked. "You can see our dinner's on the table."

"My business is with your husband."

"Why me?" Jesse said. "Why me, I'd like to know?"

"You're the nearest thing Tom Maddox has got for a father, that's why, and I want to know what's happened to Tilly."

"Yes, well," Jesse said. "That ent nothing to do with me." And he busied himself about the stove, leaving the matter to his wife and daughter. They, it seemed, found nothing amiss with the way young Tom was carrying on. They, therefore, could answer all the awkward questions.

"Tilly's run off," Betony said to Emery Preston. "Hadn't you heard?"

"I've heard a lot of funny things lately, but nothing at all from Maddox hisself, so what's he playing at, you tell me that!"

"Seems they weren't happy, so Tilly left him."

"Then why ent we seen her?" Emery said. "A girl falling out with her husband like that would surely come home to her own father?"

"Not if she left with another man."

"I ent having *that*! Not my girl Tilly. She was always a good girl and she certainly wouldn't behave like that!"

"Rubbish!" Beth said. "Tilly's no better than she should be, and well you know it, Emery Preston."

"She deceived Tom," Betony said, "making believe she was having a baby."

"She never told me she was having a baby."

"She wouldn't, of course. She knew you'd take your belt to her."

"Who says I take my belt to my children? And why shouldn't I if they deserve it? I always warned her against that boy. I tried to stop her marrying him."

"It's a pity you didn't succeed, Mr Preston."

"What'd he do to her, the swine, to make her run off without a word?"

"*He* didn't take his belt to her, if that's what you mean."

"We don't know that! We know nothing at all. He's been acting queer for some time past and I ent the only one to say so neither."

"Is it surprising, since he's going blind?"

"I know! I know!" Emery said. "It ent that I don't feel nothing for him. He's been through a lot, I daresay, but it don't excuse his ill-using Tilly and I'm going out there to see him about it."

"No, don't do that," Betony said. "Leave him alone."

"You needn't worry about my feelings! I know damn

well he's got another woman living there with him. It's no good hoping to keep it quiet, even if he does live three miles out. All Huntlip knows about the way he's going on."

"Huntlip would!" Dicky muttered.

"He didn't waste much time, did he, finding someone to take Tilly's place?"

"She was the one who walked out."

"I don't know that! That's just his story! It's like this chap she's supposed to've run away with. I don't know he even existed."

"He existed all right," said great-grumpa. "He came to my workshop, trying to sell me foreign brushes."

"Well, *I've* never seen him," Emery said, "and I'm the one that keeps the pub!"

"I've seen him, though," Matthew said suddenly. "Chap about thirty, driving a motor, sounded as though he came from Brum. I was parked beside him in the road once and he gave me some lip about my motor-cycle."

"Oh? Is that so?"

"Come to think about it," Matthew said, "he ent been around these few weeks lately, though one or two people still owe him money."

"Why didn't you say so before?"

"It warnt till they mentioned his selling brushes – "

"And it still don't prove nothing, neither, does it?"

"What're you hoping to prove?" asked Beth.

"I dunno!" Emery said. "All I know is that I don't like it and I tell you straight so's you know how I stand. But I'll say this – if Tilly turns up with this salesman fella, they'll both rue the day, I promise you that!"

He turned towards the door, shoving the boy Matthew before him, and Great-grumpa Tewke looked up from carving the joint of beef.

"I'd ask you to stop to dinner," he said, his voice laden with sarcasm, "if it warnt all gone cold while you was so busy showing yourself up for the fool you are!"

When the Prestons had gone, Jesse returned to his place at the table, next to Betony.

"All this talk!" he said, shaking his head. "I'm disappointed in that boy Tom, causing all this scandal and gossip. Whatever will people think of us? What'll the *captain* think of us?"

"You don't need to call him the captain now, father. He's not in the Army any more."

"He'll always be the captain to me."

"Even when he and I are married?"

"H'mm," Jesse said, "and when'll that come to pass, I wonder?"

He longed to see her married to Michael. He could not understand why they should wait.

"You're always so busy," Michael said, looking over Betony's shoulder at the exercise-book she was correcting. "What with your work at Chepsworth Park and now the school – I hardly see you nowadays."

"It's only temporary," Betony said. "The school, that is. It's only while Miss Likeness is ill."

"I'm surprised you teach them geometry. I'd no idea village schools were so ambitious. I thought it was all hymn-singing and sewing fine seams on linen samplers."

"Huntlip's got a *good* village school. All others ought to be like it."

"I've half a mind, the moment we're married, to whisk you off to South Africa and hide you away on my uncle's farm."

"You're always talking about South Africa."

"I had a very happy year out there, when I was a care-free boy in my teens."

"The trouble is not so much that I'm busy," Betony said, "as that you are not busy enough."

"Would you believe it!" he exclaimed. "My mother says I need a long rest and you say I need to be active. What's a man to do, between two women offering such conflicting advice?"

"He should choose for himself, every time."

"I don't seem able to settle down, since coming home from the war," he said. "I'm bored stiff with the factory and it runs itself anyway under George Williams. I think what I'd really enjoy is having a farm of my own."

"Then why not buy one?"

"You make it all sound so simple."

"Well, isn't it simple, if you've got the money?"

"Would you like living on a farm?"

"Yes, I should, though not in South Africa," Betony said.

Michael went and stood at the window, looking out at the old orchard. The plum trees were stippled white with blossom; the evening sunlight lit their trunks; and a woodpecker flew from tree to tree. Nearby, in the garden, Jesse was splitting seed potatoes and Beth was planting them in the rows, her back bent in a perfect arch, her gloved hands working swiftly and surely, opening the soil with her sharp trowel and closing it again over the seed in a movement almost too quick for the eye to see.

"I suppose South Africa is too far away from your collection of lame dogs."

"What lame dogs?"

"Oh, come, now," he said. "There's your foster-brother for a start."

"Why do you always call him that? You know his name

so why not use it?" Betony closed one exercise-book, placed it on its pile, and took another. "Sometimes I feel you resent Tom."

"Perhaps I do," Michael said, turning towards her. "He does claim rather a lot of your attention."

"You can't be jealous of someone like Tom, knowing he's slowly going blind. It's too absurd."

"I didn't say I was jealous of him."

"Then what is all this about, exactly?"

"Oh, I don't know! It isn't very easy to talk to you these days, Betony. You're always thinking of other things."

"Very well," Betony said, and swung round to face him. "You now have my undivided attention, so what is it you're trying to say to me?"

"Yes, you're very good at putting me in the wrong and making me feel ridiculous," he said. "You're always much better than I am at any sort of argument."

"But I don't want to be better at it! I don't want to argue at all. All I want is to understand you." Looking at him she could see there was something seriously wrong; some awful uncertainty in his face; some fear that lurked and flickered in his eyes. "Michael," she said, "was it very bad in the prison-camp?"

"It wasn't what I would call a picnic."

"I wish you'd tell me about it."

"No," he said. "There's nothing to tell, and you're mistaken in thinking I want to talk about it. It's the last thing I want. I'm always trying to forget about it."

Betony rose and went to him. She touched his arm and found he was trembling.

"You'll have to make allowances for me, Michael, when I don't understand things. It was so hard for us at home here to imagine what it was really like. We tried and tried – or some of us did – but we couldn't really understand.

And I must admit I stopped worrying – indeed I was thankful in a way – once I heard you'd been taken prisoner."

"Thankful? Were you? Were you really?"

"Of course," she said. "Especially after the uncertainty while you were posted missing. All I could think of was that you were safe. Safe and alive and out of it all!"

"Yes," he said, in a dull voice, and took her in his arms so that his face should be hidden from her.

The night was unusually warm for May. There were too many blankets on his bed and he lay sweating, unable to sleep, listening to the cathedral clock striking. It was half past two. The room was full of white moonlight.

He rose and put on his dressing-gown. He opened the door quietly and went out across the landing. His mother heard him and called out. Her door was half open, and when he looked in she was sitting up in bed, groping for the light-switch.

"Don't put the light on. The moon is bright enough."

"What's the matter, Michael, are you ill?"

"No, no. I just couldn't sleep, that's all. I thought a drop of Scotch might do the trick."

"I'm worried about you, not sleeping. You've been like this for weeks now."

"My bed's too cushy, that's the trouble. Perhaps I should get a wire-netting bunk."

His mother patted a place on the bed. He went and sat there, and the two of them were close together, with the moon shining on them, bright as a searchlight. Her grey hair was set in symmetrical wavelets, as orderly as in the day-time, and had the sheen of polished pewter. Her face was pale and her lips in the moonlight looked almost purple.

"Have you got something on your mind?"

"Nothing more than usual."

"Is everything all right between you and Betony?"

"If it isn't, the fault is entirely on my side."

"You can't expect me to accept that."

"It's true all the same."

"You've been home for five months, yet you grow more nervy all the time. You're drinking a lot. You never used to."

"That's what it does to us . . . lies in wait and pounces on us . . ."

"Were you ill-treated at the camp?"

"Some of the guards were pretty brutal, but most of them were all right. Hunger was the worst thing we had to bear, and I almost welcomed that in a way, as an expiation."

"Expiation?"

"Because I felt guilty at being safe."

"My dear boy! What nonsense you're talking – '

"Don't interrupt me. I want to tell you what really happened. I gave myself up, you see, because I couldn't face any more fighting. I wasn't all that badly wounded. I could have got back to our lines if I'd tried. Minching and Darby wanted to help me, but I made some excuse and stayed behind, where the German patrol was sure to find me."

His mother was silent, sitting upright against her pillows, her hands lying motionless on the quilt. For once he could guess nothing of her thoughts.

"I liked it at first, being a soldier. I was even good at it, up to a point. Promotion came quickly, as you know. But it all went on so long, so long, and the more one did the more they expected. I began to wish, like everyone else, that I might be wounded and out of it, but I was wounded three times and every time they patched me up as good as new and sent me back again for more.

"It wouldn't have been so bad, I think, if I had been just a private soldier, but I was an officer giving orders . . . blowing a whistle and sending men over the parapet . . . and when we were in a tight spot, I'd see them all looking at me, expecting me to know the answer, expecting me to do the right thing and get them all out of the mess. Sometimes their faith nearly drove me mad. I *didn't* always know what to do. Often I knew no more than they did. And there were one or two among them who were better men than I'll ever be."

From being hot, he was now shivering. The sweat lay cold on his face and body, and sickness crept on him, reducing him to nothing.

"I forgot when I gave myself up," he said, "that I'd have to live with it ever after."

His mother's face was still impassive, and yet she was reaching out to him, leaning towards him with outstretched arms. And when he yielded his shuddering body, she drew him fiercely into her bed, pressing him close, trying to give him strength and comfort, trying to protect him from the bitterness of self-recrimination. He was her child again, creeping into her warm bed, letting her wrap him round in the bedclothes, letting her press his head to her bosom. He was her child, crying after a bad dream, and her only duty in the world was to him.

"They asked too much of you. Yes, yes, they did! How could you go on for ever and ever? Nobody could. It's too much to ask. You mustn't feel guilty for the rest of your life. What good does it do? None whatever!" And a little later, as the shivering passed, she said to him: "Have you told Betony about this?"

"No," he said, "I'm afraid to tell her."

"There shouldn't be secrets between man and wife."

"I'm afraid I might lose her. I couldn't bear that."

"If she loves you, it won't make any difference. She will understand you that much better. She'll be able to help you. It's only right that she should know."

"Yes," he said. "It's only right, as you say. I'll tell her tomorrow."

But in the morning, when he thought of Betony, he knew he would never be able to tell her.

High above the woods of Scoate House Manor a kestrel hovered, taking its ease on the warm summer air, and Tom, returning with Linn along the old turnpike, a bundle of osiers on his shoulder, stood still to watch it, one hand raised against the sun.

"Can you see it?" Linn asked.

"Yes, just about, though I wouldn't have knowed it for a kestrel if it warnt for *knowing,* if you see what I mean."

"Supposing you tell me what you mean."

"Well, it's the way he's lazing about up there . . . the way he's concentrating on something below . . . ah, and now the way he's gliding around, before going off, away down the wind."

The kestrel circled three times and swooped away, racing its shadow over the treetops. Tom turned his attention to a soaring lark.

"I'm a lot luckier than folk that've had no sight at all. Take that there lark, now, up in the sky. That could be a gnat for all I can see to tell me different, but when I hear it singing, well, it means I can see it at the same time, just as plain as I ever did, rising up and up all the time into a sky as blue as blue."

They had been shopping in Norton village. Tom drew his pension from the post office there, and they rarely went to Huntlip now. He bought his osiers at Washpool Farm and sold his baskets to a dealer who called every other Friday.

The day was a hot one in late July and the sun was immediately overhead. Every few hundred yards or so, Tom dropped his bundle on the grass verge and the two of them sat on it, side by side, among the meadowsweet and sorrel. What wind there was came breathing hotly out of the east, and Linn tried to cool it by fanning herself with a bunch of ferns. Under the brim of her big straw hat, her face was shadowed, and he saw her only as a shape. Yet he knew the day had exhausted her.

"You'd have done better stopping at home. You shouldn't be walking so far in this heat."

"We spend more time resting than we do walking. It'll likely be dark by the time we get home."

"Dark or light, what does it matter? We ent catching no train, are we?"

"I left my washing on the line. It'll go too dry for ironing."

"You just rest," he said firmly. "You know what Mrs Gibbs told you. You've got to rest and take things easy."

When they reached home and were passing through the Pikehouse gate, Linn saw a man standing watching them from the edge of the woods, thirty yards off, across the road. He was half-hidden behind a tree and stood quite still, his hands in his pockets, his cap pulled low over his forehead.

"There's a man over there. Can you see him? He's standing at the edge of the wood."

"Perhaps it's a keeper," Tom said.

But then the man stepped out to the open; he crossed the grass verge and stood in the roadway: a short stocky man with a chest like a barrel.

"It's Emery Preston," Linn said.

"What's he doing hanging about here for?"

"It's not the first time I've seen him about. When I went up to Eastery last Friday, he was standing on the churchyard wall, looking down at the Pikehouse, and he stared hard at me as I went past."

"I'll go and have a word with him," Tom said.

Emery Preston stood like a post. Tom went up to him, squinting a little, for he could see better by looking out of the sides of his eyes.

"Did you want to speak to me, Mr Preston?"

"No, why should I?" Emery said.

"Then why are you out here, watching us the way you are?"

"Is there a law that says I mustn't?"

"No, there's no law," Tom said, "or none that I know of, anyway."

"There's laws about *some* things," Emery said. "There's a law against bigamy for a start."

"I ent no bigamist, Mr Preston."

"You're both a lot worser to my way of thinking, living together, the two of you, with no sign of shame in either of you. I'm a publican and a sinner but I wouldn't carry on like that."

"What d'you want of us?" Tom asked.

"I'd like to know what became of my daughter."

"Tilly went off with another chap. I dunno no more'n that."

"So you say, but I sometimes wonder!"

"What do you mean?"

"Never mind! Never mind! I was thinking out loud."

"You should try looking in Birmingham. That's where he lived, the chap she went off with."

"Have you tried looking for her your own-self?"

"No," Tom said, " 'cos I don't want her back."

"That's understandable, sure enough. A lawful wife is something of a hinderment to the likes of you. You better prefer a looser arrangement."

Linn still stood at the Pikehouse gate. Emery could see that she was with child. His glance roved over her, full of contempt.

"You yourself was begot in the hedge, Maddox, and it seems it's a thing that gets passed on!"

He turned and walked off towards Huntlip, kicking up a cloud of dust. Tom and Linn went indoors.

"Take no notice," she said to him. "Don't let it upset you."

"It don't worry me, except for your sake," Tom said, "and maybe the little 'un's, when he comes."

"You are not to worry. There's no need."

It was very strange, the way his sight varied from day to day. Some days, especially when the sun was shining, he could see the poppies red along the roadside, the apples ripening in the garden, the white clouds crossing the blue sky. But other days were bad, and once, out in the empty stretch of wasteland surrounding the Pikehouse, he came to a standstill, lost as though in a thick dark fog.

He was quite alone, and he felt that the rest of the earth had gone; he thought of it as a smoking ruin, crumbling away into a pit, leaving him on the edge of nothing; and he knew a moment of whirling terror. But after a while, putting out his hands, he felt the long feathery grasses that grew high everywhere around him, and their touch reassured him. The earth was still there, unchanged, unchanging, and he must find his way across it, through the gathering darkness. Home was in front of him. Not much more than a hundred yards. He could smell the woodsmoke, and could hear Linn beating a mat. It seemed a long way.

"You should've called to me," she said, coming to him as he groped along the hedgerow to the garden gate. "I'm sure I'd have heard you."

"I've got to get used to finding my way about," he said.

But Linn rarely left him alone after that. She watched over him and was always at hand when he needed her. Their lives were tight-linked. They shared every moment of the night and day.

Once, when she was rummaging in the cupboard, she said, "I didn't know you ever smoked."

"I did smoke, a bit, in the trenches," he said. "Why?"

" 'Cos I found this." And she put a tobacco-pipe into his hands.

"It belonged to Bob Newers, my mate in the army. I meant to send it home to his people, but what with my getting blown up and that, I never got round to it after all."

Until now, whenever he had remembered Newers, he had seen only the space left after the shell had burst in the crater; had seen only the hole in the ground, and the debris falling, bringing down bits of human remains. But now, as he held the pipe between his hands, he saw Newers as a whole man again; felt his solid bulk beside him; heard his voice; and remembered a day at Liere on the Somme, when the first tanks had been seen on the road, making towards Rilloy-sus-Coll.

Newers and he, in the reserve line, had been drumming up tea when a new chap named Worth had let out a shriek.

"God Almighty! Take a dekko at these monsters! What the hell are they, d'you suppose?"

"What, them?" said Newers, standing up to look at the tanks. "They've brought the buns."

Linn went and sat beside Tom on the settle. She saw he was smiling.

"Newers could always make us laugh," he said.

Every day now, while the summer weather lasted, Tom worked out of doors, close by the pump where his osiers lay soaking in the trough. He sat on a mat on the paving-stones with a wooden board on his lap, and often when Linn went out to the garden she would stop and watch the basket growing as his clever fingers worked the rods, or reached for the hammer to rap them home, or took up the knife to trim the ends. Human hands, when they worked and made things, always filled her with a kind of wonder.

"I know you're there," he said once. "I can see you plain. Well, plain enough. You've got your blue dress on, and the new pinny with the big pockets."

"And what am I holding in my hand?"

"I suppose it's that medicine again."

"You drink it up and no nonsense."

"All right," he said. "You're the nurse. But it won't bring my sight back, I don't suppose."

"It'll help your headaches, Dr Dundas said."

"It'd be a miracle if that was to give me back my sight. I'd drink a whole bottle every day." He emptied the glass and returned it to her. He looked up at her with his side-ways stare. "It ent very likely, is it?" he said. "Miracles ent all that common nowadays."

"No, Tom, you won't get your sight back, I'm afraid."

"No. Well. It's not to be expected, I know that. It's just wishful thinking, as they say."

One day when Linn went out to the garden, to pick the last of the kidney beans, she saw Emery Preston again, coming out of Scoate woods. He stood for a while, looking across as though hesitating, then walked off towards Huntlip. She decided not to tell Tom, but the next time her father came to call on them, she took him aside and told him in private.

"I don't know what he means by it. I suppose it's to make us feel uncomfortable. In which case he succeeds all too well, 'cos it worries me, somehow, seeing him prowling about like that."

"I'll have a word with him," Jack said. "I'll tell him to mind his own damned business."

"I don't think it's wise to quarrel with him."

"Who said anything about quarrelling?"

"I know what you are, father."

"It's no use wearing velvet gloves when dealing with men like Emery Preston. You've got to tell them out straight."

Jack went to The Rose and Crown the following evening after work. He spoke to Emery regardless of the crowd in the taproom listening.

"What're you always hanging around the Pikehouse for?"

"It's a free country. I do as I please."

"Then hear this!" Jack said. "If you cause any harm to my daughter, or to Tom Maddox, you'll have to answer to me for it, and I'm none too gentle when dealing with ruffians like you, Preston, so just you watch out!"

Jack walked out again. Emery turned to his customers.

"He thinks hisself somebody, that chap Mercybright, don't he, by God? And him just a labourer on Outlands Farm!"

"What's wrong with labourers?" Billy Ratchet said, offended. "Jack's all right. He's a good sort. I feel sorry for him, with that daughter of his turning out so unexpected, living like she do with Tom Maddox and carrying his bastard, bold as brass."

"You needn't tell me!" Emery said. "I know how they're carrying on. I been out there and seen for myself. But it's what they done, the two of them, to get rid of Tilly that bothers me, and one of these days I shall find out!"

"Why, your Tilly's as bad herself, ent she?" said Norman Rye, calling from one of the small tables. "Going off with that traveller like she done?"

"That's the story that's been put about! But I've got ideas of my own on that score, and I shan't rest till I know more about it."

"What do you mean, Emery?"

"You'll know soon enough, when the time comes."

Emery went and drew himself a pint of Chepsworth. He drank till the glass was three parts empty and froth had given him a white moustache. His three sons watched him. His customers eyed one another in stony silence.

On a warm Saturday in late September, a car drew up at The Rose and Crown, and a young man got out, red-faced and sweating. He locked the car door, made a face at the children gathering round, and glanced at his wrist-watch. It wanted five minutes to closing time. He was very thirsty.

Matthew, in the taproom, called his father to the window.

"It's him," he said. "That travelling salesman. You can see the brushes in the car."

"Are you sure it's the same one?"

"I'm positive," Matthew said.

When the young man came in, glancing round at the customers, and smoothing his hair with the flat of his hand, Emery stood behind the counter.

"Your name Trimble by any chance?"

"Upon my word! What memories you country folk have got – "

"Is it or ent it?" Emery demanded.

"Yes, indeed," the man said, and found himself half way across the counter, with Emery Preston's enormous hands twisted in the front of his jacket. "Good God! What's the matter? Are you drunk or mad or what?"

"Where's my daughter Tilly got to?"

"I don't know what you're talking about."

"The story is she went off with you, in that dinky motor you got out there, and if it's true, Mr Smarty Trimble, I'll break every bone in your soft greasy body!"

"Of course it's not true! I don't even know your daughter Tilly."

"You know her all right. You sold her brushes out at the Pikehouse."

"Did I? Did I? Good Lord, let me see! The Pikehouse, you said? Yes, it does ring a bell. It's that tiny tollhouse out towards Norton. The young lady's name was Mrs Maddox."

"And what else do you remember?"

"Nothing whatever, I do assure you. I called there three or four times, I agree, and sold Mrs Maddox a few little items, but what you're saying is simply monstrous and I insist you let go of me at once!"

"Monstrous, is it?" Emery said. "Does that mean you're saying it's a damned lie?"

"Indeed I am! And I'd like to know who's responsible for it! I'm a happily married man. I can show you snaps of my wife and kiddies. I can get people to speak for me – "

"Never mind that," Emery said. "Just answer me one more question. Why did you leave the district so sudden, with people owing you money on orders?"

"I was taken ill. I went down with 'flu and very nearly

died of it. If it hadn't been for my wife, God bless her, nursing me for weeks on end, I shouldn't be here at this moment."

"Oh, is that so?" Emery said. "And now you've come back to collect what's owing? Well, you're hopeful, I must say, after so many months gone by."

He loosened his hold on the man's jacket, but continued to look at him narrowly.

"You got a business card you can give me?"

"No, no, I haven't," Trimble said. "I've had some trouble getting them printed." He shrugged himself into his ruffled clothes and tucked his necktie into his jacket. He half glanced round at the few customers in the taproom. "But I'll write my address down if you want it and then you can verify all I've told you."

"Yes, you do that," Emery said, and watched as Trimble, with a shaking hand, wrote his address on a scrap of paper. "Seems I got the wrong man. I'm sorry I rumpled you up a bit but it ent my fault you've been blamed for something you ent done. It's my son-in-law you can thank for that."

"Is it indeed? I should like to meet him!"

"Don't you tangle with Tom Maddox. I shall be dealing with him myself."

"Right!" Trimble said. "All's well that ends well, that's what I say, and no hard feelings either way."

"Ent you having the drink you came for?"

"No, no, I think not. I'm behind-hand already and I've got an appointment at two-thirty." Trimble walked towards the door. "Let me know," he said, "if there's anything more I can do to help you."

He drove away from The Rose and Crown and chugged slowly along the Straight, but once out on the main road he opened the throttle and let her go, eager to put the village of Huntlip well behind him, together with its ugly-tempered, violent people.

At The Rose and Crown, the last customer had now left, and Emery Preston was locking up. He threw the keys to the boy Matthew.

"So now we know where we stand, by God, and it's what I been scared of all along. I warned our Tilly often-times against taking up with Tom Maddox, but she wouldn't listen, oh no, not she!"

"You reckon he's gone and harmed her, dad?"

"He's done away with her, that's what he's done, the same as his father done with his mother, only *he's* been smarter about it, the swine, and made sure she ent to be found!"

"What're you going to do, dad?"

"I'm going to the police," Emery said, "which I should've done at the very beginning."

"Detectives?" Linn said, staring at the men who stood in
the porch.

"I'm Detective-Inspector Darns, madam, and this is
Detective Constable Penfold. We'd like a word with Mr
Maddox."

"You'd better come in."

They stepped in after her and the younger man closed
the door. It was not yet six o'clock, but the lamp had
been lit and Tom sat beside it on a stool, mending a boot
on a last in his lap. Linn stood behind him and touched
his shoulder.

"It's the police. They want to see you."

"Ah, I heard. I was wondering what it was all about."
He sat up straight, trying to see them. "What am I supposed to've done?"

"May we sit down Mr Maddox?"

"You go ahead. Suit yourselves."

"We're enquiring into the disappearance of your wife,
Mrs Tilly Maddox, formerly Preston. Her father has
reported her missing."

"Has he?" Tom said. "Whatever for?"

"Is there anything you can tell us?"

"She went off with another chap. I couldn't tell you
where she is."

"What date would that be, Mr Maddox?"

"Early in February," Tom said. "I can't say no nearer than that."

"Did she tell you she was going?"

"No. Not beforehand. Not in so many words exactly."

"Can you make that a little plainer?"

"She *did* say she wished she could live in a town. She didn't like it out here. She said it was lonely and drove her mad."

"I'd like you to tell us how she left."

"I came home and she was gone. There was a note on the table there. All her things had gone too."

"Did you keep the note?"

"No," Tom said, "I threw it away."

"Perhaps you can remember what it said."

"She wrote she was sick of being so lonely. She said she wouldn't be coming back."

"Did she say she was going with a man?"

"Not in so many words exactly."

"What *were* her words, Mr Maddox?"

"Well, she said she was tired of the way I treated her, and Mr Trimble would treat her better. He would look after her, she said."

"So you assumed they'd gone off together?"

"I'm certain of it," Tom said. "They was thick together. He was here a lot. I saw them once, laughing and talking. He'd got his arm round her, squeezing her tight."

"Were you jealous, Mr Maddox?"

"No, not a jot, it was no odds to me."

"I gather you didn't get on all that well with your wife?"

"You couldn't gather nothing else, after what I just been saying."

"What was the cause of your disagreements?"

"Everything," Tom said. "It was all a mistake, our getting married in the first place. We shouldn't never ought to've done it."

The two men were sitting side by side, almost filling the small settle. Tom could see them as two dark shadows; their faces were nothing but paler blurs; but he sensed that the young one was making notes.

"You writing it down, what I'm saying?"

"My constable is writing it down."

Inspector Darns was a man of fifty, quiet-spoken, easy-going. He sat relaxed, his hands clasped on the hat in his lap. He was rather interested in the half-cobbled boot on Tom's last.

"I'm surprised you can see to mend boots. I'd heard you had trouble with your eyes."

"I can see if I feel," Tom said. "But it's true what they said about my eyes. I got blown up during the war."

"He's going blind," Linn said.

"Were you going blind when your wife was with you?"

"It had started," Tom said, "but she didn't know it."

"Were you resentful, Mr Maddox, when this misfortune came to you?"

"Wouldn't you have been resentful?"

"You haven't really answered my question."

"Haven't I? I thought I had."

"Were you upset, Mr Maddox?"

"I wasn't exactly over the moon."

"And did you take it out on your wife?"

"Maybe I did. I wasn't too nice to her sometimes."

"Did you hit her by any chance?"

"No, never."

"Not even once, in a temper, perhaps, when she was nagging as she probably did?"

"I never touched her," Tom said. "Is somebody trying to say I did?"

"Mr Preston is not quite satisfied that his daughter left you for another man. He thinks you killed her, Mr Maddox."

"He's off his hinges!" Tom said.

"I take it you deny the allegation?"

"I do deny it! It's a bloody lie!"

Tom sat rigid on his stool. He felt imprisoned; trapped by his blindness; and a great anger ran through his blood, threatening destruction. He felt it would break him; that he would go to pieces like a man driven mad; that the darkness would engulf his mind. But he felt Linn's hand on his shoulder again, and her touch steadied him. He wished he could see the two men's faces.

"Why now all of a sudden? Tilly's been gone for months and months. Why don't Emery look for her in Birmingham, together with that Trimble fellow?"

"The man Trimble's been seen in Huntlip. Mr Preston asked him about your wife and the man denies that she went with him."

"But she must've done! She took all her things. She couldn't have took 'em if she'd gone alone. She couldn't have took 'em if she didn't have a car to drive away in. It's three miles to the nearest bus. Supposing Trimble is telling lies?"

"If somebody's lying, it's up to us to find out, Mr Maddox, and that's what we are aiming to do."

The two men stood up. They were very tall and their heads touched the rafters. Tom could feel them towering above him.

"You ent arresting me nor nothing, then?"

"Your wife has been reported missing and a certain allegation has been made. We have no choice but to follow it up. That's all there is to the matter at present, Mr

Maddox, and I hope we'll succeed in tracing your wife in Birmingham as you suggest."

"What happens if you don't?"

"We'll cross that bridge when we come to it. But one last question if you don't mind. Do you know the name of the firm this man Trimble worked for?"

"The name," Tom repeated, and thought about it. "It was Bruno," he said. "Bruno Brushes of Birmingham. It was on the dustpan and broom Tilly bought. You can have a look at them if you like."

"No need for that," Darns said. "It merely confirms what we've already heard. Thank you for answering our questions, Mr Maddox. We'll let you know if we have any news."

The two men went. Tom and Linn listened as they drove away. He turned towards her.

"*You* don't think I murdered Tilly?"

"Don't be foolish," Linn said.

"I should like to know."

"No, Tom, I don't believe it."

"What about them? Did they look as though they believed me?"

"I think so, yes. In fact I'm sure."

"Seems like I bring you nothing but trouble. I make a mess of things all the time."

His hands were still clenched on his cobbling hammer. He was breathing hard, and trembling a little. Linn took the hammer and the boot on its last and put them aside. She knelt before him, taking his hands between her own.

"You must try not to worry about it," she said. "The police will soon find her, I'm sure of that. I know how you feel, having Emery Preston spreading this lie, but you mustn't let it poison you. You must try and put it out of your mind."

Tom made no answer, but drew her gently into his arms.

At The Rose and Crown, when the two detectives entered the taproom, the gathering of customers fell silent. Emery Preston, sitting at one of the crowded tables, got up at once.

"Well?" he said. "Have you arrested Tom Maddox?"

"Mr Preston," Darns said, "I'd like a word with you in private."

"No need for that. I don't mind my customers hearing. I ent got nothing I want to hide."

"I'd sooner we were private," Darns said, and Emery, shrugging, led them into the back room.

"I'll ask you again. – Have you arrested Tom Maddox?"

"No, Mr Preston, for there's no evidence as yet that a crime has been committed at all."

"Evidence? It's your job to find it! Though there won't be much, I don't suppose, 'cos he'll have made certain of that, you mark my words. Out there in that lonely place, he could've buried her in them woods and no one the wiser, and I'll stake my last penny that's just what happened."

"If there's anything to be found," Darns said, "we shall find it, be sure of that."

"How long'll it take?" Emery asked. "From now to Christmas?"

"The only fact so far is that your daughter has disappeared. Everything else is speculation and I would advise you to be more careful in what you say or Mr Maddox could take you to law on a charge of slander."

"I'd like to see it!" Emery said. "A murderer taking me to law because I tell the world what he is?"

"What reasons have you for your suspicions?"

"Where's my daughter if he ent killed her?"

"Apart from that, Mr Preston?"

"His father was a murderer, did you know that?"

"That's no reason," Darns said, but he was interested all the same.

"It is to *me!*" Emery said. "I know the stock Tom Maddox comes from. His father was a wrong 'un. Anyone will tell you that. He attacked my poor old mother once and she was over eighty years old. He had a murderous temper always. He turned on the woman he lived with in the end and hit her over the head with a poker. He went and hanged hisself afterwards and saved the hangman a lot of swither."

"Yes, I remember the case, now you mention it," Darns said, "but is the son as violent?"

"Sure to be. It runs in the blood."

"But he's never actually been in trouble?"

"Not that I know of. He's been away. But he'll have got used to killing, won't he, out there in the war, fighting the Germans?"

"That could be said of thousands. But what I came for, Mr Preston, was to ask for the address of Arthur Trimble."

"I've got it here," Emery said, and passed over a piece of paper.

"I'd also like a photograph of your daughter."

"What for?"

"To help us trace her, Mr Preston."

"Trace her! Trace her!" Emery muttered, beginning to search a sideboard drawer. "How'll they trace her if she's under the sod?" But he found a photograph and handed it over. "That was took on her wedding day and a bad day it turned out to be for her, too, poor girl."

"She looks very happy in the picture."

"She didn't know what she was in for, did she?"

Emery followed them out through the taproom and saw them off the premises. He returned to his customers with a scornful face.

"A lot of use *they* are, going about so dilladerry, as though they got all the time in the world. Tom Maddox could vanish while they play about."

"Have they seen him, Emery?"

"Seen him? Yes! They been passing the time of day with him, just as though they was all good pals, or so it seemed from what they said."

"That's the way they go about it," said Emery's cousin, Humphrey Bartley. "They let him feel he's pretty safe and then when he goes and gives hisself away they pounce on him like a cat on a mouse."

"If I had Tom Maddox alone in my yard," Emery said, hard-faced, "he'd be telling the truth in ten seconds!"

Betony was away in Wiltshire when the rumours started. She returned to find them in full spate.

"Who started all this? Emery Preston, I suppose! And no doubt the village is all agog!"

"No doubt it is," her mother said, "but the best thing is to take no notice."

"Has anyone been to see Tom and Linn?"

"Dicky and me went a day or two back but your father's busy all of a sudden and can't find the time."

"Yes, well," Jesse said, not quite meeting Betony's eye, "what good can I do, going to see them?"

"I always said it!" granna exclaimed. "I always said he'd end up badly. It's the bad blood in him. He can't rightly help it."

"So he's tried and condemned already, is he?" Betony said, fiercely angry. "By his own family too!"

"We ent his family by rights," said great-grumpa. "We

took him in as an act of kindness."

"Yes, and it's him that's cut hisself off," said Jesse, "living over the brush with the Mercybright girl and making us feel ashamed to know him."

"I'm not ashamed," Betony said.

"Don't mind your father," Beth said. "Go out and see them. They need to know they've got a few friends."

"Yes, mother, I'll go now."

Driving along the main road, she overtook Jack Mercybright, and he rode with her the rest of the way. When they got to the Pikehouse, Tom was sitting in the open doorway, watching the sun going down in splinters of crimson light behind the church on Eastery ridge.

"Can you see it?" Betony asked.

"I should think I can!" he said, smiling, and the sunset colours were bright on his face. "Such sunsets we been having lately! Almost as good as the winter time. But I don't see much, besides lights."

In the lamplit room beyond, Linn, big with child, moved slowly to and fro, setting supper on the table. Tom rose from his chair and carried it in. He set it by the table, feeling his way.

"You heard what they're saying about me in Huntlip?"

"I've heard it all right. This fairy tale!"

"You don't believe it, then, Bet?"

"Not a single word."

"There's plenty that will," Jack said, and stood lighting a broken clay pipe, watching Tom through the smoke he was making. "As for myself, well, if you *had* upped and murdered Tilly Preston, I dunno that I'd really blame you. Her sort of girl often asks for trouble."

"Father!" Linn said, rounding on him. "What are you saying?"

"I reckon he's trying me out," Tom said. "The policeman

did the same thing. But I ent going to be catched that way 'cos I never touched her, neither by accident nor on a purpose, though I'd hardly admit it if I had, would I?"

"You needn't worry," Jack said. "I'd sooner believe what you tell me than anything the Prestons is putting about."

"The police are trying to trace Tilly, but what'll happen if they don't? What'll they do if she don't come forward?"

"What can they do when there's nothing to go on except a rumour? If you're innocent you got nothing to fear."

"It's the waiting and wondering," Tom said, "and the fact that the rumour might never get scotched."

"Forget about it," Jack said. "Gossip of this sort is not worth fretting over. It's less than the smoke going up that chimney. Meantime, we must look on the bright side, and hope that wife of yours turns up."

"I don't think she will," Tom said.

"Oh? Why's that?"

"I dunno why. I just don't, that's all."

Jack said no more, and Linn at that moment called on him to put out his pipe, for the soup-bowls were filled and on the table. But Betony noticed how, during supper, his gaze often rested on Tom's face, and, driving home later that evening, she asked him if he had any doubts.

"Doubts? Yes. Ent you?"

"I've never known Tom tell a lie."

"Everybody tells lies, especially when they're in trouble."

"Then you think him guilty!"

"I never said that. I *don't* think it. I only said I'd got my doubts. I'll have them for ever, I daresay, if that Tilly ent found."

"They can't be very serious doubts or you'd be frightened for Linn's sake."

"No, I ent frightened, 'cos it's like I said – if Tom did kill Tilly she very likely drove him to it."

"I don't think he killed her. He wouldn't, I'm sure." And she cast her mind back to that day early in the year when she had called on Tom at the Pikehouse: the day he had told her Tilly was gone and that he was beginning to go blind. "I'd have *known*," she said. "I'd have felt it, somehow, in my bones."

A few days later, Michael called for Betony at Chepsworth Park, and took her to lunch at The Old Plough.

"There's good news about Kingsmore Farm. I'm taking over the lease at Christmas, so by the time we come back from our honeymoon, there'll only be a month or two to wait before we move in. We'll live at King's Hill until then. D'you think you can bear it?"

"If your mother can, so can I."

"You don't look all that delighted," he said. "Aren't you pleased about Kingsmore?"

"Of course I'm pleased. It's just that I'm worried about Tom."

"Ah, yes, I might have known. So much for my little celebration!" He raised his glass, sardonically, and sipped his champagne. He tried to purge himself of his irritation. "Is there any truth in the allegations?"

"No, there isn't. None whatever."

"You seem very sure."

"It's just wicked gossip. Huntlip has bouts of it from time to time." And, after a pause, she said: "I'm afraid this is all very unpleasant for you, Michael. You're not only marrying beneath you – you're marrying into a family that's getting talked about in a hateful way."

"Huntlip gossip is nothing to me, though I agree it's a very unpleasant thing to happen. Still, I'll have you out of it quite soon, and you'll be able to put it behind you."

"You don't understand," Betony said. "I don't want to be out of it. Not while this thing is hanging over my family. I think we should wait a little longer."

"Haven't we waited long enough? Hell and damnation! Your vicar has started publishing the banns."

"It's the going away I don't like."

"Look," Michael said, and he was suddenly very angry. "I'm not giving up my honeymoon for anything or anyone, least of all that foster-brother of yours. He got himself into this God-awful mess and he's only got himself to blame."

"I don't agree. None of this is his own doing."

"How can you be sure of that?"

"How can we be sure of anything?"

Betony's anger was as fierce as his. They stared at each other across the table. But, aware that people were watching them, they ate for a while in complete silence, until they were in command of themselves and could speak calmly.

"If Tom is innocent, you don't need to worry."

"But he's a sick man. It's the strain and the worry that will do the harm."

"He's got other people looking after him."

"Yes. That's true."

"Can you do more for him than they can?"

"No," she said, "perhaps not."

For a moment she was tempted to tell him the truth: that Tom was now a dying man; but she could not. This secret she shared only with the Mercybrights and old Dr Dundas out at Norton. It was better that it should remain so.

"You're right, of course, there's nothing much I can do for him."

"Well, then?" Michael said, and reached across to refill her glass. "Perhaps now I can have a few minutes of your time in which to discuss our future lives? Just trivial things, you know, like the wedding arrangements and the honeymoon and making Kingsmore fit to live in."

Betony smiled.

"Dear Michael," she said. "You're very patient."

One morning, when Tom awoke, he could see nothing, not even outlines. When he stepped out into the garden and turned his face towards the sun, its light was concealed from him, as though in eclipse. It fell on dead eyes.

He sat on the old backless chair against the wall and yielded to the darkness. He felt it surrounding him, pressing in on all sides, as though it would squeeze him from the face of the earth. Nothing was left of him, only a central bubble of fear, and if that burst he would be destroyed.

Then suddenly the fear was gone. He could not have said why. But it was as though he had been away from his own body, lost in a no-man's-land of nothingness, and now he had come upon himself again, sitting on this seat in the autumn sun, with the overgrown garden all around him, smelling of mint and marigolds and apples eaten-out by wasps.

"What is it?" Linn asked, finding him sitting there so still.

"I was thinking of Grannie Izzard," he said, "and how she used to tend this garden."

"Are you coming in to breakfast?"

"Might as well, if you've got it ready."

He was reluctant to tell her that the last of his sight had gone completely. It would only grieve her. But Linn knew without being told, and she took his arm to lead him indoors.

Betony often called at the Pikehouse. She brought him a white-painted walking-stick and a whistle for him to hang round his neck. She brought things, too, ready for the baby.

"No more visits from the police?"

"No. Nothing."

"I was thinking," she said once. "It might be as well if you were to see a solicitor. Great-grumpa's man, perhaps, young Mr Hay. I would go with you if you like."

"But I ent done nothing," Tom said.

"Think about it all the same, if the police come pestering you again."

"I reckon it's all blowing over now," he said.

But a few days later, on the fifteenth, the two policemen came again.

"Is it news of Tilly?" Tom asked.

"I'm afraid not, Mr Maddox. There's been no response to our poster so far, nor to our enquiries. But I'd like to ask a few further questions. What, for instance, was Mrs Maddox wearing the day she left home?"

"I dunno. I wasn't here."

"But what about in the morning, early, before you went to work? Can you recall what she wore then?"

"She was in bed when I left the house."

"And you did say, I believe, that she left no clothes behind her?"

"Not a stitch," Tom said. "Is that all you wanted to know?"

"Unless there's something more you'd like to tell me."

"No, there's nothing," Tom said.

Darns turned to Linn.

"Were you acquainted with Mrs Maddox?"

"No," Linn said, "I never saw her in my life."

"Would you mind telling me your name, Mrs –?"

"Mercybright," Linn said, "but it's Miss, not Mrs."

"May I ask what relation you are to Mr Maddox?"

"It's none of your business!" Tom said.

"I don't mind answering," Linn said. "We live together as man and wife."

"Thank you," Darns said. "It's always a help when people are perfectly frank with us. Were you acquainted with Mr Maddox before his wife disappeared?"

"Yes. I was."

"How long after her departure did you come and take her place as it were?"

"About a week," Linn said, and met the man's gaze with only the slightest change of colour.

"I'm just wondering," Tom said, "if I ought to see a solicitor."

"And what do you think he would do for you, Mr Maddox?"

"I dunno," Tom said. "I dunno what they ever do. Somebody said it, that's all."

"I shouldn't worry, Mr Maddox. Not yet, anyway."

"What do you mean, not yet?"

But Darns and his constable left without another word.

Betony, hearing of this visit, became very angry.

"That settles it!" she said. "I'm going to Birmingham to look for Tilly."

"There's no point in that," Tom said. "If the police can't find her, what chance have you?"

"Perhaps they're not trying hard enough."

"They've got posters out, or so they told me."

"I'm going there all the same."

But although she spent two whole days in Birmingham, tramping all the busiest streets, asking at shops and boardinghouses, she learnt nothing. "We've been asked already," a shopkeeper told her. "The police've been round trying to find that same young woman." And she saw the posters everywhere, asking for Mrs Tilly Maddox, of the Pikehouse, Eastery, near Chepsworth, to present herself at the nearest police station, as her next of kin were anxious about her.

At the Bruno Brush Company in Hall Street, however, Betony discovered an interesting fact: that the travelling salesman, Arthur Trimble, had left their employ at a day's notice on September twenty-ninth and had talked of taking his family to London. His wife, is seemed, had relations there. Her uncle was offering him a job.

Betony returned home and went to the Pikehouse. She found Tom alone, for Linn had gone up to Eastery, to see the midwife, Mrs Gibbs.

"September twenty-ninth! Don't you see? It means Trimble left Brum immediately after Emery Preston had asked him questions about Tilly. So obviously he must have been mixed up with her, just as you said, and was frightened his wife might hear about it."

"We're still no nearer finding Tilly."

"No, she probably parted from Trimble quite soon, and she might be anywhere by now. But at least the police must know all this. They'll know he went off in a terrible hurry and they'll draw the same conclusions as I have done."

"I hope you're right," Tom said.

"Of course I'm right!" she exclaimed, and went on to talk of her wedding instead. "Will you be coming, you and Linn?"

"Better not," he said, undoing knots in a piece of string. "What with her being pretty near her time, and the things folk're saying in Huntlip at present, we'd only spoil it if we was there."

"You could come to Cobbs, though, afterwards. Dicky could fetch you in the trap."

"Better not," he said again. "We ent really wanted there, Linn and me. "

"*I* want you," Betony said, "or I wouldn't be asking."

But she knew he was wise to keep away. Only Dicky and her mother accepted him now. To the rest of the the family he was an outcast.

"All right," she said. "I won't press you if you'd rather not come. But I hope my present is ready in time!"

"It will be," he said. "There ent a lot to do on it now." He was making her a wickerwork chair. "Jack comes out to watch me at it, so's I don't make janders of it, but that'll be ready in time, you'll see. Honest John! as William always used to say."

Often, when he was unable to sleep, he would lie on his back, utterly still, afraid of disturbing Linn beside him. He would think of things to make himself sleepy, such as counting the cost of his osier rods, and the profit remaining when he sold his baskets. Sometimes he was back at Etaples during inspection, going over in his mind all the items laid out before him. Respirator. Field-dressings. Iron rations. Mess-tin, water-bottle, Tommy's cooker. Rifle, ammunition, ground-sheet.

Then the names would start coming. Newers. Ritchie. Glover. Braid. Danson. Evans. Privitt. Rush. Until, in a state between waking and sleeping, he wandered alone in a vast empty space, over ground much cratered by shells and mines, looking for men he knew were lost, while a

voice kept whispering in his ear: Where are they? Where
are they? Where are they *gone?*

Often Linn herself was awake, because of the baby
moving inside her, or because she sensed his wakeful-
ness. She had nursed many men during the war; had
heard them groaning, sobbing, swearing; had held them,
writhing, in her arms while they screamed out the sub-
stance of their nightmares. But Tom never tossed about
in bed; never moaned or screamed; he lay quite still and
silent always, and if she turned her head on the pillow,
she would find that his eyes were wide open, twitching a
little now and then, intent, it seemed, though they saw
nothing.

"Tom? Can't you sleep? Is your head hurting?"

"It's throbbing a bit, but nothing much."

"What were you thinking about?" she asked.

"Oh, this and that. Nothing special. It's harder to
sleep, you know, now that day and night are the same."

But sleep when it did come was often pure and sweet
and clean, and sometimes his dreams were happy ones.

"I was up on Lippy Hill and the sun was shining. The
berries was red on the rowan trees, and there was dozens
of thrushes there, mostly gathered on just one tree. I had
a little lad with me. He brought me some berries that the
thrushes had shook down onto the ground and he
showed them to me in his two hands."

"What did he look like?" Linn asked. "Perhaps he was
our son."

"I never properly saw his face. Just the berries in his
hands. Then we was sitting on a little hummock and all
the rabbits was out playing. It was evening time. Still and
warm. And some of the rabbits came so close, they was
eating right between our feet, mine and the boy's, as we
sat on the hummock side by side."

Tom was lighting the fire for breakfast. He liked to be able to do these things, and Linn, though she watched, never interfered. He was always careful, handling the matches, and the fire was always beautifully laid.

"The berries was just as red as red, and the thrushes was yellow, with great fluffed-up chests speckled all over as smart as you please."

He put a match to the laid fire and it crackled up. He crouched before it, the light of it flickering in his eyes.

"It's a funny thing, but I ent never blind in my dreams," he said.

One morning, early, when Linn was shaving him and trimming his hair, she thought she heard a dog barking, somewhere in the woods across the road.

"It's probably MacNab's spaniel," Tom said. "Maybe he's out after rabbits."

At half-past-nine, Jimmy Winger's milk-float stopped at the gate, and Linn went out with the quart jug.

"I see you got company," Jimmy said, and pointed to a car drawn up on the grass at the edge of the woods. "The police are rooting about in there. I seen 'em as I came round past Tyson's. What're they up to, do you reckon?"

"Haven't you heard the gossip, Jimmy?"

"I might've done," Jimmy said. "But I wouldn't stand for it if I was you. There should be a law against policemen."

Jimmy had once been fined ten shillings for riding his bicycle without lights. Policemen were worse than game-keepers and needed something better to do.

"I'll lend you a loan of my shotgun if you like, so's you can send 'em packing," he said, "and if I should meet one of 'em on the road, I shall let old Twinkler ride him down!"

When Jimmy had gone, Linn stood looking towards the woods, but could see no sign of the searchers there. Only, once, she thought she heard the same dog barking, somewhere deep among the trees.

She said nothing to Tom about it, but later in the morning another car drew up behind the first, and four policemen in uniform got out. One of them sounded a blast on the horn and after a while the first party emerged from the wood. Detective-Inspector Darns was among them. There were seven men altogether, one of them with a wolfhound on a leash, and they all stood talking for about five minutes. Then the newcomers went to their car and each took a spade and a sack from the dicky. All seven vanished together among the trees.

"What's the commotion?" Tom asked.

"The police are searching the woods," she said.

His face became bleak. He stood as though turned to stone. Linn went to him and took hold of his arm.

At one o'clock, the searchers assembled at the edge of the wood and sat on the grass, eating sandwiches and drinking tea from vacuum flasks. Tom went across to them, using his white walking-stick and making towards the sound of their voices, but they stopped talking as he drew near, and he stood in the roadway, hesitating. Darns got up and went to him.

"Yes, Mr Maddox, did you want me?"

"What d'you hope to find in there?"

"What are you afraid we'll find?"

"You're wasting your time. You won't find nothing."

"Then there's no need for you to be worried."

"Who said I was worried?"

Tom turned and walked back home, very slowly, counting the paces. Darns went and sat on the running-board of the first car, and one of the uniformed constables offered him a cigarette.

"Is he as blind as he seems, that chap?"

"What a suspicious mind you've got, Ryelands. You're very nearly as bad as me."

"You got any intuitions, sir, one way or the other?"

"Not reliable ones," Darns said. "But if he has done his missus in, well, the sight of us turning the place upside down may well poke a chink or two in that armour of his."

Towards the end of the afternoon, when the searchers again mustered on the turnpike, they found they had an audience there: three women and a man, all elderly, who had wandered down from Eastery.

"Is it true," the old man asked, "that you've found a grave in them there woods?"

"No, it's not true," Darns said.

"What *have* you found?"

"I'm afraid I can't answer any questions."

"Then they ent found nothing," the old man said to the three women. "I knowed it was all a pack of lies."

"Who spread these rumours?" Darns asked.

"Not me, not me!" the old man said.

"Have you got permission to search them woods?" one of the women asked Darns. "Have you spoken to Mrs Lannam?"

"Yes, and we've got a warrant," Darns said.

"What, signed by the king and his chancellors?"

"Move away, please!" a constable said. "Can't you see we're trying to turn?"

As the first car moved off, back towards Huntlip, a tall figure came striding down the field-path from Eastery and stepped out into the road. It was the Reverend Peter Chance, vicar of Eastery-with-Scoate, a big man with a shock of white hair, and he stood waving the car to a standstill.

"What is the meaning of this?" he asked, stooping to speak to Darns through the window. "Why are you persecuting Tom Maddox? Has he done something wrong? Is there any truth in these wild rumours?"

"It's our job to find out, vicar."

"Have you questioned the boy? Does he admit harming his wife?"

"People don't generally admit such things, until they're obliged to," Darns said.

"If he denies it, I'm quite sure he's speaking the truth."

"But just supposing he isn't, vicar?"

"Then God will punish him, without a doubt."

"I'm afraid that won't satisfy the law."

"The law takes too much on itself in these matters. Revenge belongs to God alone. 'Thou shalt not kill,' the commandment says, and it makes no exception of any kind. The hanging of murderers is therefore wrong."

"It has one advantage," Darns said. "It stops them doing it again."

He motioned the constable to drive on.

The next day, Saturday the twenty-fifth, was cloudy and dull and rather cold. Tom stepped outside as always, first thing, and stood for a while sniffing the air. The wind was blowing from the northwest.

"Betony's wedding day," he said, "and it smells like rain."

"What time is the wedding?"

"Two o'clock this afternoon. If we listen carefully we may hear the bells, though it ent very likely with the wind as it is."

"It's certainly a dark old day," Linn said, "but perhaps it'll brighten by this afternoon."

At ten o'clock two cars turned into the old turnpike and parked as before on the wide grass verge. Linn went to the gate and saw the policemen go into the wood. There were five altogether, four in uniform, one in plain clothes. Inspector Darns was not among them.

Linn for once was filled with hatred. She wanted to rush out after the men and pummel them. She wanted to strike their cheerful faces and see them crumple. She wished she and Tom could run away.

"Is it them?" he asked, when she went indoors. "They're deadly determined, I'll say that, when they once get a notion in their heads."

"Why must they stop just opposite? They could just as well stop in Tyson's lane."

"They want me to know they're there," he said. "They want to scare me and whittle me down."

"You mustn't let them," Linn said.

"I shan't, don't worry. But I wish it was over all the same."

By eleven o'clock, there was a gathering on the turnpike road of people from Eastery, Huntlip, Middening, and Blagg. Two newspaper men drove over from Chepsworth and took a photograph of the Pikehouse. They talked to all the local people. Emery Preston came with his sons, the four of them packed onto Matthew's motor-cycle and sidecar, so that when Darns arrived at half-past-eleven he was appalled at the growing crowd. He turned to Penfold.

"Send these people about their business! What the hell do they think this is?"

"I'm taking no orders from you, young fella," an Eastery man said to Penfold. "You ent even wearing a uniform."

But the crowd moved off eventually. The newspaper men drove away. Only the Prestons lingered on.

"Mr Preston," Darns said. "I must ask you to take yourself off and your sons with you. You've got no business hanging about here like this."

"It's *my* daughter you're looking for, remember, and I aim to give you a helping hand."

"Enter those woods," Darns said, "and I'll have you placed under arrest."

"Why, what've you found, for God's sake?"

"Nothing whatever so far, Mr Preston, but I'm in charge of this investigation and I will not tolerate interference."

"You can't turn me off the road, however. I've got a right to stand here if I so choose and so've my boys."

"I thought you had a public house to manage."

"My cousin's looking after that. I've got more important business here."

"Was it you who summoned those reporters?"

"What if it was? People got a right to know what's happening."

"We don't even know if anything *has* happened, Mr Preston."

"No, nor you never will, neither," Emery said, "if you don't shift yourselves better than this!"

Darns and Penfold turned away. Their work was often distasteful to them.

"I reckon he'd *like* it," Penfold muttered, "if we *were* to dig up his daughter's body."

The day remained darkly overcast, and from midday onwards a small rain fell, light but drenching. Emery Preston and his three boys took shelter just inside the wood, staring across at the tiny Pikehouse, where firelight flickered at the window and smoke blew downwards from the chimney.

"Sitting comfortably by his fire! – The murdering bastard!" Emery said, and turned his collar up to his ears.

At one o'clock, when Darns thought of cancelling further search, Penfold came to him with a cotton scarf, found in the deeper part of the wood, among the oaks and beeches. It had lain in the undergrowth a long time; its printed pattern was almost gone; and it had a dark brown stain upon it that could have been blood.

Penfold had marked the place of its finding, and Darns went with him to look around. Many trees had been felled during the war. Their stumps were still pale and clean-looking, and heaps of brushwood still lay around. Darns gave orders for the search to continue. He wanted the heaps of brushwood moved. Then he and Penfold went to speak to Emery Preston. They showed him the scarf, carefully folded with the stain inside.

"Have you ever seen this before, Mr Preston?"

"Seen it? Yes. It belonged to Tilly."

"Are you sure of that?"

"How sure must I be? She had one like it. That's all I can say. I bought it myself at the Christmas bazaar last year." Emery looked from one to the other. He swallowed hard. "Did you find anything else besides?"

"Nothing else, Mr Preston, and the scarf of course means very little. Your daughter could have dropped it at any time, if she happened to take a walk in the woods."

"Tilly never walked if she could help it. Not by herself, at any rate."

"I think we'll have a word with Mr Maddox," Darns said to Penfold.

"About time too!" Emery said. "I'll come with you."

"No, Mr Preston. You'll return home."

"I ent budging till it damn well suits me, so you might as well get used to the fact."

"Please yourself," Darns said, "but you're not seeing Maddox."

When Linn let them in, Tom was sitting at the table, finishing a meal of bread and cheese. He pushed back his chair a little way and crossed his legs. Darns put the scarf into his hands.

"We found that in the woods, Mr Maddox. Can you tell us anything about it?"

"I dunno what it is, do I? I can't see it." Tom felt the scarf between his fingers. "Is it a handkerchief?" he asked.

"It's a cheap cotton scarf, Mr Maddox, printed red and white, with a stripe at the edge and spots in the middle. Did your wife have such a scarf?"

"I dunno. I don't remember."

"Mr Preston said she did."

"Maybe she did, then. He ought to know. Why ask me if he's already told you?"

"It appears to be stained with blood," Darns said. "Does that help you remember?"

"It ent Tilly's blood, if that's what you mean. It's the blood of a dog that got catched in a trap."

"So you do remember the scarf, after all?"

"Yes," Tom said. "It's coming back. Charley Bailey was out after rabbits and his dog, Shorty, got catched in a trap. Charley called on me to help and I took that scarf to tie the dog's leg with."

"But the scarf has just been found in the woods."

"Shorty must've shook it off."

"Laboratory tests will show whether the blood on that scarf came from a dog or a human being."

"If there's human blood on it," Tom said, "that'll be mine, not Tilly's, 'cos Shorty took a bite out of my hand when I was trying to get him free."

"Mr Maddox," Darns said, "I'd like you to come with us to the police station."

"Why?" Linn demanded, stepping between them. "Why does he have to come with you?"

"He's not obliged to," Darns said. "I'm asking for his co-operation."

"What if I don't?" Tom said. "What if I refuse to go?"
He was very pale.

"It's only for questioning, Mr Maddox."

"Why can't you ask your questions here?"

"Yes! Why can't you?" Linn exclaimed. "He's blind and
helpless. Why do you have to take him away?"

"It's customary procedure," Darns said. "A refusal
could constitute an obstruction of the law."

"But you said he wasn't obliged to go!"

"It's like the Army," Tom said. "Our N.C.O.'s used to
say to us, 'I want volunteers for a listening party – you five
in front will suit me fine!' " He got up and went to the
door. He felt for his jacket and put it on. "I'm ready," he
said, and stood waiting.

"Can I come with him?" Linn asked.

"I don't advise it," Darns said.

"No more don't I!" Tom said. "That won't do no good
at all." His hand rested on Linn's arm. "You stop at home
and don't worry. You must think of the baby – you
mustn't let yourself get upset. They'll bring me back.
You'll see."

"But when? When? How long will it take, asking these
questions?"

She was looking at Darns, and he found it difficult to
meet her gaze.

"It all depends. But we'll let you know if any developments occur."

"What d'you mean, developments? What developments *could* there be?"

"Come along, Mr Maddox," Darns said.

"I asked you a question!" Linn said, following them
out along the path. "What developments do you mean?"

"Please! Linn!" Tom said, in distress. "Don't fret yourself. You must take it easy."

"Tom, I'm afraid! I don't think you ought to be going with them."

"Don't be afraid. They can't hurt me. They're just hoping I'll let something slip. You go indoors out of the rain and don't worry. I promise you I'll be all right."

But Linn continued to stand in the garden, her hands clenched in the pockets of her apron, watching as they led him away.

Outside, when they got to the car, the Prestons were waiting.

"Are you arresting him?" Emery asked.

"No, we're not!" Darns said, snapping. "He's coming to the station of his own free will. He's agreed to answer some further questions."

"But you will be arresting him when you get there?"

"Out of the way, please, and let us pass."

They got into the car and drove off, and Emery was left swearing. He hurried over to the motor-cycle and sidecar.

"Come on, you three. There's no sense in waiting here. Matthew, you can drop us off at home first, then go on to Chepsworth, to the police station. I want to know what happens next."

"But I ent even had my dinner yet!"

"You can buy yourself a sandwich when you get to Chepsworth. But mind you remember what I said! – Don't come away till you know what they're doing with Tom Maddox!" And Emery, waiting while Matthew adjusted his goggles, looked back to where Linn still stood in the rain. "She should think herself lucky they've took him away, before he turned nasty and done for her like he done for our Tilly."

Matthew stepped hard on the starter and the engine roared. They drove off towards Huntlip. Behind them, in the woods of Scoate House Manor, the police search continued.

Linn, going back into the kitchen, was struck by its look of emptiness. Tom's chair set sideways at the table; his dinner plate with its few crumbs; his empty teacup askew in its saucer: these things cried out to her like ghosts, and she could scarcely bear to see them.

Sitting upright on the settle, she made herself breathe very deeply and slowly, till the tightness eased from around her heart. She wished with a kind of sick longing that her father were with her, for she felt, as she had always felt in childhood, that he would know just what to do. So intense was her longing that she sprang up and went to the window, convinced she had heard his step on the path. But she was mistaken. He was not there. She knew she would have to go to him.

She got up and put on her coat. She drew a shawl over her head. She stepped into her rubber galoshes. The clock on the mantelpiece said five to two. She went out into the rain.

At Cobbs, when the clock on the workshop roof struck the hour, a crow took off from the weathervane and left it swivelling against the wind. Jesse stood at the parlour window. He watched the crow flying off towards Anster.

"That's two o'clock striking. We're going to be desperate late, ent we?"

"A bride is expected to arrive late. Granna said so. It's the done thing."

Betony smiled at him, seeing him frowning at his watch. She went forward and took it from him, and slipped it into his waistcoat pocket, where it belonged. She held his hands between her own, to keep them from fidgeting with his collar and tie.

"Just look at that rain!" he said to her. "That vexes me so's I could bost! Why did you have to choose October?"

"Today is my birthday. I'm twenty-four. It seemed as good a day as any. What does a drop of rain matter?"

"It'll spoil your dress. That's why it matters. Now where's that cloak you're going to put on?"

"It's here, handy, on the back of the chair."

"Do I look all right in this new suit? Is my parting properly straight? Have I shaved myself nicely, would you say?"

He got his hands free and touched his hair, which was well greased down and shone like straw. He touched his chin, feeling critically for traces of stubble.

"You look very handsome," Betony said, "and far too young to be my father."

"The church'll be crowded. D'you realize that? Folk have been going up forever. I seen 'em as early as twelve noon."

"I hope there's room for them all to sit."

"There won't be," he said. "No lections of that! A lot'll be standing about outside. The rain won't stop them. You mark my words."

He turned from her to the dining-table, extended as far as it would go, caparisoned in a white damask cloth, and already spread with the wedding breakfast.

"There's cold roast venison. Have you seen it? Mrs Andrews sent it yesterday." He took up a spoon and polished it on his jacket sleeve. "Of course," he said, "the men'll be eating in the kitchen."

"The men from the workshop, do you mean?"

"The table in the kitchen's more fuller than this one. Your mother and granna have worked very hard, and your sister, too."

"I suppose *you'll* be eating in the kitchen, then, seeing you're a carpenter just like them? Dicky, too, and great-grumpa."

"Not us! Laws, no! Not the bride's own family!" And,

turning away from her teasing glance, he said: "The men'll be happier, keeping theirselves to theirselves out there. They wouldn't be properly come-for-double, mixing with the captain and his mother and all the guests on *their* side."

"Michael will see that they mix," she said, "and so shall I."

"Glory be, just look at the time! Where d'you think that boy can've got to?"

"It's only five minutes past, father. Try and relax and stop fussing."

"That's all very well," Jesse muttered. "We should've hired another carriage. Ent I been saying so all along?"

Michael and his mother, with his uncle and aunt from Ilton Lye, and his best man, Major Peter Thomas, had gone to the church in the King's Hill carriage, with a King's Hill servant in livery driving. The Cobbs family had gone in the trap, and Dicky was returning for the bride and her father.

"What's the betting Duffer's cast a shoe?" Jesse said. "Or gone lame, even. It's always at times like this, ent it?"

A door slammed at the back of the house, and Jesse snatched up Betony's cloak.

"Here he is! Here he is! Better late than never, I suppose." And as Dicky burst into the room: "Good heavens, boy, how's it you've been so long a-coming?"

"It's Tom!" Dicky said. "The police've took him away to Chepsworth."

"Who told you that?" Betony asked.

"I seen it my own-self. They drove past me as I came from the church. They'd got Tom sitting in the back of the motor."

"Didn't you stop them and ask why?"

"There wasn't no chance," Dicky said. "By the time I

realized what was happening, the motor-car had gone right past. I did draw up straight away and while I was stuck there, wondering what I ought to do, the Prestons came up on that motor-cycle. Seems they was out at the Pikehouse all morning and saw our Tom get took away."

"Did they say he'd been arrested?"

"No, they didn't say that, or not exactly."

"What *did* they say, for God's sake?"

"They said he'd got what was coming to him. They said we'd be reading it in the papers."

"What about Linn?" Betony asked.

"Left at home," Dicky said.

"Laws!" Jesse said, looking anxiously at Betony. "That this should happen on your wedding day! Was ever anything so unlucky?" He felt he could scarcely look at Dicky. If only the boy had had the sense to keep the news until after the wedding! "Never mind, my blossom. Try not to let it spoil your day." He moved towards her with the cloak.

Betony was staring at the clock in the middle of the mantelpiece. Her mind worked with great clarity. The wedding ceremony would take perhaps an hour and a half. It would all be over by four o'clock. Not very long, she told herself, if she went from the church immediately afterwards. And yet it was *too* long. Some part of her said so. Some part of her had already settled all the questions.

In fancy now she saw Michael's face as he waited for her inside the church. He seemed to know what she was thinking; his grey eyes were worried, intent on hers; he was asking her to come to him. Then she saw Tom's face, his eyes deep and dark and hollow-looking, staring past her, asking nothing.

"Come on, my blossom," Jesse said. "We're late enough as it is already."

"No, dad, I'm not going. The wedding will have to be postponed."

"Postponed? Are you mad? You surely can't mean it! It's out of all reason!"

"You'll have to go to the church and tell them. I'll drop you there on my way to Chepsworth. But first I must go and change my dress."

"Betony, no!" he said, outraged, and stepped in front of her, barring the way. "You can't go and do a thing like that! Think of all the people waiting! Think of the captain and Mrs Andrews! What in God's name are they going to say?"

"Don't you care what happens to Tom?"

"I care all right. A whole lot more'n he deserves. But what can you do to help matters?"

"There must be something I can do."

"Well, afterwards, then, when it's all over. We can go and see about it then."

"No, father, I'm going now."

"I don't understand you!" Jesse said, following her out across the hall. "I don't know how you can do such a thing! I'd never've believed it! You of all people – my favourite daughter!" He continued to shout at her as she hurried upstairs. "What if the captain don't forgive you? I'm sure I shouldn't, in his place! I shan't forgive you anyway! – You're making us a byword in this village, you and Tom between you."

When Betony descended again, having changed into an ordinary dress, her father sat on the bottom stair and Dicky stood over him, arguing with him. Jesse's face was averted from her. He had never been angry in his life till today. She could see he was sick with disappointment.

"I ent going to the church to tell them. You needn't think it."

"Then Dicky must go instead," she said.

"That's up to him. I can't stop him. My children take no account of me."

"If you won't go to the church, will you go to the Pikehouse and see Linn? She must be worried out of her mind."

"Not me. Oh, no! That young woman is nothing to me. I'm just stopping where I am."

"Come on, Dicky," Betony said, and Dicky followed her out to the trap.

Driving briskly through Huntlip, they passed little knots of villagers, who turned and stared as the trap went past them. Further on, when they got to the green, she could see the people gathered in the churchyard, standing under the yews and birches, sheltering from the rain. The bells were ringing out loud, and the rooks, disturbed, were floating in circles round the tower. Betony stopped to let Dicky down, then she drove on towards Chepsworth.

Linn walked as fast as her heavily burdened body would allow. She tried to keep fear from clawing at her mind. It was three miles by road from the Pikehouse to Huntlip, and another two and a half from Huntlip to Blagg, but by taking the footpath to Millery Bridge and the old drove road over Puppet Hill, she was able to cut off a mile.

The rain was now a steady downpour, and she felt glad of it, soaked though she was, for it meant her father would surely be at home, sitting with his leg up, beside the fire. He hated wet days, for his bad knee became swollen and caused him much pain, and only the heat of a good fire brought him any measure of relief.

So strong was her faith that he would be there, reading his paper and smoking his pipe, that when she found the

cottage empty she stood for a moment in shocked disbe-
lief. A terrible weakness flooded through her, and a great
anger. Why couldn't he be there when he was needed?
What business had taken him out of his home on a wet
Saturday in October? A boy scaring birds in the field
below came to the hedge and gave her the answer.

"Mr Mercybright's gone to Upham. The master sent
him to look at a boar."

"How long'll he be, Godwin, do you know?"

"He said he'd be home by six o'clock. He said for me
to light his fire and he'd give me tea when he got in. He
generally does on Saturdays."

"Then I'll write him a message," Linn said.

She went into the cottage and sat for a while, shivering
in her wet clothes. She felt sick and giddy, hot and cold
at the same time, and pain burnt in the small of her
back, as though her spine were splitting and breaking.
She thought of putting a match to the fire; of resting
and warming herself for an hour; even waiting for her
father; but she was afraid the police might return with
Tom to the Pikehouse and that he would be worried at
finding her gone. Or, she thought, they might call to say
he had been arrested. So she got up, found paper and
pencil and wrote her message, and went out again into
the rain.

Just past the farm, at a bend in the lane, where it was
narrow, she had to stand aside for a herd of bullocks.
They had just come down from Puppet Hill, and the man
in charge of them, Frank Kendrick, was driving them too
fast down the steep track. Linn, though she pressed herself close into the hedge, was bumped and buffeted several times and had to hold tight to a hawthorn branch to
avoid being spun out into the lane and trampled under
the cloven hooves. But the last bullock lumbered by, and

Frank Kendrick came panting behind, his stick on his shoulder, his dog at his heels.

"Bloody cattle!" he said as he passed. "I could shoot them sometimes. I could. Honest."

Linn walked on, up the steep track and through the wicket, out onto the open hill. At the top of the rise she stopped to rest, leaning with her back against a tree, her hands on her stomach, seeking to still the throbbing there; seeking assurance that all was well within her womb. Then, having felt her child moving vigorously under her hand, she walked on over the hill.

All the way along Cricketers Lane, where the horse-chestnut trees hung over the hedge, the ground was strewn with the fallen chestnuts, bursting out of their spiky shells. Passing that way earlier she had met not a soul, but now a ragged figure crouched there, shuffling along low on his haunches, the skirts of his overcoat trailing in the mud. Although a man of forty or more, Jumper Lane had the face of a schoolboy, smooth-skinned and pink, with little arched brows over eyes a brilliant china blue. He looked at Linn with a gap-toothed smile and sprang upright, showing her the chestnuts crammed to the tops of his overcoat pockets.

"Yes, Jumper, they're beautiful. You're going to be busy, collecting all these."

"Look at this one!" he said, and snatched up a chestnut still in its skin, pressing it open to show her the dark-shining nut inside. "Look at *this* one and *this* one and *this* one and *this*!"

He was shuffling after her, stooping repeatedly to snatch up the chestnuts, then jumping up to thrust them at her.

"Yes, they're lovely," Linn said. "But I must hurry. I've got to get home."

"No need to hurry. The clocks are slow. Stop and help me collect the conkers."

"Not now, Jumper, I'm in a hurry."

"You always used to play with me."

"Not today, however. There's no time."

"I shall tell on you if you don't stop. I know what you done. You're just as bad as Alice Quinton."

And, blocking her way, he made his arms into a cradle, rocking slowly from side to side and uttering croodling noises in his throat. Then, his whole body squirming suddenly, he leapt high into the air, his knees going up like the blades of a jack-knife.

"Can't be helped! Can't be helped! What's done is done and can't be undone!"

"Please let me pass, Jumper," Linn said. "I'm tired and wet and I want to get home."

"Not till you let me have my way. I ent so simple as you seem to think."

"If you don't let me pass I shall speak to your auntie, Mrs Tupper, and tell her you were behaving badly. You won't like that, now, will you, Jumper?"

"Play conkers, then. I'll thread one for you."

"I told you before. I haven't got time."

She had never been frightened of Jumper Lane. There was no harm in him beyond a boisterous playfulness and the lewdness he learnt at The Rose and Crown. She was not frightened even now but she couldn't get past him and tiredness was bringing her close to tears. She made a great effort to keep her composure.

"Look here, Jumper, what about seeing me half way home? I'm passing not far from your Auntie Tupper's. We can walk together as far as the bridge."

"All right," he said. "But people will talk, you know. People will say I'm to blame for the babby."

"Never mind. Talk never hurts us, does it, Jumper?"

"They was asking me at the public once if I was to blame for getting Alice into trouble. But I ent saying. Oh, no, not me! I ent so green as I'm cabbage-looking."

Walking beside her along the lane, he kept kicking the chestnuts and leaves on the ground, but now and then he would turn towards her, putting both hands on her right arm and giving it a hard squeeze. He was plainly enjoying his walk with her.

"My auntie's got a mangle. She lets me turn the handle for her. She gives me a penny if I don't turn it backwards."

"You're always very good to your auntie. I've heard people say so oftentimes."

"I want watching, though. I'm a dark horse. Joe Wilkes says I'm as sly as the devil. He wouldn't leave his missus with me for five minutes . He said it hisself. So did she."

"People talk a lot of rubbish."

"They do, they do, they want sewing up!" Jumper said. "They want their gobs stopped, that's what I say."

On reaching the stile at the playing-field, he vaulted over in a single bound, slithering a little in the mud. Linn followed, slowly and awkwardly, and Jumper watched her in some concern.

"The trouble is, you've gone too fat. You're as fat as a landlady, that's what you are. Now, easy does it, that's the ticket. Easy and over and down and round."

He reached for her hand to help her down, but the moment his fingers closed on hers, he was seized by a sudden spasm of mischief.

"Statues!" he said, and pulled her headlong off the stile, so that she fell with great force, face forward onto the ground.

The pain was worse than anything she had ever

experienced. The scream of it echoed on and on, in her mind and her body, shrilling along every nerve. She thought she was going to lose her senses, but she lay on her side in the long wet grass and fixed her gaze on a marguerite that hung, drenched with rain, about eighteen inches from her face. She made herself think of it, concentrating with all her will, focusing on it until she could see every clean white petal sprouting from the yellow middle. And after a moment the faintness passed. But the whole of her body shrieked with pain. It was spreading out from the core of her being, where her child lay coiled like a spring in her womb. It made her powerless to move.

Jumper was bending over her, trying to look into her face. His big clumsy hands were locked together.

"I never done it! Oh, no, not me! She was climbing the stile and she tumbled off. It's not Jumper's fault she went such a whomper. He warnt nowhere near the playing-field."

He ran off, whimpering, back along Cricketers Lane, plunging his hands into his pockets and scattering the chestnuts as he went.

When Linn got up, raising herself little by little, he had vanished completely. It was useless calling him back to help her. He would be at the marlpits by now, or even at Outlands, hiding in one of the farm buildings. She stood for a time holding on to the bar of the stile, waiting while the sickness ebbed and flowed; waiting till her sight no longer rippled. Then she went on her way, across the playing-field and out at the gate by Millery Bridge.

Every step she took was a step homewards. Pain must not be allowed to matter. The sensible thing, as she well knew, was to turn into Huntlip and ask for help. Fifty yards off, if she turned left, there was a row of cottages, but she shrank from the thought of appealing to strangers. In half a mile, if she turned right, she would come to Cobbs where she was known, but there, she thought, the wedding party would be under way and her arrival would spoil it all. So she crossed the main street of the village and took the path up through Millery Wood.

But now a new kind of pain took hold of her, and she stood still, as though listening to it, as though her stillness would smooth it away. It was different from the pain she was already suffering: it was one sort of pain underlying another: the sudden clenching of a savage fist and then the slow, reluctant unclenching, leaving nausea in its wake. There was also a terrible liquid warmth and she knew that the waters protecting her child in the womb were breaking and moving.

But if animals could hold back their young without any harm coming to them, then so could she, for her will was surely as strong as theirs? And she went on steadily as before, up the steep slopes of Millery Wood, over the open fields at Peckstone, out onto the Norton road. When the pains came she stood quite still, gripping the fence with both hands, breathing great deep measured breaths. Fear and pain were working together. They would pluck her down if her strength failed, and she would be like a hare in its form or a vixen creeping into its hole.

"Please, God," she whispered, "don't let my baby be born at the roadside."

The Pikehouse was as empty as when she had left it, the fire dying on the hearth. She took a white sheet from a drawer, went out to the garden, and pegged it securely on the line. It was a signal to the midwife, Mrs Gibbs, who lived in a cottage near Eastery church. The cottage could not be seen from the Pikehouse because it was hidden among the trees; nor could the Pikehouse be seen from the cottage; but if Mrs Gibbs stepped out to the churchyard and looked down between the two elms as she had promised to do every morning and evening, she would see the signal very plainly.

Linn went in and closed the door. She reached for the bellows to revive the fire. But then, since darkness was not very far away, she lit the lamp with the pink-frosted shade, took it upstairs into the bedroom and placed it in the window facing towards Eastery church.

"Please, God," she said, as she turned up the flame, "make Mrs Gibbs step out to the churchyard."

She went downstairs again into the kitchen, to rebuild the fire and shed her wet clothes. The pains were coming more frequently now. Fear could no longer be shut out.

When Betony arrived at the Chepsworth police station, she found Matthew Preston sitting on a form in the main hall.

"What are you doing here?"

"My father sent me. He said to wait and see what's happening."

"Isn't your father satisfied with the trouble he's caused already?"

"It ent my dad that's caused the trouble. It's him in there – Tom Maddox."

"Tom never hurt anyone in his life."

"The police don't think that. Or why've they got him in there?"

"Why indeed!" Betony said.

At the desk in the hall sat a uniformed sergeant, writing in a ledger and drinking a cup of tea at the same time. He stopped writing and looked at Betony over his cup.

"Yes, miss?"

"I want to know why Mr Thomas Maddox is being held here."

"Ah," he said slowly, and put down his cup, looking at her with sharper interest. "Are you some relation to the man Maddox?"

"*Mister* Maddox is my foster-brother."

"And your name is?"

"Miss Betony Izzard."

"Well, Miss Izzard, Mr Maddox is here to answer questions concerning the disappearance of his wife. Inspector Darns is in charge of the matter, and Constable Penfold is helping him."

"I would like to see Inspector Darns."

"I'm afraid that's impossible at the moment. The inspector is with Mr Maddox now and he won't relish being disturbed."

"That's nothing to me. I insist that you tell the inspector I'm here. It's very important."

"Very well, Miss Izzard, I'll send in a message as soon as I can."

"When will that be? After you've had another cup of tea?"

"If you will kindly take a seat – "

"No, no. I'd sooner stand."

She walked about the hall, reading the notices on the boards. The station was a big one, newly built. A corridor ran from the back of the hall, with five doors at either side. She watched people coming and going for a while, and, with growing impatience, returned to the desk.

"I've got a pony and trap outside. If I'm going to be kept waiting – "

"I'll get someone to see to it for you," the sergeant said, and beckoned to a constable who was crossing from one door to another. "There's a pony and trap outside, Simmonds. Drive it round to the stables, will you?"

"I'm obliged to you," Betony said.

"All part of the service, miss."

"Is it part of the service to keep a man in custody when he's done nothing at all to deserve it?"

"Mr Maddox is not in custody, miss. He came along of his own free will."

"Did you send in my message to Inspector Darns?"

"Yes, miss, but I doubt if he'll see you for a while yet."

"Which room are they in, out of all those?"

"Third on the left," the sergeant said, and eyed Betony with some suspicion. "You weren't thinking of just walking in, were you, miss?"

"I might," she said, "if I don't soon get satisfaction."

"I wouldn't advise doing that, miss. It'll only draw things out that much longer. Why not sit down and wait patiently?"

"It's very important that I see Inspector Darns."

But she went and sat on one of the forms, watched by Matthew Preston, sitting nearby.

The clock on the wall said ten past three. She thought it was probably rather slow but five minutes later the cathedral clock was striking the quarter. At twenty past four a man in plain clothes emerged from a door in the corridor and stood talking to the desk sergeant. Betony rose and went to him.

"Miss Izzard?" he said. "I'm Detective-Constable Penfold. I gather you're enquiring for Mr Maddox."

"How much longer do you intend keeping him here?"

"That depends on what he tells us."

"And what has he told you so far?"

"Nothing much," Penfold said, "but it's often surprising what a man will tell us when he's been here for a few hours, and we've had time to wear him down."

"Perhaps if you wear them down enough, they may even confess to things they've never done!" she said.

"That's hardly likely, Miss Izzard. We don't employ the thumbscrew, you know."

236 Mary E. Pearce

"Tilly went off with a man named Trimble. Why don't you try finding him?"

"Arthur Trimble is proving elusive."

"Exactly!" she said. "Because he had an affair with Tilly and doesn't want his wife to know."

"Not necessarily. People often take fright for nothing at all. But, of course, it may be that Trimble was indeed having an affair with Mrs Maddox and Mr Maddox took exception to it. In which case, if jealousy was the motive, and provocation could be proved, the charge would be manslaughter, not murder."

"Aren't you being a little previous?"

"I was theorizing. Nothing more."

"Mr Penfold," she said. "I want to see Inspector Darns. There's something important I want to tell him."

"Is it directly concerned with the case?"

"It's directly concerned with my foster-brother. That's all that matters to me. But it *is* important."

"All right, Miss Izzard, I'll see what I can do."

Penfold went along the corridor and back into the room on the left. He emerged again with an older man and they stood talking in quiet voices, glancing often in Betony's direction. Then they went off down the corridor and into a room at the far end. Betony took a few steps forward but the desk sergeant stood in her way. She returned in great anger to her seat against the wall.

"Take their time, don't they?" Matthew Preston said to her.

Betony glanced at him but made no answer. He was, with his dark curly hair and thick stocky body, the very image of his father, and she hated him for it.

"Wasn't you getting married today? I thought the wedding was two o'clock. Did you leave the chap standing on account of Tom Maddox?"

"Don't speak to me!" Betony said. "There's nothing I want to say to you!"

She would not allow herself to think of Michael. Not yet, anyway. Such thoughts would have to wait.

Tom sat in a room that smelt of hot water pipes and floor-polish. It was stuffy and airless, and he wished they would open the window wider, but he couldn't bring himself to ask. The silence, ever since Darns had gone out, was too sweet to break, and he sat quite still in the chair at the table, his ankles crossed, his hands in his lap, his head turned in such a way that the current of air coming in, teasing though it was, blew directly into his face, bringing with it the smell of rain.

He knew he was not alone in the room. He knew that a constable sat in the corner and watched him. But so long as the man remained silent, Tom could pretend he was not there; could pretend the room was utterly empty; could picture the walls receding, receding, until they were gone altogether, giving way to open country where the rain blew like smoke on the wind and the clouds rode low on the backs of the distant hills.

Some little way off he could see the Pikehouse, lonely beside the old turnpike road. He was walking towards it, down the slope from Eastery, across the wasteland known as the Chacks, with the long tawny grasses brushing against him, leaving him dusty with their pollen. He had been on an errand to Mrs Hurst's shop. He carried flour, yeast, sugar, matches, candles, soap, rock salt, in a sack slung on his shoulder, and a can of paraffin in his left hand. Linn would be waiting for the yeast. It being Saturday, she was going to make bread.

Now, in fancy, he saw the tiny Pikehouse kitchen, with its scrubbed deal table and two varnished chairs, its oak settle and corner-cupboard and brass-topped fender round the hearth. And yet there was something that worried him. He could not picture what Linn was doing. The fire was burning brightly enough. The kettle, on its hook, was puffing steam up the chimney. The whole place was neat and trim and spoke of Linn's recent attention, yet she herself was somehow absent, and he heard his own voice calling, "Linn? Where are you? Are you upstairs?" But although he listened carefully, inside his mind, there was no answer.

"What time is it?" he asked sharply.

"Half-past-five," the policeman said. "Would you like a cup of tea?"

"No, I'd like to go home," Tom said, and when Inspector Darns came into the room, he sat up straight and turned his head. "I reckon you've kept me long enough. I've answered your questions. It's time I went home."

"We'd all like to go home, Mr Maddox, but there are just a few more questions I'd like to ask you before we finally call it a day."

"A few more? Or the same ones all over again?"

"You saw your wife with Arthur Trimble. You walked in and found them, in your own home, in something of a compromising situation. That's what you said, I think, when I first questioned you some weeks ago?"

"Oh no it ent!" Tom said. "I never said nothing of the kind!"

"What *did* you say, Mr Maddox?"

"I said I saw them. I never said I walked in. I didn't walk in. I went away."

"You mean you spied on them, without their knowing?"

"Not on purpose. It just happened."

"What were they doing when you saw them?"

"She was seeing him off at the gate. He had his arm around her neck. It looked like they was pretty friendly."

"That must have made you very angry."

"Not me," Tom said. "I was past being angry by that time."

"But you had been angry in the beginning?"

"When I found out she'd lied about having a baby, that made me angry, right enough. I could've struck her."

"Quite natural, I'm sure. Any man would have felt the same. But when you struck your wife, Mr Maddox, what exactly did you use? A stick? A hammer? A fire-iron snatched from the hearth?"

"I didn't use nothing!" Tom said.

"Just your bare hands, is that what you mean?"

"No. It ent. I never touched her."

"Perhaps you only meant to slap her. Just a light blow with the flat of your hand. Or a bit of a push that sent her reeling, so that she fell and hit her head."

"Seems to me you're getting muddled. You been listening to tales about my father."

"Did it happen at home or did you persuade her to walk in the woods?"

"No more questions!" Tom said. "We been over and over it time and again. You won't get me saying nothing different, not if you try from now to domesday.".

"You certainly had plenty of time," Darns said, "to decide what story you would tell."

He drew a chair from under the table and sat down opposite Tom. He opened a folder and turned over a few of the papers.

"About this court martial when you were in the Army."

"Yes? What about it?" Tom said.

"You were charged with refusing to obey an order. You were found guilty and given five days' F.P."

"You should know. You're the one that's looked it up."

"What was the order you refused to obey?"

"Don't it tell you in my record?"

"The details are sparse. Even at the court martial itself they don't seem to have asked what the order was."

"No. That's right. It didn't suit them."

"What was the order, Mr Maddox?"

"I was told off as one of a firing-party."

"What made you refuse? A delicate stomach?"

"I didn't hold with killing my mates. They'd no right to ask me. They knew that."

"What about sergeants, Mr Maddox? Did you hold with killing them? Or one sergeant in particular, say, by the name of Townchurch? A man you fell foul of, I understand."

"Me and a few score others, yes."

"A man who was mortally wounded in the back, although he was facing the enemy, and who died making certain accusations. Or so I was told at Capleton barracks."

"I never killed him, if that's what you're saying. It was more than likely an accident."

"An accident! That takes some believing."

"Them things happened," Tom said. "I was blinded by an English shell but nobody says it was done on purpose."

"You look a bit groggy," Darns said. "Are you feeling ill?"

"I'm all right," Tom said. "I'm just wondering what else you're going to try and blame me for."

"You do look groggy all the same. Perhaps you'd like a cup of tea."

"I'd like to go home," Tom said. "That's all I want. I just want to be took back home."

Outside the room there was a sudden loud commotion; a scuffling at the door and voices upraised; then a woman's voice ringing out above the rest. Darns got up and went out quickly. The policeman in the corner moved to the door. Tom sat listening as the voices outside slowly died away. His head felt hollow, like an empty shell, and the usual pins-and-needles feeling was spreading out from the back of his skull. Perhaps he was having strange fancies, but he could have sworn it was Betony's voice he had heard outside in the corridor.

Betony and Darns stood facing each other in a small room with barred windows. They were quite alone.

"Well, Miss Izzard, now you've got your way, what is it you have to say to me that's so important?"

"My foster-brother is a sick man. It's very wrong that you should keep him here like this, and I have come to take him home."

"A sick man? Are you referring to his blindness?"

"It's not only that. Tom was badly blown up in the war and there was some damage to the brain. The doctors who saw him last February gave him a year at the outside. Too much strain could be very harmful and perhaps shorten his life still more."

"I see," Darns said. "And he himself doesn't know this?"

"No, nor mustn't, ever!" Betony said, with great passion.

"Don't worry, Miss Izzard," Darns said. "We aren't monsters here, you know."

"You can check what I've told you by telephoning Dr Dundas at Norton."

"I may do that, but at present I'm willing to accept your word."

"Then I can take him home?" she said.

Before Darns could answer, Penfold knocked and

looked into the room, waving a piece of paper. Darns excused himself to Betony and stepped outside.

"It's Waring's report on that scarf at last," Penfold said. "The blood is animal's blood, sure enough, so we're left with precious little to hammer Maddox with, aren't we?"

"I'm losing the desire to try," Darns said.

"Feel he's innocent, do you, sir?"

"I don't know. I've got no feelings either way. He certainly isn't easy to rattle."

"One other thing," Penfold said. "Blackmore's back from searching Scoate. He says it's getting too dark to see. But he reckons he'd bet his last penny that there's nothing to be found in those woods."

"That settles it, then. I'll tell his sister she can take him home."

A few minutes later, Betony and Tom walked out through the hall. Matthew Preston rose from his seat. He looked past them at Inspector Darns.

"You letting him go? My dad won't like that! I thought you was going to arrest him for murder."

"There is no evidence whatever against your brother-in law," Darns said, "and you can tell your father I said so."

"I'll tell him all right, but he ent going to like it! I reckon he'll just about raise the roof!"

Matthew ran out, leaving the glass door swinging, and they heard him ride away on his motor-cycle. When Betony followed, guiding Tom down the steps, the pony and trap stood in the roadway with a caped policeman in attendance, and the two lamps had been lit ready. The sky was very dark now, but the rain was little more than a drizzle.

"Smells good," Tom said, as they drove off. "I thought I should likely smother in there." And, after a while, he said: "I don't understand about your wedding. I don't, that's a fact."

"It's perfectly simple," Betony said. "It's been postponed till another day. Such things do happen sometimes, you know. There's nothing extraordinary about it."

As they journeyed homeward dusk became night, although it was not much later than six o'clock. Tom was silent, sitting hunched behind her, and whenever she turned to look at him, his face in the glow of the lamps looked worn, his eyes anxious.

"Are you all right?" she asked once.

"Right as rain," he said promptly.

"I thought you looked tired."

"I was thinking of Linn, left alone all this time. She'll be worried sick."

"We won't be long now. We're almost in Huntlip. We've just passed Steadworth Mill."

At Carter's Bridge, where the road crossed a bend in the Derrent Brook, a light was glimmering through the drizzle, and as she got nearer Betony saw that a man stood in the middle of the bridge, swinging a lantern.

"What is it?" Tom asked, as the pony slowed to a hesitant walk.

"Someone with a lantern. I don't know who."

Betony halted and was at once sorry, for out of the darkness stepped four more men, and now she realized who they were. The man with the lantern was Harry Yelland, who had once been "engaged" to Tilly Preston. The others were Emery and his three boys. They had chosen a good place for their ambush. The nearest house was half a mile.

"It's Yelland and the Prestons," she said to Tom. "We're at Carter's Bridge and they're blocking the way."

"Can't you drive through them?"

"No. I've left it too late."

She drove forward a little way, up the incline onto the bridge, hoping the Prestons would give ground before her, but Emery caught at the pony's bridle and jerked him to a standstill. Betony took the whip from its socket.

"Step aside and let us pass or you'll be sorry, I promise you."

"*He's* the one that's going to be sorry. Him there behind you, who murdered my Tilly."

"The police have sent him home because there isn't a shred of evidence against him. If they're satisfied, why aren't you?"

" 'Cos I know Tom Maddox better'n they do. I know what sort of stock he growed from. His father was a murderer and everyone knows it and the old saying speaks the truth – like father, like son, every time."

"If that were true, we'd all be murderers," Betony said, "seeing we're all descended from Cain."

"I'm not wasting time in arguments. Just hand that man over and you can get home."

"Do you set yourself above the law?"

"He may be able to fool the police, but he'll soon tell the truth when I get hold of him, you may be sure of that, by God!"

"I've already told the truth!" Tom said. "I've told it and told it and it ent going to change!"

"Supposing you step down from there!" Yelland shouted. "Instead of hiding behind a woman!"

"This man is blind!" Betony said. "Have you lost all sense of pity?"

"We know he's blind," Emery answered, "but it don't mean he's going to get away with murder."

"You will not set hands on my foster-brother unless you deal with me first!"

"We mean you no harm, being a woman, but if you

choose to hinder us, it's your own fault if you get hurt."

Emery let go of the bridle and came alongside the trap. He tried to step up onto the wheel. Betony struck at him with the whip-stock and he fell back, swearing, one hand covering his eyes. She flicked the reins and tried to drive on, but Matthew had taken his father's place and was pulling hard on the pony's bridle. The pony reared up and danced a little, the white sparks flying as his shoes scrabbled the smooth-worn cobbles. Alfie Preston got kicked on the knee, and his twin, Victor, was squeezed between the wheel of the trap and the low stone parapet of the bridge.

Harry Yelland set down his lantern and took a stone from the heap he had ready between his feet. His arm went back and the stone flew close past Betony's face. Tom, behind her, gave a cry of pain, and when she turned to look at him, the blood was dark on his left temple. At the same moment, Emery Preston came forward again, but this time when Betony lashed at him with the whip, he caught hold of the thong and wrenched it clean out of her hands.

"Now, then!" he bellowed. "I've had about enough of this! Come down from that trap, Tom Maddox, or it'll be worse for you in the end 'cos I'm just about running out of patience!"

Approaching the trap, he was trying the whip in his right hand. He looked as though he would use it on Tom. But now, suddenly, there came the sharp crack of a shotgun, which set the pony dancing again but brought the five men to a standstill. The skitter of shot went into the boughs of a willow overhead, and in the little silence that followed, a few spent pellets fell among them, pattering down like extra heavy drops of rain. Then a voice spoke and Jack Mercybright came up onto the bridge, into the light shed by the lantern. His shotgun lay in the crook of his arm, smoke curling from one barrel, and he turned it full on Harry Yelland.

"Come away from that trap, all you others, or he gets the next lot in his guts. Make haste about it! No dilladerrying or trying tricks. The sort of day I've had today, I'm in the right mood to murder someone, and I'd just as soon it was one of you as anyone else I can think of offhand."

"This is none of your business!" Emery shouted. "We've got a score to settle with Maddox and it's no concern of yours whatever!"

"It is now," Jack said. "Move out of the way or Yelland gets it."

His wet bearded face was grim and ferocious. They decided he meant every word he said. Emery twisted the whip in its thong and threw it onto Betony's knees. He motioned his sons away from the trap, and led them back over the bridge, picking up the lantern as he went. Yelland followed, and the five of them stood at the side of the road, watching as Jack climbed into the trap.

Betony gave a flip of the reins and the pony pulled off over the bridge. As the trap passed him, Emery took a step forward, but at sight of the shotgun pointing towards him, he thought better of it and vented his feelings by pounding the panelwork with his fists.

"We'll get you, Tom Maddox, even if we do have to bide our time! No murderer yet ever went unpunished. Your crime will catch up with you, mark my words!"

"Take no notice," Jack said, and, peering closer into Tom's face: "Are you all right, boy? It looks like you've had a crack on the head."

"I'm all right," Tom said. "I just want to get back to Linn."

"We shan't be long now," Jack said.

"How did you happen to come by just then?" Betony asked, over her shoulder.

"I got a message from Linn, that's how, saying Tom'd been took away, so I set out to go to Chepsworth to see the police like she asked me to."

"Armed with a shotgun?" Betony said.

"I saw the Prestons come jumbling out of The Rose and Crown and I judged they was up to some sort of mischief. So I went along to the haywarden's office and borrowed this gun from Billy Ratchet."

Tom, sitting hunched against the rain, could feel the blood from the wound on his forehead trickling down the side of his face. He wiped it away with his handkerchief. The wound was not hurting overmuch, but his whole head ached in a dense way, especially the back of his skull.

"How did Linn manage to send you a message?"

"She brought it herself," Jack said. "Godwin saw her."

"What, walked all that way?" Tom exclaimed, and gave a groan, pressing the knuckles of his fists together and squeezing them hard between his knees. "But I *told* her not to go out of doors! She had no right to go walking so far! Supposing she was took ill going back? Supposing she was to lose the baby?" And then suddenly, from the depths of his darkness and helplessness, he cried out in a great trembling voice, "For God's sake, Betony, get me home!"

Betony whipped up the little pony and they drove fast through the stinging rain.

"It's all right," she said, when they came at last within sound of the Pikehouse. "It's all right, Tom, there's a light in the window so she must be there."

*

In the Pikehouse kitchen, Mrs Gibbs removed her soiled apron, wrapped it in newspaper, and stowed it away in her leather bag. She heard the sound of the trap approaching and stood listening for it to stop. She went to the door and opened it wide.

"My dear life!" she said, seeing the blood on Tom's forehead. "The policemen never done that to you, surely?"

"Mrs Gibbs! How come you're here? Where's Linn?"

"Linn's all right. So's your little baby son. They're both pretty fine, all things considered, and now they're having a well-earnt rest. Here, sit down, young fella, you look as though you're about all in."

"No, no," Tom said. "I want to see her."

"Well, you can't go up dripping wet, can you? Nor with your head all bloody neither."

"Of course he can't," Betony said. She drew him towards the blazing fire. "A minute or two won't make much difference. You must shed a few of these wet clothes."

He took off his cap, jacket, and bloodstained shirt, and Mrs Gibbs received them from him. She hung a towel round his shoulders.

"Are you sure she's all right?" he asked. "You ent keeping nothing from me?"

"I give you my word," Mrs Gibbs said, and touched his arm.

"How long ago did the baby come?"

"Half an hour or thereabouts, and if he'd come sooner he'd have stood a chance of getting hisself born between here and Blagg."

"You sure she ent done herself no harm?"

"She's used up every ounce of strength for the time being, but she'll be all right, I promise you."

"Oughtn't we to get the doctor?"

"Yes," Jack said, "I'll go and fetch him."

"It might be as well, to be on the safe side," said Mrs Gibbs. "It's Dr Dundas down in Norton. Second house past the post office."

"Tell him it's urgent," Tom said.

"I'll bring him, don't worry," Jack said, and the door closed behind him.

Mrs Gibbs was warming a shirt at the fire. She gave it to Tom and he put it on. He was trembling all over and his fingers could scarcely fasten the buttons. She had to help him. Betony brought a bowl of water and cleaned the blood from the cut on his temple. He bore it in silence, only dimly aware of what she was doing. He tucked his shirt into his trousers and ran a hand through his hair.

"Am I tidy enough? Can I go up to her now?" he asked.

"Go, you," Mrs Gibbs said, "and I'll come in a minute to show you your baby."

In the tiny bedroom, Linn lay in bed feeling she would never move again. Close beside her, her baby lay in its wickerwork cot, a doll-like shape under the blankets, a smudge of dark hair just showing above. She could hear the voices in the kitchen below, and when Tom came up the steep stairs into the bedroom, she turned towards him, putting out a hand.

"You've hurt your head," she said, in a weak voice.

"It was an accident," Tom said. He did not want to tell her about the Prestons. "I hit myself on a low rafter."

"You look pale and tired. They had no right to keep you so long."

"I wish I could see how *you* are looking, after all you been through today."

"I'm not too bad. Mrs Gibbs was wonderful. Did she tell you we've got a son?"

"Oh, I've heard about *him.* Is he there beside you? Does he like the cot I made for him?"

"Come round," she said. "Seems to me he's heard your voice and he's listening to it. He's turning his head this way and that."

"Is he?" Tom said, and felt his way round to the cot. "Does he know I'm his father, d'you suppose?"

When he touched the blankets covering his son, and felt the warm body moving, small, under his hands, something leapt at his throat and took his breath away completely. Until this moment the baby had merely been part of Linn's body; a part of the life they had together; something that made him fearful for her. But now as it stirred beneath the blankets, and he felt the warmth of it throbbing against the palms of his hands; felt the shape of it, and the way it squirmed, trying the strength of its small limbs; he knew it had a life all its own, its own heart and soul and obstinate will, its own place under the sun.

"Pick him up," Linn said. "He's your own son."

"I'm afraid to," he said. "I might hurt him, being blind."

The stairs creaked and Mrs Gibbs came into the room. She took the baby out of his cot and placed him, in his blankets, in Tom's arms. And now, with the small warm face nuzzling with such surprising strength against his own, the small hands pushing against him, Tom stood for a while feeling that he and this baby son of his were alone together in the dark. Alone together as one flesh. But, right at the heart of this shared darkness, there was a sunny picture forming.

"I can see you," he whispered. "I can see you, little boy, one summer's day, after rain, reaching up with both hands to touch a wild pink rose in the hedgerow, and you're laughing the way your mother laughs, 'cos one or two raindrops is splashing down into your face."

Mrs Gibbs took the baby and laid it back again in its cot. Tom returned to Linn's bedside and sat with her hand between his own.

"Your father was here. Did you hear him? He's gone to fetch Dr Dundas."

"Yes, I heard him."

"You went against me, didn't you? You left the house and went all them miles to Outlands Farm. That frightens me to think of, your going all that way."

"Did father come and fetch you home?"

"It was Betony that done that. She put off her wedding, would you believe it? I dunno what she said to the policeman, but they let me go, whatever it was. Then we picked up your father on the way home."

Tom felt Mrs Gibbs beside him. She was touching his shoulder.

"We should ought to let her rest. The doctor'll be here before long. You can come up again in an hour or two. I'll sit up here while she has a sleep."

"I reckon that's right," Tom said. "I'm gabbling on like an old goose."

He rose from the stool and leant over to kiss Linn's forehead. He felt her fingers touching his face. He turned and went down into the kitchen.

"How is she?" Betony asked.

"She says she's all right. And Mrs Gibbs don't seem too worried about her, does she? Anyway, Dr Dundas will be here directly."

"How's the baby?"

"Oh, he's a masterpiece, he is! I daresay they'll let you see him later."

"Sit down here," Betony said. "I'm going to clean that forehead properly."

"All right," he said, and sat on the edge of the rocking-chair, his back quite straight, his hands folded between his knees. He was thinking about his baby son. "Maybe he'll be a carpenter, the same as me. Maybe they'll take him on at Cobbs." And after a while he said, "D'you think he'll mind overmuch, having a father that's stone blind?"

"No, he won't mind, I'm sure of that."

Betony was swabbing the deep cut, wiping away the dried blood.

"I don't like the look of this at all. It's very ugly."

"It's a funny thing, but I can't feel it. I felt it all right when the stone hit me. I thought I was going to fly to bits. But I don't feel nothing any more." He put up a hand and touched the wound with the tips of his fingers. "No, not a thing," he said, pressing. "My head just feels numb, that's all."

"Numb all over, do you mean?"

"Pretty well all over. I ent sure. It's like pins-and-needles inside my skull."

"I wish the doctor would come!" she said. "Surely he ought to be here by now?"

"Maybe he was out some place else. Maybe Jack has had to wait. Are you worried about Linn?"

"I'm more worried about this cut."

"I told you, that's nothing, I don't hardly know it's there at all. I'm a bit muzzy, but I'm used to that."

"I think you ought to try and rest."

"Can a man rest when he's just this minute become a father?"

"They haven't all spent such hours as you have, under police questioning."

"No," he said, and, after a pause: "I never murdered Tilly, Bet, and that's the truth as God's my witness."

"I never thought you did for one moment."

"I wish she'd come forward and put an end to all this talk. I don't want my son growing up in the world with people saying his dad's a murderer."

"Lean back and rest," Betony said. She was worried and frightened by the colourless, leached-out look of his skin. "Lean back in the chair and take it easy."

"All right," he said, and leant his head against the flat cushion that hung on tapes from the back of the chair. "I am a bit tired, now that I think of it, I suppose."

Betony lifted his booted feet and put the stool underneath them. She fetched a blanket and spread it over him, up to the chin.

"Sleep if you can. You'll be better for it. Linn and your baby are in good hands."

"We're going to call him Robert, you know, after Bob Newers, my mate in the Army. We was going to ask if you'd be his godmother."

"I'd be cross if you asked anyone else!"

Betony went about the kitchen; turned the napkins airing on a string above the fire; eased the kettle out on its bracket; set the teapot on the hob to warm. The lamp on the table was burning crooked. She went and turned the wick down low. Then she took up scissors and an old newspaper and sat down with them in her lap. She began making spills, cutting and folding carefully, making hardly any noise.

"I know what you're doing," Tom said. "You're making spills."

"Yes," she said, "I noticed the jar was almost empty."

"That was always a favourite job of yours, even when you was a little girl. You wouldn't let nobody else make them. Nobody else done a proper job."

He could picture her plainly at her childhood task and somehow the thought of it made him smile. Sitting back

in his chair, wrapped in his blanket, he had the heat of
the fire in his face, could hear the small sounds it made,
and could smell the sweet smell of old mossy applewood
burning on it. But slowly the world was slipping away.
The picture inside his mind was fading. His blind eyes
were closing of their own accord. And because he was
really very tired, death came to him disguised as sleep, so
that when he gave himself up to it he was still smiling.

"Michael's not here," Mrs Andrews said. "He motored up to London this morning and is staying the night with Major Thomas. Tomorrow he sails for South Africa."

"How long for?" Betony asked.

"He may decide to stay for good. If he does I shall probably go out and join him there. But should he decide to return to England he would prefer not to see you again. That was the message he asked me to give you."

"Yes. I see. In that case I think I'd better leave this with you." Betony took the ring from her finger and placed it on the hall table. "I came as soon as I could," she said, "but it seems I'm too late."

"It wouldn't have made a scrap of difference however soon you had come. He wouldn't have seen you."

"I'm sorry he feels so bitterly."

"*Are* you sorry? – I very much doubt it, Betony. You never really loved Michael. I always thought that, from the very first." Mrs Andrews was unyielding. "You could never have done such a thing," she said, "if you'd really loved him."

Armistice Day was cold and sunless. A bitter wind blew in the churchyard yews and birches, and a few dry snowflakes fell on the people below. The war memorial, cut from a piece of Springs Hill granite, was a tall Celtic cross surmounting a rough-hewn pedestal, and stood inside the main gateway. Huntlip had given thirty-six lives. The names were cut on three sides of the stone. Some were repeated twice or three times. Hayward. Izzard. Mustoe. Wilkes.

"Thirty-six young men," the vicar said, at the end of his address, "whose courage and sacrifice will live forever."

People stood very still, during the two minutes' silence, and their heads were bowed. The silence would last in many hearts. But heads were raised again during the singing of the hymn, and the frail human voices rose defiantly round the cross, strong because they sang together. The people, singing, all looked up, and the cold wind dried the tears on their faces.

Afterwards, walking home through the village, Dicky said: "Tom's name should be on that stone by rights, along with the others."

"Yes, perhaps so," Betony said.

She and Dicky walked with their father. The rest of the family came behind. Jesse was staring straight ahead. He found it difficult to speak.

"No 'perhaps' about it. Dicky's right. Tom gave his life for King and Country, just the same as William and Roger."

Betony took her father's arm.

The following day, she spent three hours at Chepsworth Park, where all the invalid veterans wore sprigs of greenery in their coats, remembering their dead comrades. There were many "helpers" there that day: every wheelchair case had been taken for an outing through the park, all the bedridden men had someone to talk to, and several ladies had banded together to put on a concert in the evening.

"Oh, we've got floods of helpers at the moment!" the superintendant said dryly to Betony. "Armistice Day has made them remember, certainly. But it'll fall off by the end of the week and then we'll be left short-handed as always."

"Perhaps it would help," Betony said, "if I came more often."

Afterwards, on her way through Chepsworth, she stopped to look at the new memorial standing in the cathedral grounds. It was the figure of a private soldier, bareheaded save for a bandage, and he stood with his rifle in front of him, the butt on the ground, the barrel clasped between his hands, staring at the ground as though bowed down with weariness. All around the monument, the steps were strewn with laurel wreaths.

As Betony left the cathedral precincts, a column of unemployed men passed by, each with a placard on his chest and back. "Hundreds more where we come from!" "We take charity but what we want is work." "Old soldiers never die, they only fade away – from starvation!" And one man, seeing Betony coming away from the war memorial, called out to her: "The dead are remembered all right! It's us live ones that get forgotten!"

Sipping a glass of Madeira wine in the vicarage drawing-room, Betony could easily guess why the vicar, Mr Wisdom, had summoned her there. Miss Emily Likeness, headmistress of Huntlip school for forty-three and a half years, was retiring at Christmas, reluctantly, due to a general decline in health.

"Am I correct," the vicar asked, "in thinking you will not be marrying Captain Andrews after all?"

"Quite correct," Betony said.

"I am very sorry, Betony, that it has worked out so sadly for you."

"Thank you, vicar. You're very kind."

"I was wondering whether, in view of your changed circumstances, you'd consider taking over from Miss Likeness as headmistress of the village school. I can think of no one more suitable. Miss Likeness herself hopes you'll agree. But, of course, you needn't give your answer tonight. You will probably wish to think it over."

"Yes, I will," Betony said, "but I think the answer will probably be yes."

As she was leaving, the vicar said: "There's a rumour in the village that Tilly Preston's been seen in Warwick. Is it true, d'you suppose?"

"Yes. It's true. Jeremy Rye saw her there, serving in the bar of a public house. She's been living there for some time as the wife of the landlord."

"Why did she never come forward, then? Surely she must have seen the posters?"

"Jeremy Rye asked her that. She claimed she knew nothing at all about it."

"I never doubted that your foster-brother was innocent."

"Neither did I," Betony said.

Her sister Janie had been ill with 'flu. She was now recovering, sitting up in bed, eating the grapes Betony had brought her.

"Have you heard from Michael?"

"No, not a word."

"Mother tells me there'll be no wedding but surely – "

"Yes. That's right. Michael's gone abroad. He doesn't want to see me again."

"Oh, Betony! Are you sure?"

"Don't be upset. I'm not. I feel, somehow, that it wasn't really meant to happen."

"But what will you *do*?" Janie asked. She could not imagine her own life without her husband and her three children. She could not imagine such emptiness. "Whatever will you *do*?"

Betony smiled. She thought of the school, where she would soon be mistress-in-charge, with over a hundred small children in her care. She thought of the invalid veteran soldiers needing help at Chepsworth Park, and she thought of the grey-faced men she had seen walking the streets because they had no work to go to. She thought, too, of Linn Mercybright and her fatherless baby.

"There's always plenty to do, Janie. It's only a question of where to begin."